THE
TRUTH
OF
WHO
YOU
ARE

SHEILA MYERS

Black Rose Writing | Texas

ISBN: 978-1-68433-934-1
PUBLISHED BY BLACK ROSE WRITING
www.blackrosewriting.com

Printed in the United States of America
Suggested Retail Price (SRP) $20.95

The Truth of Who You Are is printed in Baskerville

*As a planet-friendly publisher, Black Rose Writing does its best to eliminate unnecessary waste to
reduce paper usage and energy costs, while never compromising the reading experience. As a result, the
final word count vs. page count may not meet common expectations.

To the men and women of the US Conservation Corps
who continue to preserve and protect
our nation's natural environment.

THE TRUTH OF WHO YOU ARE

HICKORY RUN, TENNESSEE 1959

From the window of my small office at the Hickory Run Press, I watch people go about their lives, running errands, nodding greetings to friends and acquaintances. And I wonder, do they know what their families might say about them when they die; what they'll tell me to write in the obituary column about their loved ones' brief existence on earth?

Mrs. Stewart steps out of her husband's store, hat lowered half-mast as if we won't notice the black eye. She crosses the street to the post office while on-lookers nod their heads at her in greeting, then quickly look away. Mr. Stewart, the culprit, comes outside and wipes his hands on his bloody apron, observing people as his wife scurries away, daring anyone to disrespect her as he holds the credit for so many families in town. His eyes narrow as his gaze lands on me; he pivots on his heel and goes back to butchering.

The Stewarts show up weekly at church, holding hands, smiling as if his bouts of alcoholic rage don't matter. And we all let him be because he was in the war and we all know how the war can change a man. It's a small town that I live in. Half the men here have been in either the first or the second war, and no one will pass judgment on a veteran.

We all believe what we want to believe if it will make our lives easier. To do otherwise means facing some uncomfortable truths. That's what I've come to realize after writing people's obituaries for over twenty-five years. But I learned that lesson much earlier while growing up in the shadow of the Great Smoky Mountains.

Now, I'm not so sure if hiding the truth is the best option. My doctor told me yesterday to look for solace, because I've been writing everyone else's stories after they die, and soon someone will be tasked with writing mine. I thought I'd give them material to work with.

To do that I have to reveal some uncomfortable truths I've tried to forget. Everybody has regrets. Everybody wishes they could go back in time to change things. What if my brother hadn't gotten sick? What if I hadn't given my mother that satchel of herbs? And what if my father had saved his old forest? All what ifs.

What if I'd stopped my cousin from using that defective jack lift? The trajectory of so many lives would've pivoted. And there's only one man who, besides me, knows the truth about what I did. And that man is dead.

PART ONE
1926
TAYLOR VALLEY

1

I grew up in the Smoky Mountains, where distances are measured in hours instead of miles. My father could point out the nearest cabin just by scanning the horizon, seeking a tendril of chimney smoke snaking its way past the tree line. His family owned Taylor Valley, and an extended family of sisters and cousins all made it their home. As a result, I was never more than a day's hike from a family relation.

His sense of direction was uncanny. We would hike up the side of a mountain, and when we came to a clearing, he'd point in any direction and tell me what lay in that direction.

"See over there, Ben?" he'd say. "That's the State of North Carolina."

I'd focus in the direction he pointed and see nothing but waves of green forest, capped with blue haze. "How do you know it's not still Tennessee?"

"Son, you live in these mountains, and you just know where one thing ends and the other begins."

Every spring Pa took a trip to check on his ginseng plants in a grove of old trees high above a ravine. The year I turned thirteen, I went with him. We left while the moon and stars were dim memories, in the brief time between night and dawn, the wind talking to the trees, the mountains— phantoms in the mist. We took Cherokee trails that plunged into the thick woods, following the path of least resistance, razor-backing along precipices that brought my stomach to my throat whenever I glanced down.

I thought hiking would tire him out, but he never wavered during the trip. He kept up his banter as he loped along, informing me about the history of the Taylors and their adventures. Pa was good at storytelling because he had learned the only way to maintain a position in a family so large was to entertain people.

We reached a juncture in the path where Hickory Creek cascaded over large boulders, creating plunging pools, and we stopped to fish.

After a good hour of wasting bait, Pa said, "Let's git going."

I started downstream, thinking that was the direction to take, and he said, "Not that way. That way leads to town."

I followed him along the creek up a steep hill, past boulders, and waterfalls as tall as our cabin. The roaring water drowned any other sounds. I could barely make out what he was yelling at me. Then I glimpsed where he pointed—a grove of trees above the falls—and gasped in wonder. He waved to me to follow him as he scaled the vertical outcrop of rocks alongside the falls.

Pa had the dexterity of a mountain goat, but I was not as nimble. My shoes were so worn that I couldn't get a hold of the slippery rocks, so I pulled them off and wedged them into a crevice to retrieve on the way back down. Every once in a while, Pa looked back to make sure I hadn't fallen and gave me an encouraging wave of a free hand. I waved back, grasping a limb of a mountain laurel bush for balance, my feet scraped raw from the rocks.

"Keep climbing and don't look down," he called.

Just as he finished his sentence, I slipped and tumbled. A laurel bush ripped the back of my shirt, and my bare feet scraped against the sharp stone as I tried to maintain purchase. I landed with a thud on a rock ledge. The fall left me winded; my back ached, and the soles of my feet burned.

"Ye all right down there?" Pa called.

"I guess so," I called back weakly.

Pa grinned and kept on going. I had no choice but to follow. We finally reached the top at the headwaters of the falls. A wide ribbon of water slipped over the granite before plunging over a bank of smooth rock. I stepped into the water to cool my throbbing feet; the icy water stung, then numbed them.

"Come on," Pa said, walking away from the creek toward the forest.

As we entered the grove of trees, it felt as if a door to a room had shut behind me, hushing the world outside. Pa motioned for me to look up.

That grove of trees above the waterfalls was as close to heaven as I'd ever seen.

Trees so large they towered over us. Tangled limbs reaching for the sky, stretching toward a place no human could reach, their leaves so distant I could barely make them out. Sunlight was sparse, and where a ray did poke through, small plants strained for a taste of it.

I gazed at the ground. Dark, green, lush, it throbbed with moisture. Dead trees, the height of tall buildings, cluttered the forest floor. I clambered up the side of one, slipping on moss as thick as a carpet, and soaked it all in. The quiet was like a church service before the preacher started his sermon. After sitting for a few moments without talking, my ears buzzed. "Hear that?" I said.

Pa chewed on the stem of a plant. He took it out of his mouth and said, "Insects. They's eatin' away at that log you're sittin' on. This here is one of the oldest forests you'll ever see. It's called Taylor Grove. Been this way since your grandpa came here. He never cut these trees, and I'll neither."

He beamed with a joy I hadn't seen since Nellie was born, a look of pride and wonder as if he couldn't believe something so beautiful existed in the world, but here it was right in front of us. A ray of light landed on his head, making his silver hair shiny. I swear it looked like a halo surrounding him.

"Who knows about this?" I asked.

"My sisters. Our pa left me the deed, but my sisters come here a lot. Your aunt Cornelia used to climb that cliff with me, up until she got married. She'd help me collect 'seng and goldenseal for Bertie." He pointed to a patch of ginseng. "That 'seng fetches ten dollars a pound if we can git it to the right market. Grows slow, though."

"It must take a lot of plants to make a pound."

"It's the roots, son. You pull the plant, and it has white roots like an old woman's fist. That's what we sell to the store in town, and they ship it to Knoxville or someplace, where Chinamen buy it for medicine."

"Chinamen want our plants?"

"Bertie says they think it has magical powers."

"Does it?"

He shrugged. "I dunno."

That knowledge gave me a new appreciation for my pa. He was a hard worker, but as far as I could tell from our humble lifestyle, his ventures were just enough to keep us in clothes and food.

I lay back on the log and felt the cool sponginess of the moss beneath me. Pa climbed up to sit next to me, and I gazed up at the dome of trees above, swaying gently in the afternoon breeze. They were giants.

"Seems like it might be awfully hard to get these trees down into the valley," I said.

Pa nodded in agreement. "Yep. Sure would be. But that don't mean the Beaufort Lumber Company ain't tried to git me to sell this place to 'em." He slapped my pant leg lightly as if I was a grown-up who understood these things.

I sprang up to a sitting position. "How'd they think they're gonna get these big ol' trees down into town?"

Pa pointed at the waterfalls. "Alls they have to do is cut a railroad up here and drag them with a skidder to the water. The falls would do the rest. All that water would land them in a spot where the railroad could take 'em to town."

It was hard for me to grasp that trees the size of churches could be cut down and dragged to the mill in Hickory Run. If just one of them was cut, it would take the rest of them down in the process.

Sensing I didn't believe him, Pa said, "I've seen 'em do it on the other side of this mountain."

2

Ma had painted a picture of a foxes' den and wanted me to take it to Hickory Run and sell it to the owners of Foster's Inn. She'd been working on the painting for weeks after Sam and I discovered the den while wandering in the woods looking for firewood. The den was in a clearing of older gnarled trees, their roots growing over boulders that scarred the mountain landscape as if they'd been tossed there by giants. One of the boulders was tilted, leaving a passage for the foxes' den. Once I'd found them, I kept strict vigil over the henhouse because I liked the idea that this little family had made themselves a home in our woods, and I liked to watch them play. We didn't dare tell Pa about it because he'd kill them.

Instead, we told Ma, and she wanted to paint the fox pups. One day, we all hiked there and perched ourselves on a ledge of rock overlooking the spot where they lived. Ma spread a blanket on the ground, arranged her easel and canvas, and organized her paints.

Sam and I sat patiently on the edge of the ledge, listening to the sounds of the woods, while Ma painted the scenery. Then it happened. A little red head popped out of the hole in the ground. And another. Ma never said a word. She knelt in front of her canvas; glossy brown eyes determined. Her brush hung poised over the canvas, her mouth parting slightly in concentration.

She toiled over the painting after putting Nellie to bed, dabbing with her brush, recreating the scene and the way the sunlight shafted through the forest canopy, the tinged gray and blue boulders, the darkness of the foxes' den, capturing the mischief in the pups' eyes.

At the time, Pa was living in town, helping to build the community hall, so he didn't know about the painting or the den. She wanted to sell it before he came home. We asked Cousin Floyd, who lived up the road and went to town regularly, if we could catch a ride on one of his twice weekly visits to town. Ma wrapped the painting in burlap, placed it alongside Floyd, and Sam and I climbed into the flatbed of his truck one morning. The road was bumpy, even though Floyd and some of Pa's other cousins had recently cleared it of vines and brush and patched up the holes that formed after spring storms. We clutched the sides of the flatbed, staying put as best as we could, but it didn't help much. By the time we got to town, I had dust in my mouth, my head pounded from being tossed around, and I was dizzy.

Floyd dropped us off in front of Foster's Inn. "You boys meet me back here at exactly four o'clock. Got it?"

"Sure thing," I said.

"And stay out of trouble," he said.

We retrieved our packs, which Ma had filled with sandwiches and apples. Floyd put the truck in gear and left us in a cloud of smoke.

Foster's Inn had a large sign in the window, calling for the development of a National Park in the Smoky Mountains. "A park will bring clean air, tourism, and economic opportunity!" it said in bold letters.

Sam tugged my arm impatiently. I followed him inside to find Mr. Foster. The inn was just as I remembered it: plush, warm, golden, with ceilings as high as a young beech tree. I warned Sam not to talk as we walked to the front desk with the painting.

Mr. Foster stood behind the desk in a sharp suit and tie. He slicked back his hair with oil and wore cologne I could smell from five feet away. At first, he didn't recognize me—it had been over a year since I'd last come with Ma—but when he did, he glanced over our heads in search of her.

I lowered my voice, so he knew I was serious, and laid the painting on the counter between us. "Hello, Mr. Foster. I'm Ben Taylor. My ma asked me to give this to you. She couldn't come this time."

He hesitated at first, then opened the burlap to reveal the painting, which was about the width of his shoulders. He contemplated it with admiration. "This will surely sell," he said. "Tell her I'll hang it in the parlor and see if we get any offers."

"Thank you," I said.

I pulled Sam along behind me toward the exit, but he was lured into looking into the parlor, just the way I had been last time I visited. It had a chandelier covered in glass pendants that twinkled in the electric lights, several wingback chairs, a velvet couch, and a fireplace that would fill up the back wall of our cabin. People drank their mid-morning tea.

"Holy smokes!" he said, gaping into the room.

"Come on," I said. "We can't go in there."

Tired and hungry from the long ride, we planted ourselves underneath a large oak outside the inn to eat our sandwiches and watch the comings and goings of the town-folk. The late June sun beat down on the unpaved road. Cars, horses, wagons, and people kicked up the dirt, sending it into the air in clouds of honey-colored dust that swirled in the wind. The inn sat on the main street of Hickory Run. Pa had told me once that Hickory Run was like a teenager busting out of his pants. There was so much energy. A few men ambled by on crutches, some with missing limbs as a result of their service in the Great War. Mrs. Reed, our Cherokee neighbor, and her daughter passed by with baskets on their backs filled to the brim with plants from the forest, headed to the general store to barter for supplies.

A group of tourists stepped off the porch of the inn, carrying large packs on their backs. I hadn't thought women had the time to go on leisure hikes in the mountains, but they bounced off the steps with their bobbed hair, knickers, long wool socks, and sturdy boots, dressed just like the men they flirted with.

The ladies of the town bustled with children in tow, in and out of the general store and the post office. We gawked at the children. How similar to us, yet different. Their clothes store-bought and new. They didn't wear dreary browns and grays made from rough-hewn wools and cotton as we did. The girls wore dresses the color of the sky, the boys plaid shirts. The ladies wore fancy hats with feathers sticking out of them. As they passed us, I saw the children watching us with a mixture of envy and contempt. One boy said to his mother, "Hillbillies."

The mother's eyes narrowed to slits as if we'd jump up and steal her bag. I don't think Sam heard because he was gawking at everybody, his mouth was half-open as he munched on his sandwich.

"Come on," I said. "Let's go see the general store. Ma gave me a nickel and told me to buy her some thread and a needle for sewing."

The Stewart general store was first built in 1850 and dominated the main street until it burned down in 1920 (some say it was arson), then was rebuilt the following year with the insurance money. Its pine plank floors creaked when walked on and it ran the length of a large barn. It was filled with gadgets, household goods, and foods that we had never had the luxury of trying.

A woman sat at one of their new sewing machines, watching a demonstration by Mrs. Stewart, the owner's wife. The customer asked a lot of questions as she tested the device. It was attached to an electric motor, and the lady gasped, astonished by its speed. At one point, she bungled up the fabric she was stitching because she couldn't keep up. I thought about Ma at her machine, which was operated by a treadle and thought how this new machine would save her lots of time.

Because I'd dawdled so long, I lost sight of Sam. I ran from one end of the store to the other, searching until I found him at the counter, wantonly staring at the big jars of candy sticks.

"Can we buy one of these?"

"No. I gotta get this needle and thread Ma wanted."

The nickel Ma had given me was burning a hole in my pocket. How I would have loved to buy one of the bright red, green, or caramel candies with swirls of taffy. My mouth watered, remembering the sweet gooey taste of them from Christmas.

I handed the paper Ma had given me to the clerk, and he found what she sought, placed the items in a small bag, and took my nickel. That was the end of it as far as I could see. But as we swung around to leave, we found ourselves smack in front of Pa's sister, Aunt Cornelia Beaufort, and her twin sons, Jimmy Jr., and John. Our cousins.

"Why, hello," she said, startled. "Aren't you Bob's sons? Ben and Sam?"

"Yes, ma'am," I replied. "Hello, Aunt Cornelia."

We didn't see much of Aunt Cornelia or her family, even though her husband, Jimmy Sr., owned the local lumber company. They lived in a fancy house at the end of the lane and never invited us over. I'm not sure my Pa would've accepted an invitation anyway. He didn't talk as if he liked Jimmy Beaufort Sr.

Aunt Cornelia's head canted back. "You remember me, then?"

"Yes."

It had been a long time since I'd seen her. She never came up the mountain anymore, even to visit her sisters, but the last time I was in town Ma had pointed her out to me, walking in the distance. She had seen Ma and me, standing at the bottom of the porch steps at Foster's Inn, but she hadn't made the effort to cross the street and say hello, and neither had Ma.

"I don't think you've met your cousins. This is Jimmy Jr., and this is John."

They were my age with icy blue eyes that penetrated like arrows. Each mumbled a hello, peering around us toward the candy.

"Show your manners, boys. Shake hands," Aunt Cornelia instructed.

We reached out to shake half-heartedly. Jimmy Jr. wiped his on his trousers after shaking my hand, so I did the same.

"What brings you to town?" she said, her eyes like Pa's, dark brown and framed by lush lashes, but shadowed. And unlike Pa's eyes, hers were flat; they lacked joy. She was a decade younger than Pa but appeared older.

"Cousin Floyd brought us. We had to deliver a painting for Ma at Foster's Inn and buy her something here at the store."

"Your mother still finds time to paint with all of you children scurrying underfoot?" Aunt Cornelia's lips curled into a crooked smile.

"Yes, ma'am," I replied.

"Where are your shoes?" Jimmy Jr. said so loud that other people looked down at my feet.

I felt the blood rise to my cheeks.

Sam came to my defense. "He ain't got any. Left them at the cliff where the big trees grow!"

This made the twins burst out laughing, until Aunt Cornelia, sensing my distress, shushed them.

"Your Pa still goes up there 'sengin', does he?"

I was shocked by how she said that, with a twang like Pa. I had forgotten for a moment that she was a Taylor and had visited the grove of trees above the waterfall, with its crop of ginseng.

"I, uh…don't know," I said, keeping Pa's secret.

She smirked. "Would you boys like a candy?" I supposed she was making amends for her twins' bad behavior.

"Theys…theys…" John spoke so quietly it was hard to grasp that he had a stutter, but he was trying to say something to Jimmy Jr. "Gon…"

It was painful to watch him try to express just a few syllables.

"Of course, they want some candy," Cornelia said, sighing.

"No, thank—" I started, but Sam interrupted me. "Yes!"

I elbowed him, which made him cry out and the twins laugh.

Aunt Cornelia didn't wait for me to protest; she sashayed to the counter, her dress the color of a goldfinch flowing like sheets in the wind. The hem showed off her calves, as thin as a willow branch.

What a contrast she was to her sisters. Aunt Bertie and the others wore stiff gingham dresses that fell to the floor. Even Ma's skirts didn't show much of her legs. And the shoes! My aunts' and Ma's shoes were made of dark leather that buttoned in front; their heels low to the ground so they didn't teeter over while doing their chores. Cornelia's, however, were blue and high-heeled, and the top of each one festooned with a bow.

My other aunts were stocky, but Cornelia was as thin as a rail. And she had a nervous energy, skittish like a hen. She asked for a jar of Aunt Ophelia's honey, then motioned to the candy jars. The owner reached in and took out four sticks. She turned to hand us each one with a false smile.

We thanked her, and I shoved Sam out the door, ashamed of taking it, ashamed of not having shoes. I pulled Sam along as we went in search of Pa.

The new hall was a two-story structure by the railroad station. Beaufort's Lumber Company was financing the building, a community service, or so the signs staked into the ground around the building claimed. Quite a few men worked on the roof, hammering, and shouting at each other. We saw Pa coming down a ladder to retrieve more shingling and ran to him.

"Pa!" Sam shouted, throwing his arms around Pa's legs.

"What're you two doing here?" Pa said, joy mingled with worry in his voice. "Is Ma ok? The girls?"

"Everything's fine, Pa," I said. "Ma wanted me to take a painting to Mr. Foster and Sam wanted to see the town. Cousin Floyd gave us a ride in his wagon."

Pa didn't appear reassured, but he scooped up Sam anyway and gave him a bear hug. "I wish I could spend the day with ye both, but I gotta work. We're almost finished with the roof, and I'll be home soon."

"Where are you living?" Sam asked.

Pa pointed in the direction of the woods. "Back in there, we all set up tents. It's not so bad."

"We saw Aunt Cornelia, Pa. And she bought us candy!" Sam said.

Pa turned stern. "Is that so?"

"Yeah." Sam wouldn't shut up. "And we met her boys, the twins. They weren't very nice to Bennie. They laughed because he didn't have shoes on."

Pa's mouth puckered, and he was about to say something when a burly man with a greasy hat came up and barked at him to get back to work. Pa shooed us away. "Tell Ma I miss her and the girls," he called to us.

I missed him dearly and hoped he'd make enough money so that he wouldn't ever have to work in town again.

We sat back under the oak by Foster's and licked our candy until our hands were sticky. Sam dozed off as I watched the world go by. Ma told me once that if I wanted to go to school in town, I might be able to live with Aunt Cornelia. If only Pa would ask. But how would I ever be able to manage at school living with Aunt Cornelia and those awful boys?

When Cousin Floyd came by at four, the passenger seat of his cab was filled with something, and his flatbed covered with a canvas tarp. "Don't touch anything," he said as we squirmed our way to the back of the flatbed, grabbing onto the sideboards. I heard the tinkling of the glass and snuck a peek under the canvas to find four crates of empty jugs.

3

By the time we got to the place where Hickory Creek sliced the road in half, the skies had darkened. We mistook the rumble of the thunder for the motor as it crossed over the slats of the wide plank bridge. Moisture-laden clouds loomed, dipping low into the forest.

"Storm coming!" Floyd twisted around and hollered from the cab. "Pull that canvas over your heads."

We huddled under the canvas. As we climbed higher up the road toward our cabin, the rain pelted us. Sam began panting, clutching my arm. He scooted closer to me whenever there was a clap of thunder. I wondered if Floyd would seek shelter.

As if reading my thoughts, he shouted. "Ain't nowhere to go, boys! The trees are swinging like crazy in this wind. We'll just keep on moving."

After that, we couldn't hear anything besides the howling wind and occasional crack of thunder. We clutched the canvas over our heads as best we could, but the rain seeped through along the seams, soaking into our clothes. Sam shivered. I couldn't put my arm around him because I was holding on for dear life. My arms ached from the effort, and my knuckles turned white and cold from clutching the canvas. A burst of wind caught a corner and it flapped wildly. I shot up and grabbed the end of it before we lost the whole thing to the wind. Sam's head was drenched. I braced myself against the wind and rain. Finally, I saw our cabin coming in and out of view in the watery distance.

"Hold on, Sam. You'll be all right," I tried to assure him.

Ma came running out to greet us, her skirts flailing in the wind. She didn't bother to speak to Floyd or me, she reached for Sam, wrenched him out of my arms, and carried him into the cabin. I jumped out, and

Floyd cut the engine. When I got inside, Ma sat by the hearth in front of Sam, stripping off his clothes and rubbing him down with a blanket.

"Get your clothes off," she said to me.

I gladly obliged. Floyd stepped inside quietly, shame-faced, his clothes dripping, and his hat in hand.

"Why didn't you seek cover?" Ma snapped.

"I couldn'," Floyd said. "It would have been dangerous to stop in the forest."

"You could have found a cave or something," Ma said. "My boys are soaking wet and cold and Sam…" She choked back tears as she pulled Sam onto her lap, wrapping her arms around him, rocking and cooing. His lips turned blue, and his teeth chattered.

I draped our wet pants and shirts over the iron grate by the fire and went to the loft to retrieve dry clothes for Sam and me. While I was up there, I heard Ma scolding Floyd and him replying defensively, then the door to the cabin slammed shut, which meant he was either waiting it out in the barn or taking a chance and continuing his journey another five miles up the road to his cabin. I thought it was not very kind of Ma, considering it was still raining.

Sam's cough came back that night. His skin was cold and clammy, and he shivered. When his coughing got so loud it woke my sisters, Ma came up and carried him downstairs to the sick room. As I fell in and out of sleep, I heard her speaking softly to him. In the morning, I went to find them, and Ma was still by his side with dark shadows around her eyes. Sam slept but his breathing was labored as he struggled to get air in and out of his lungs. His small face peeped out from under the covers. His lips weren't blue anymore, but his complexion was like ash.

"Floyd should have found cover," she said accusingly.

Nellie started to cry. I went to get her out of her crib and the smell of urine made me gag. She had soaked through the mattress. I pulled her out, changed her diaper, and yanked the mattress out to the front porch to air. Mary and Rachel sensed the tension and made breakfast without a fuss. We ate in silence as Ma came in and out of the kitchen to fetch warm water for Sam's tea. Without being told, we went to the fields to see if the corn hadn't washed away in the rain and to hoe while the ground was soft.

"Why'd you have to go to town anyway?" Mary said as we dug and pulled at the weeds around the corn.

"Ma asked us to go. How was I supposed to know it would rain?" It felt good to sweat. As the drops fell from my brow, it relieved my tension.

Rachel walked in front of us, on the lookout for snakes, so we didn't inadvertently step on any while hoeing. She was better at it than any of us. Being three feet from the ground had its advantages. When she spied one coiled in a ball ahead of us, she'd tug at my arm and I'd whack it with my hoe then pitch it to the side. I must've killed six snakes that day. Admittedly, I took some pleasure in taking out my frustration on the poor critters.

When we got back to the cabin, we about collapsed on the front porch. None of us wanted to go inside for fear something terrible happened while we were gone. It was quiet. Ma came out, taut-faced, exhausted, Nellie gripping her skirt.

"Ben, you need to go to Aunt Bertie and get some medicine for Sam."

It took me all day to get to their cabin. Aunt Peg was at the front steps of their porch, waving her arms in welcome at the sight of me loping over the hill.

"My you're all grow'd up, Ben! Just look at ye standin' thar, almost as tall as me. How old are ye now?"

"Thirteen."

"My, my. You look older than that!"

The yeasty smell of baking bread permeated the air. The cabin was clean and tidy. The main room had an enormous fireplace and hearth that could have fit two small children standing up. The aunts had blue curtains in the windows, a spinning wheel, and a loom resting in the corner. There were four bedrooms off the main living area. The sisters each had the luxury of occupying their own room with one open for guests. And the kitchen was built off the back end of the house so that the smoke from the stove didn't clog the air.

It was apparent my aunts lived well. They had stocked cupboards, dresses without patches, leather shoes without holes in them.

The Taylor sisters were industrious. They kept bees, and their honey was renowned in the region for being the best. Aunt Ophelia had shown me the magic of beekeeping in a grove of black gum tupelo trees. The hives occupied the hollow center of sawed-off logs from rotted gum trees. Ophelia capped the top of the stumps with pieces of wood. She anchored sticks inside so the bees could build combs and carved two holes, one for the entrance, one for the exit.

She took a jar of honey out of her apron pocket and mixed some of it with water in a bucket. I watched, fascinated, as she poured the honey water over her head, soaking her hair. She told me to stand back while she lit an oil-soaked rag at the end of a stick, and she smoked the bees out from their hive, then reached inside the stump with a gloved hand, pulling out a comb filled with bees. They swarmed her head, feeding on the honey water that dripped off her hair.

She wasn't scared, just brushed them off and dumped the comb into a bucket without making a sound, the bees simply a nuisance, and repeated her actions at several stumps until the bucket filled with combs.

Back at the cabin, a pot of boiling water sat above the fire. We placed the combs over a linen cloth, steamed the wax off and crushed the combs, filling a large bucket with the gooey, rich golden honey. It dripped through my fingers and when I placed a finger in my mouth, the honey coated my tongue like a warm blanket. She took the combs to the stove where she boiled them down to make candles.

After we had extracted all we could from the combs, the aunts put the rich liquid into glass jars. They tied strips of red calico cloth they cut from an old dress around the lids and placed them in boxes for transport to town and Stewart's General Store. Mr. Stewart paid them a dollar a jar and resold it for two. Selling the honey to the local store wasn't the only way they managed. Honey was a commodity to be bartered. They paid the men that brought the hollowed-out gum tree stumps with honey. If a local fellow cut a supply of wood for them for a week, he got a jar of honey. Heck, even the jars and cans they used were paid for with honey. If they needed a new roof, they paid for it with honey.

If it wasn't honey, it was herbs. They had several gardens, including an extensive herb garden that Aunt Bertie maintained. She was famous for her herbal remedies, and people came from miles away for cures. And if they didn't go to her, she went to them. I'd seen her at Sunday services, yapping away with fellow churchgoers about what ailed them. She'd reach into a burlap pouch she carried full of herbs and pass them out like candy to a child. If a woman was having a baby or a neighbor was dying, they called on Bertie before they called on a doctor.

Aunt Bertie took me to her garden to collect the herbs for my brother's cough. She was covered head to foot in a gingham dress, stained at the hem with mud and dirt. Her sturdy shoes clomped along the footpath made of large cobblestones. She had a wide-brimmed straw hat clamped over her brow. Her girth took up most of the path, and when she bent over to pinch off the end of a plant, I could barely see around her. Her brows turned into one dark line across her forehead when she frowned. As we walked the cobble path, she told me what each plant was good for.

"That thar is where I grow Bee Balm to cure sore throats." Her pointer finger was stained sickly yellow from pulling at weeds.

On and on she went about her herbs to the point that I started yawning.

"Am I keeping you up, boy?"

"Sorry, it's just I'm tired out from all the knowledge you're trying to stuff my head with. I'll never remember it all."

"Well," she clucked. "Not everybody is made for this type of thin'. Maybe one of your sisters would like to learn. I'd like to pass down the knowledge to somebody."

"Why don't you write it all down for somebody, so you don't ever lose it?"

She regarded me, sideways, like I had committed a great sin.

"I don't have to. It's all in my head. Why'd you even suggest such a thin'?"

"Well, then," I said. "You could ask Mary to visit and she might be able to write things down for ye. She could even draw the herbs while you describe what they're good for."

Aunt Bertie scratched her chin. "Hmmm."

I noticed she clipped off the last syllables of her words. "It" became "Hit" and "Just" "Jist". Pa would do the same thing, and my ma would correct him.

He would point to a field. "Thars where my pa planted his first patch of corn."

"You mean *there is where*," Ma would say.

"I don't need ye correctin' me," he said. "You're from the north. Ye'll talk funny."

I thought about that. Ma had shown me on a map once where she was from, a state named Pennsylvania. That's where she went to school, a teacher's college she called it, where she studied math, English, and art. She told me it was much colder there, and the snow was so deep in places you could ski down hills on it. She said they had ponds bigger than our spring pools. They called them lakes and people could skate across them when they froze.

I figured that's why she talked so fast. Maybe up north people were in such a hurry to speak about things because it was cold outside, and they didn't have time to linger on the front porch for long to tell everybody their news. Ma said mountain people 'drawl', and I knew the way she said it she didn't approve. Maybe it was because it could take half a day when a neighbor or family relation stopped by to tell you the news.

That night Bertie sat in her rocker by the fire stroking the back of the orange tabby she'd found yowling on the path that led to the church. "Hit was half-starved and needed a home. That's good luck," she told me. "To bring a starvin' cat home. Means your house won't never burn down."

I had no idea how she knew that, but it was just one of the many tidbits of knowledge she'd learned throughout her life. Another one I heard from her was if a bird built a nest with a strand of your hair, you'd have headaches until the nest fell apart. I wondered if she used this one as an excuse if her potions didn't cure someone who had headaches.

Aunt Peg glanced down at my bare feet.

"You outgrew your shoes?" she asked.

"Yes, ma'am," I said. "I outgrew them fast. I'm getting some new ones for school."

Aunt Peg tssked and turned her attention to a quilt she was stitching. "You packed that medicine for Sam?" she asked Aunt Bertie.

"Yes, I did. Tell your ma to steep the herbs in hot water. When it cools, she can give him some tea. Best to wait an hour for the tonic to bleed out of the plant."

"My ma could use some medicine," I said. All attention turned on me.

"What d' ye mean?" Aunt Bertie said.

"Well, she's been…uh," I stammered, suddenly self-conscious about my decision to inform my aunts about my ma's recent bout of vomiting.

My aunts all knit their brows.

"Well, it's nothin', I guess," I said. "She's been sick before. I'm gonna go to bed now." And I headed up into the loft but stayed awake long enough to overhear their conversation. They talked about Ma and what was probably ailing her, although I could only catch snippets of what they said. They talked about a woman who wanted to live with them, a scientist who knew about Aunt Bertie and her magic herbs and wanted to record them. Since they had an extra room to stay in, she'd pay them room and board.

And then I heard them talk about Aunt Cornelia and my ears pricked.

"I tell ye I saw her in Hickory Run, she tried to avoid me, but I caught up to her." I heard Aunt Peg say. "One of her eyes were half shut and black and blue. Jimmy Beaufort is no better than a varmint! And we shoulda never let Cornelia run off with 'im!"

"The Devil!" Aunt Ophelia chimed in.

While I packed to leave in the morning, Aunt Bertie pulled me aside and told me to follow her to the garden. There, she placed a small satchel of linen filled with an herb that smelled like mint when I crushed it in my hand.

"Give this to your ma," she said to me in a conspiratorial tone. "She'll know what to do with it."

"Is it for Sam?" I asked.

She shook her head. "I put his medicine in your pack. You keep this in your pocket until you find a time to give it to her in private. She'll know what it's for. Just don't tell yer pa."

4

While walking home, I recalled the way Aunt Bertie had handed me the satchel of herbs for Ma, looking sideways to make sure no one was watching her, putting it into the palm of my hand, curling my fingers around it for safekeeping. I felt the satchel burning a hole in my pocket. I clasped it protectively and caught a waft of mint.

I heard Sam's racking cough as I approached our cabin. Ma stood on the edge of the porch, baby Nellie on one hip, and a broom in the other. Relieved to see me, she barely asked me to recount my journey, just took the package of herbs for Sam.

"It's not getting any better," she said. "If this doesn't work, you'll have to go into town and get the doctor."

I followed Ma to the kitchen; my mind filled with all of the images from the past day that needed to tumble out. Ma handed me Nellie. "Watch her while I boil the water."

I began telling her about the honey-making and how nice the Aunts' cabin looked, and she shushed me. "Get Nellie out of here. Go play," she said.

I carried Nellie with me to the loft to retrieve the journal Ma had given me for my thirteenth birthday, then out to the porch and sat her down at my feet.

"Stay put," I said. "And don't put that dirt in your mouth. Here." I handed her an old rag doll. "Play with this instead."

She took it gingerly out of my hand and whipped it around in the air before tossing it. Laughing, she picked herself up and waddled after it to throw again.

"Just stay put," I commanded again. Keeping track of her out of the corner of my eye, I turned my attention to my journal. After what only seemed like a few minutes, Nellie was bored with the doll. She came to where I sat and tugged at my pencil. Frustrated, I went to search for my sisters Mary and Rachel, to put them in charge. I found them in the back of the cabin feeding the chickens.

"Here, take care of her," I said.

"We don't want to!" Mary cried.

Mary was a year younger than me and didn't like being bossed around. Rachel was only five and easier to persuade.

"I gotta help Ma," I lied. "Here." I handed Nellie off to Rachel. "She can help you chase the chickens into the coop."

I went back into the cabin to find Ma. She was in the sick room, where they kept my brother Sam when he wasn't feeling well. He was gagging on the tonic Ma prepared using Aunt Bertie's herbs. Poor Sam, ten years old and he looked the same age as Rachel. The consumption was wasting him away. On his good days, he would trail behind me, and we'd scout the woods for nuts and berries. He was never cross and hardly cried except when the pain in his lungs was unbearable. Even then, it was more like the mew of a lamb.

I watched Ma coax him into drinking the tonic. He sipped, sputtered, hacked up phlegm that Ma caught in a small handkerchief she kept by his bedside. Then he lay his head back on the pillow and gasped. "It tastes like dandelion," he said.

"I'll stay with him, Ma," I said.

Her hands trembled, and she choked back a sob as she pressed her lips on my head. "Thank you, Bennie. I have to make supper, but I'll be right here if you need me."

The skin around Sam's eyelids was yellow, and his chest heaved air in and out of his lungs in raspy waves.

"You want to hear about the aunts?" I whispered in his ear.

His eyes popped open. Sam had the longest lashes of anyone I'd ever known. They lay like feathers on his face when his eyes closed. He nodded his head.

I told him how Aunt Ophelia coaxed the bees out of the hive using smoke and honey water; how I helped fix their fence because the groundhogs tore it up; how they sheared the wool off the sheep that roamed the mountain; and about the big spinning wheel they used to spin the thread. His face relaxed, and I got him to smile, which made his lips crack wide open and bleed a little. He licked his dry, cracked lips, and I brought the tonic to them. He waved it away.

"Can you get me some water?"

I filled a glass from the pitcher on his bedside table and helped him drink it.

"Aunt Bertie said you have to finish. She said it will take away your coughing," I told him.

I placed the tonic back to his lips, and he grimaced.

That night was one of the first in a long while that Sam slept soundly. He made it through without a coughing fit. Ma was up before everyone cooking breakfast. She was humming, floating around the kitchen. I yawned and sat down at the table to watch her knead bread.

"We've got flour," she said with a broad smile on her face. "Cousin Floyd stopped by while you were gone. He had our mail, and I got eight dollars from Foster's Inn. Someone bought a whole assortment of my cards. So, the next time he went into town, I asked him to pay our bill at the store plus buy flour, sugar, butter, and salt. Floyd said the Fosters are planning to build another inn."

"Really?" I said. "There ain't that many tourists needing a place to stay in Hickory Run are there?"

"Don't say ain't." She furrowed her brows and pummeled the dough.

"Why it's just an old lumber mill town," I muttered.

"It won't always be that way," she said, "That community hall will bring in preachers and speakers. There's a new shop that sells bolts of fabric and a free library."

"I can see why we'd want to listen to a preacher, but why a speaker? What's to speak about?"

She didn't answer the question, continued humming while tossing and punching the dough. Suddenly, her face changed. She pressed her fist to her mouth, gagged, and ran out the door to vomit over the porch rail.

I rushed up behind her and patted her back. "You all right, Ma?"

"Oh, dear. I'm sorry about that," she said.

Her face was pale, and her thick brown hair had come loose from the pins. I left her leaning over the rail while I went into the kitchen to retrieve some water.

"Here," I said, holding out a rag soaked with the cold spring water. She pressed it to her head. As the color returned to her face, I thought about the satchel of herbs from Aunt Bertie. I knew I should offer it to her, but I had a strange feeling that the minty concoction smelling up my bed wasn't any good. Why else would Bertie tell me to keep it a secret from Pa?

"She'll know what to do with it," she'd whispered in my ear.

Nellie woke up and started crying to be let out of her crib.

"Where's Pa?" I asked.

"He's still working in town," she said. "Since he's not back yet…" She glanced at the dirt road that led to town as if she thought her luck would run out any minute, and he'd come tramping back with nothing. All clear. She turned her attention back to me, brightening. "He must have gotten hired for another day."

"But you just said you made eight dollars—"

"We needed that for food," she said sharply. "I don't want to talk about it."

I was mad at Ma, not just because she'd been short with me since Sam got sick, but because Pa was still working in town and I was responsible for his chores. Like making sure there was always wood stacked by the hearth, and the hencoop was closed up tight every night to prevent foxes from getting at them, that the water buckets were filled and—

"Bennie," Ma's voice startled me. "You're daydreaming again. I have to get Nellie out of her crib. Go wake your sisters up and start your chores."

I trudged back to the loft to wake my sisters up. Sitting down on the edge of my bed, I reached under my pillow and felt the lump of herbs in the satchel.

"Wake up!" I called.

Mary stretched like a cat. "What's that delicious smell? Is that bread?" Mary had the prettiest eyes of all of us. She took them from Pa and enhanced the glint.

"Ma says we have to fetch water from the spring," I said.

Their faces fell. "Where's Pa?"

"Still working in town on that community hall," I said.

Rachel's faced scrunched in confusion. "Work?"

I tousled her golden hair, soft like sheep wool after it'd been carded. Rachel reached up. I pulled her up in my arms for a hug then set her down on the bed. "Come on, let's eat some of Ma's bread with Aunt Ophelia's honey."

Nellie was already strapped into her chair, slobbering on a piece of bread. I couldn't help myself from observing our kitchen and sizing it up against the aunts'. It was smaller, which seemed unfair, given that we had a bigger family.

"How come Pa's sisters got his grandpa's cabin?"

Ma's eyes went wide. "What?" she said.

My face felt hot. "Well, I was just wondering that's all. Seems like we could use that extra bedroom since Sam and me have to share the loft with our sisters, and Nellie's crib is in your room." Ma's glare had me sinking in my chair. Mary and Rachel went on eating, not understanding what I was getting at.

Ma sniffed. "It's just the way it is. When me and Pa married, Pa moved out. His sisters stayed. That's all."

"I heard them talking last night that some science woman wants to rent their extra room."

Ma's brows lifted. "A scientist?"

I nodded. "She heard about Aunt Bertie and her herbs and wants to record them. They don't want her to come."

"They call people who study plants *botanists*." She emphasized the word so that I would understand she was teaching me something, then turned her back to me and muttered, "They don't need the money."

"Well, I heard Aunt Bertie say—"

"No more talking." I had worn her out with my jabbering. "Eat! And then take Rachel with you. I have chores to do and can't watch her."

5

My mother was one of the few in the Taylor family who could read and write past the fifth-grade level. Her parents were teachers who once worked at the school in Hickory Run before returning to Pennsylvania. That's how she met Pa. She said they met at a church gathering, and he pestered her into marrying him. The way he told it *she* fell for *him*. I think Ma just didn't want to go back to Pennsylvania. I never met my grandparents on her side, but she never said anything nice about them.

One thing she did learn from them though was that having an education would improve our opportunities and she was determined that all the children would receive as good an education as possible.

My father and his sisters had attended school sporadically throughout their childhood. But it took a huge effort on their part to travel the distance to town. And when the weather wasn't cooperating, or there were chores to be done so they could eat, school was the last thing they worried about.

What they learned about reading and writing was just enough to sign and pay a bill. Even then, they quite often traveled miles to see my mother and had her read over any legal documents, court summons, certificates, and that sort of thing to make sure the government wasn't hoodwinking them. Suspicion of educated people ran strong in the Taylor family, although more than once they depended on my mother's education to get them out of a bind.

She also taught me the importance of observation, which came in handy when conjuring up a feeling or image experienced hours, days, or weeks prior. Sitting out on the porch one morning, we'd stolen a moment away from household chores. Ma searched the woods for inspiration and asked me to describe the scene in front of us. I followed her gaze.

"I guess I'd say it is real pretty. So pretty, I wish I could draw it just like you can," I said.

She clucked and stayed focused on the woods. "That's not what I mean, Bennie. How would you describe the scene if I had to draw it and couldn't see it for myself?"

I observed the leafless forest. The lacey dogwood flowers were hope in a sky filled with gloomy clouds. Bursts of purple flowers from the redbud competed with the dogwoods for attention. Below them, the forest floor was a carpet of hepatica and violets with dots of yellow trout lily reaching for the sun.

When I told her what I saw, described exactly that way, her eyes glowed, and she tussled my hair. "That was good," she said.

. . .

Pa worked in town most of that spring, coming home on Sundays. So, it was a surprise when he showed up one evening during the week. I was sitting on the porch with Sam helping him learn his numbers when I spotted Pa coming up the path from the direction of town in the early evening.

"Ma!" I ran inside to tell her. "Pa's home!"

I sprinted off the porch to fling myself at him. The girls all came out with Ma, baby Nellie perched on her hip as usual. The look on Ma's face wasn't particularly friendly. The first thing she said to him when he reached the porch was "Did they fire you?"

He picked up Rachel and swung her around. "Nope," he said. "We finished what we could today and ran out of planks. They told us we could take the night off." He reached for a kiss, and Ma obliged.

We sat around the fire that evening and listened as Pa gave us the latest on the town folk. I could tell by the way he described everyone he thought them odd. "The ladies walk around with the funniest-looking hats," he said.

Mary perked up. "What kind of hats?"

"Oh, they come down on their foreheads like this." He flapped the brim of his hat down and pressed it against his cheeks. "And they have all kinds of fancy decoratin' on 'em. The young girls are wearin' 'em too. And their hair is cut short."

"How short?" Ma fiddled with her hair.

He brought his hand to her neck and placed it right under her chin. "To here."

"You'd have to cut off all your hair to look like them, Ma," Mary said.

"I almost forgot!" Pa said, jumping out of his chair and reaching for his pack. He pulled out a newspaper. "I got the Knoxville Tribune for ye."

Ma spread the paper over her lap and opened it up. Advertisements took up half the page. I leaned over her shoulder, trying to catch some of the headlines, feeding on the excitement that jumped off the pages, a glimpse into the comings and goings of the people that lived and worked outside Taylor Valley.

There were pictures of ladies in hats too big and clumsy for work around the cabin, men in suit coats and ties which looked ridiculous. One headline, in particular, caught my attention: *For Weak Women* – shouted the headline. *Take Cardui, the Woman's Tonic. You can rely on Cardui. Surely it will do for you what it has done for so many thousands of other women!*

And one testimony from a Mrs. Veste of Madison Heights, Virginia: *"I got down so weak, could hardly walk... just staggered around."*

My thoughts went to Ma, did all women have her problems too? And if all women had her problems, how did they survive? Well, according to this ad, Cardui was the answer. Mrs. Veste of Madison Heights had this to say about it: *"I read of Cardui, and after taking one bottle, I felt much better. I had an appetite and commenced eating."*

"Ma, what does commenced mean?" I asked, pointing to the word.

Ma slapped the paper shut. "Thank you for the paper," she said to Pa. "Bennie needs new reading material, but this isn't what I had in mind."

"You haven't been to town in a while," Pa said.

"I know I haven't." I could tell she wanted to say more but glanced at Sam and stopped.

"I'll give you a list of things to purchase at the store. With the money you're making, we can order a few books. And new shoes for Ben."

I was just as happy reading that paper as I was *Moby Dick*.

"You're better off here than in town anyways," Pa said. "It's noisy and dirty, and the water ain't clean."

Ma frowned at him.

"Well, it *isn't*," he said.

"Go wash up," Ma instructed us. "We're going to eat."

Sensing we might be missing something big, we reluctantly left to wash our hands. That night Sam got to sleep in the loft with us. He didn't cough as much, and his cheeks stayed rosy pink instead of deadly gray. As his mood brightened, so did everyone.

We settled into bed; Sam next to me. He pulled the satchel of herbs out from under my pillow.

"What's this?" he said, holding it up to his nose. "It smells funny."

I snatched it out of his hands and in the process, infused the air with the minty smell. "It's nothin'. Aunt Bertie gave it to me in case I get sick is all. Go to sleep."

He nestled down next to me, and I felt his soft, warm breath on my arms. It eased my worry to hear him breathing normally again. I put the satchel up on the shelf above our bed, wondering why I was torn about giving it to Ma. That ad for Cardui made it clear that women were weak and needed tonics. I wondered if I could talk Pa into letting me help him harvest those ginseng plants and make some money myself so I could buy her Cardui. It was in the newspaper. Educated people wrote the news. It must be safe. I wasn't sure why I didn't trust Aunt Bertie; she had after all saved Sam. But what made Sam sick was his consumption. That wasn't the same thing as what Ma had. What did Ma have anyway? Aunt Bertie was so secretive. Maybe, if I just asked Ma what was wrong with her, my mind would be at ease.

As I was about to doze off my eyes jerked open when I heard Ma say something sharp to Pa. I sat up in bed listening to Sam's soft breathing and strained to hear what was going on below.

"You can't take it to town," Ma said.

"It's not much to draw attention," Pa answered.

"You'll get us in trouble."

Pa said something I couldn't make out. Ma replied with angry words.

"You can't tell me what to do," Pa said. And that ended it.

He left the next day, but I didn't get to see him go. Ma kept a far away, fretful look about her all day.

▪ ▪ ▪

Our stores of dried herbs, beans, and cabbage leaves that Ma had hung up on lines around the cabin had been pulled down and used for cooking over the winter months. Just a few measly stems and a clove of garlic remained. It was time to harvest ramps. We scoured the woods behind our cabin for the bright green leaf poking through the dead stuff left over from fall. When we found a patch, we pounced on it with the spoons Ma gave us, careful to pull the root out with the leaf. This was the part Ma used in stews and soups. She said it had the ingredients to help make us all stronger after a long winter. I lifted the plant out of the ground, and it smelled like earth, strong with decay and life all wrapped up in a white bulb like a sheep's teat. I told Sam, and he barked with laughter.

"What are you two doing over there?" Ma asked. A shaft of light angled over her, tree pollen dancing in its wake. Her hair was pulled back in a bun, covered with a bonnet, a streak of dirt crossed under her eye where she had wiped at her cheek with a soiled hand. She was beautiful, sitting down on the forest floor, the pollen like sun-dust, her skirts splayed out, relaxed. She reminded me of an angel.

"Bennie told me ramps—" I clamped my hand over Sam's mouth.

"It's nothin' Ma," I called to her. "I was just sayin' the ramps smell like stinky feet."

Ma smiled brightly, put the stem of a ramp to her nose, and said, "Pungent. The word you're looking for is pungent." Suddenly the smile left her face as she noticed Sam's bare feet.

"Where are your shoes?" she said.

"I…I took 'em off. Bennie don't have any on."

"Bennie *doesn't*. Put your shoes back on, Sam. Right now." Her tone startled all of us. Rachel, Mary, even Nellie looked up.

Ma picked herself off the ground and brushed the leaves and debris off her skirts. "Let's get back to the cabin," she said. We walked back in silence: me barefoot, Sam with his shoes on.

Ma cooked the ramps in a stew with chicken, and their *pungent* odor filled the cabin. While we waited for dinner, Mary and Sam pulled out their McGuffey Readers, and I scanned the newspaper to write down new words on my lap-sized chalkboard. The chalk was down to a nub, another needed supply, because we shared the chalk. I had botanist and pungent and was searching for new words in the Knoxville paper when I came across something that wasn't familiar. I asked Ma to interpret.

"It says here that some moonshiners were caught making joy water," I said.

Her face twitched, and I knew I was on to something.

"What's joy water?"

"Whiskey," she said scornfully.

I turned back to the paper. "Says the revenue officers caught them making whiskey in their smokehouse and arrested them. They have to pay $500 for a bond. What's a bond?"

"A bond is what you have to pay to get out of jail."

"And why are the revenue officers arresting people for making whiskey? I thought everyone drinks whiskey."

"Because it is illegal," she said forcefully. "Write that word down." She planted her finger on my blackboard under the words I had already written. "You can't make illegal whiskey, and you can't sell it because of prohibition."

I went back to the papers looking for the word prohibition and found it in more than a few headlines. Seemed like the whole country was worried about prohibition. "What's prohibition?" I asked.

"It's the law," she replied, "that our Congress passed that says you can't sell or drink alcohol."

"But Pa does it, the aunts do it. You even put it in our medicine!" I protested.

"Well, it's one thing if you're taking it with your medicine."

I mulled over the newspapers, scanning the headlines, writing down words I didn't recognize, and quizzing Ma on what they meant. I realized the power the news had to bring the world into our little cabin and that I'd been cooped up like a hen for my whole life, my world no bigger than the circle of distant relatives—large as that circle was—on our lonely mountain road. When I had finished reading that paper from one end to the other, Ma pinned it to the wall, adding to the collection of newspapers she used as wallpaper and to keep the mountain winds from whisking through the chinks in the logs. I spent the rest of that week reading the walls of faded, yellowed papers, wondering why I hadn't taken notice of the headlines before: *Booze and Bolshevism*, *Tuberculosis Here in Your Own County*, *Two Negroes Lynched by Mob*.

∎

It was Saturday night, and Pa told us he'd be back, but as shadows crossed the cabin, Ma gave Sam and the girls soup and told them to get ready for bed. Her brow was creased, and she was out of sorts, cross with Sam and Rachel about minor things they'd done wrong. I offered to go down the road to see if Pa was coming.

"No," she said. "You stay put. It's getting too dark." She rested her palm on her belly and rubbed it absently, staring out the cabin window at the road.

"Are you feeling all right, Ma?"

She shook herself, sat down. "I just need some rest is all."

I went to the porch, hoping to see Pa coming with his pack on his back and a grin on his face. But as the sun crept behind the mountain casting everything into darkness, I knew he wasn't coming home that night. I glumly went back inside to eat with Ma.

I tossed and turned all night worried about him but woke up to hear his soft voice rising to the loft. I sprung out of bed, glad to hear Ma talking to him normal, like she wasn't mad. I thought that was a good sign for us as we headed to the Baptist church.

Pa and his cousins built the church, which also served as a school at one time. When Ma married Pa, she pioneered the idea of setting up a school. She petitioned the local government to make it official and was paid twenty dollars a month. She collected money from the wealthy people in town, people like the Beauforts, Fosters, and Stewarts who owned all the businesses, and used what she collected to pay for McGuffey Readers and chalkboards for the pupils. Everything went well until Ma got pregnant with me. That's when the parents made her quit. She was upset about it; I know because she told me she had wanted to bring me to school and keep teaching. But our kin and neighbors didn't approve and, according to Ma, didn't appreciate an education either. So, when they stopped coming, the schooling stopped as well.

The church sat along the side of a hill, in a central location for most of the mountain families. A large stone fireplace stood at one end, used only on the coldest days. Rows of uncomfortable wooden benches, enough for a small congregation, and a pulpit made of oak filled most of the space. Other than that, it wasn't much of a church. Not like the elegant ones I'd seen in picture books in cities like New York and Boston, where the church spires spiked the air like fir trees on the top of the forest. We had some regular preachers in the spring and summer months, but once winter came, you never knew who'd show up. The weather was always a deterrent.

That day we had Preacher Joe. I liked Preacher Joe. He'd been to our cabin a few times for dinner. I knew Ma found him interesting to listen to, though she didn't believe in always following his advice. She said he was a foot-washing Baptist and had nothing against that, but she had been brought up a Methodist and had no mind to try it herself.

Preacher Joe was rambling on about sin. He said it was sinful for a wife to contradict her husband. It was sinful for a husband to stray from his family responsibilities. He said to keep harmony in a house, the family had to agree to a whole lot of rules.

Ma sat with her hands folded in her lap, pressing her lips tight. She was wearing her bright blue bonnet, her favorite, the one she only wore to church so that it wouldn't get dirty. Nellie was on the floor playing with a rag doll. Sam fidgeted next to me picking at his fingernails. Rachel and Mary didn't pay attention either.

"And so," Preacher Joe boomed in a voice that could be heard up and down the mountain, "let us consider now, are we behaving as God wants us to? Has *commanded* us to?"

I saw the men nodding: some, the hard of hearing nodding off, others nodding their heads in agreement.

Pa had a big smile on his face. "Amen," he shouted as he wrapped his arm around the top of Ma's shoulders and squeezed. She wasn't smiling.

Afterward, everybody walked to the creek and picnicked in the cool glen at the bottom of a waterfall. Aunt Bertie and the other aunts came as well. Cousin Floyd showed up. We played hide and seek, and tug of war with a long grapevine someone cut down from a tree, enacting epic battles in the forest using tree limbs as swords with our cousins. The ladies brought canned beans, apple butter, bread, salted pork, dried meat, corn pones; we feasted on blankets laid on the ground by the waterfall.

On the way back to our cabin, Ma walked fast ahead of us. Only Mary was able to keep up with her, and she was skipping the whole way back. As we entered, I could hear Ma retching over the kitchen sink.

When Pa packed up to leave the next morning for town, I followed behind, begging him to let me go with him. "I could help you carry that pack," I said hopefully.

"No," he said. But I didn't give up. As he started down the road, I tagged along.

"But if you let me go, I may be able to work on the new hall with you, and we can make more money that way. Maybe buy some of that Cardui tonic for Ma!"

He braked for a moment and peered down at me, his brown eyes piercing. "What are you talkin' 'bout?"

"Ma," I said, blushing. "She's sick to her stomach all the time. She needs some medicine. I read about it in that newspaper you brought home."

He chuckled, and the lines next to his eyes crinkled. "Ma doesn't need no medicine."

"How do you know?" I said with a touch of anger.

"Cuz I'm her husband, that's how. And besides, you're too young to be spending time in town. There's some bad people there." He started walking again, his long strides kicking dust into my eyes.

"But Ma says I'm gonna have to live with Aunt Cornelia and Uncle Jim next year and go to school there."

He swung around, putting his face close to mine. "That hasn't bin decided yet, Bennie. So, don't git yer hopes up 'bout it." He gestured toward the cabin. "Now, git back home and help Ma with the chores."

I felt the heat rising to my face and wanted to contradict what he said but knew it was no use, so I swiveled on my heels and stormed back home. Sam came out to greet me, asking if I wanted to go look for the foxes in the den.

"No!" I said, pushing past him. The idea that I'd never get off this mountain, never make it to school, burned in my gut.

6

I lay on my bed, staring at the ceiling in the loft, thinking about the women's tonic, Cardui. It sounded like magic, and it might stop Ma from throwing up all of the time. I figured if Pa wasn't going to spend the money on it, and I couldn't pay for it, the next best thing was to trust Aunt Bertie, strange bird that she was. Sam slept quietly next to me. His breathing wasn't labored anymore. Hadn't Bertie cured him?

At dawn, I woke to the sound of Ma moving about in the kitchen below. I crept down the loft stairs to peek in on her. She had made herself some coffee and was pouring it into a cup when she stopped, put her fist to her mouth, clutched her stomach, and ran out to the porch. I found her there, sitting in a chair, her face as pale as the moon.

"What do you want?" she said between gasps of air.

"Nothin'" I waited for her to control her breathing. "You all right, Ma?"

She offered a weak smile. I could see sweat beading on her brow. I ran into the kitchen and found a rag, soaked it with water, and brought it to her.

"Wait here." I ran back up to the loft. Everyone was still asleep. I grabbed the satchel of herbs and brought it to her.

"Aunt Bertie said to give this to you, but I forgot." I was worried she wouldn't believe my lie but didn't seem to care one way or the other. She took it from me, brought it to her nose, and sniffed. A look of dread spread over her face.

"You ok? Aunt Bertie said you'd know what to do with this." I wanted to tell her that Aunt Bertie also told me not to tell Pa. But I figured it hardly mattered since he didn't seem to care enough to buy Ma the real tonic she needed, the one he could get in town that Mrs. Veste from Madison Heights, Virginia said worked wonders.

She waved me away. "I'll be fine, son."

"You gonna take it?" I was eager for her to agree and get better. All of this retching and fretting made me anxious.

She shook her head. "Maybe. I can't say now. We'll see how I feel."

I didn't know what she was talking about, but Nellie started howling from her crib.

"I'll get her," I offered. As I turned at the door, I watched her eyeing the satchel of herbs and crushing it in her fist. She appeared to have the same misgivings I did.

While seated to eat breakfast, Ma listed off a litany of chores for all of us to tend to: milk the cow, clean the chicken coop, fix the wire fence around the garden, weed the garden, fetch water from the springhouse. Just listening to her made me tired.

"How 'bout we go out to the woods later for a picnic and watch the foxes' den?" I said hopefully.

Ma swiped drool off Nellie's face. "Too many chores," she said. "Maybe when Pa gets back."

"But if we got everything done early, can we?"

"Oh, that sounds like fun, Ma," Sam said.

Ma bit her lower lip, contemplating.

"Oh, please, Ma," Rachel said. "I wanna see the foxes' den!"

"All right. Now get going and get those chores done."

We scrambled out of there fast.

I knew I had made the right decision giving her that tonic this morning. As we were feeding the chickens, Cousin Floyd pulled up in his truck and jumped out of the cab. He had some supplies.

"From Bob," he said to Ma as he pulled things out of his flatbed and handed them to us.

Pa had sent us some chicken wire to fix the fence around the garden; that didn't cause too much excitement, but the flour, sugar, butter, and a bolt of cloth for the girls did.

"Any shoes?" Ma said.

Floyd scratched his head. "I didn't see any. Maybe he forgot."

Ma scowled and instructed us to unload the supplies. Even though Pa had taken my foot measurement before he left the cabin, I had a feeling he was only doing it for show. While he was measuring, using his belt as a guide by placing my foot on it and notching where it stopped, he had muttered under his breath so Ma wouldn't hear him, "Ain't no use getting new shoes now anyways, yer just gonna grow out of 'em by the end of the summer."

"I wanna go to town with Cousin Floyd next time he goes," Mary said. "Pahlease." She tugged at Ma's skirt. "I'd be so good."

"Well, now. Thar's the problem," Floyd said. "I've got grown-up business to do when I'm in town and can't be bothered."

"I could go with them," I offered.

"I need you here," Ma said. "Forget it, Mary. Not 'til Pa gets back."

"But when?" she pestered.

"Take this inside," Ma handed her a sack of something to take into the cabin.

7

We forgot about the lure of town when Sam got sick again a few weeks later.

"Is he gonna be all right?" Rachel said, tears pooling.

"I don't know," Ma whispered.

Rachel and Mary jumped up and wrapped their arms around Ma, whose face crumpled as she started weeping.

"Can't we just get more of Aunt Bertie's medicine?" I said.

"We're all out, and I don't think it will work this time. It's real bad," she said. "Ben, you need to find Pa."

"I'll take care of it, Ma," I said. I went to the barn to saddle up Bess.

It had rained the night before, and the road was pitted with jagged rocks and stones which had magically doubled in number and surfaced after the water eroded the dirt. Bess avoided the rocks as best she could, but she put up a fuss when we went to cross the bridge. The swollen creek was thundering below the bridge. Tree limbs floated past, snagging on boulders, creating dams where pools of water formed. I jumped off to guide her over the rickety bridge, and as I did, I got a splinter. It stabbed into my foot with each step. The mud stained my feet.

In town, people went about their business like nothing was the matter—even though my heart was racing with a rising panic—ignoring me as I hurried down Main Street to the building where Pa was working. He was shocked to see me and knew immediately something was wrong.

"Pa, Ma said we need a doctor for Sam."

He dropped everything he had in his hands, the tools, nails, everything, and told a fellow worker he was leaving to tend to his sick boy, didn't even wait to talk to the foreman. I followed him through town, limping from the splinter, to Doctor Sloane's house on Main Street.

A girl about my age came to the door. Her amber eyes and auburn hair reminded me of an autumn morning in the mountains. I couldn't recall her name, but I remembered Doc Sloane mentioning his only daughter on the few occasions he came up the mountain to tend to us.

"Hello Emma, is your Pa in?" Pa asked.

"Why no." She glanced at my blackened feet. My cheeks flamed. "Is there an emergency?"

"Might say so. My son, Sam. He needs a doctor. I can go fetch him if you know where he is," Pa said.

"He's at the Pharmacy."

Pa turned to me. "You stay put until I come back and git ye."

For an awkward minute, Emma and I watched Pa step off the porch and stride toward the pharmacy. She folded her arms over her chest and tried to avoid staring at my feet. "You thirsty?"

"Yes, Ma'am."

"You don't have to call me ma'am." Her laugh was like summer rain. "You need to wash your feet?"

I attempted to act as if I didn't care. "No point in it, I guess. They'll just get dirty again."

"Nonsense. Wait here." The way she said it reminded me of my aunts, but her lips held a hint of a smile. She went inside and I stood there awkwardly, my heart thrumming against my chest in anticipation until she came back with a pan of water.

"Take this over there and wash your feet."

There was no Mrs. Sloane. She died while giving birth to Emma, a fact that made Doc Sloane appear perpetually sad as if something was missing. The only time he brightened was when speaking about his daughter. And here she was, standing only two feet away so that I could almost feel her warm breath on my collar. I now understood why.

I was embarrassed but thankful. I limped to the back of the house with the pan.

By the time I was done, Pa and Doc Sloane had returned. Doc went inside to retrieve his bag. When he came back out, he said, "It'll be quicker for me to go by horse. The roads are all washed out from yesterday's rain, and my car will get stuck."

"I'll follow you then," Pa said as he took hold of Bess's reins and mounted her. "Ben, we'll see you back at the cabin."

It was a long journey back, and I had wasted my energy washing my feet. But it didn't matter because of the warm feeling I had inside when I gave the pan back to Emma. She must have thought she was Florence Nightingale or something because her face lit up at the sight of my clean feet. I wanted to tell her my foot was still throbbing, and what I really needed was a tweezer to pull out the damn splinter, but I was in a hurry to get back to the cabin and didn't want to bother her any more than I already had. By the time I reached the cabin, Doc Sloane was outside talking with Pa, heading toward his horse.

"Is he gonna be ok?" Pa said.

Doc Sloane fastened his black doctor bag to his saddle looking, as always, grim. "For now, he's settled. I gave him a heavy sedative to calm his cough and allow him to sleep easier. But he needs rest. And he needs to be put in a sanitarium. A place for children with his condition. They have a few in Knoxville. You might want to consider it, Bob. My medicine is no better than Bertie's at treating his condition."

My foot was screaming in pain, each footfall causing a searing jolt up my leg. I stumbled to the porch steps and collapsed there.

"I don't know how we'd afford such a place, Doc."

Doc Sloane tugged at the leather strap that held his bag in place. "You might consider selling some of that land you've got. Beaufort Lumber Company is buying." He shot a look over at me. "I saw you limping, what's wrong with your foot, Ben?"

I lifted my bad foot in the air and tried to discover the culprit piece of hickory that was lodged in my skin, but I couldn't see anything with all the mud.

"I got a splinter is all."

Doc Sloane frowned. "Here, let me take a look." He took a gourd of water from the bucket on the porch and poured it over my foot then examined it with these eyeglasses he had with a magnifier in them.

"Be right back." He went to his bag, took out a special tool, came back to me, and gingerly tugged at the splinter until, heaven's relief, it came out. Then he washed my foot with peroxide, which made me jump at the sting, wrapped a big piece of white cotton around my foot, and tied it in place with a string. "You need shoes, boy," he said.

"When I get back to town to collect my pay, Doc, I'll stop by," Pa said.

Doc Sloane heaved himself onto his horse with considerable effort, swung his leg in the air to the other side of his saddle, and flapped his hand at Pa. "Don't worry about that right now. I know you're good for it." He tugged at his reins and steered his horse toward the road back to town. "I can always use some ginseng or ask Floyd to stop by my office next time he's making a delivery," he called over his shoulder.

I knew what that meant, and so did Pa from the looks of it. Doc Sloane needed some of Cousin Floyd's joy water.

■　　　■　　　■

That night my parents got into an awful argument over what to do about Sam. Pa insisted he stay put, the mountain air and clean water being all he needed to get better. That and some rest. But Ma put up a fight and told Pa to find a way, any way to send her and Sam to Knoxville and the sanitarium. Doctor Sloane had told her that the doctors there could cure consumption. She was tuckered out from working so hard trying to keep up with us children, the daily chores, and taking care of Sam. She needed some rest as well. Mary and I sat at the top of the loft steps listening to the whole thing while the others slept. Mary stiffened beside me when they began talking about what to do with us while Ma went away with Sam.

"Mary can live with your sisters. They took in that woman botanist as a boarder, and I heard from Bertie at church last week she's looking for someone to take notes for her book. She'll pay. It would be good for Mary. Ben is ready for school. If you'd just ask Cornelia—"

Pa stopped her. "I ain't asking my sister Cornelia for anything. And Ben ain't livin' in a house with that low-down Jimmy Beaufort. Besides, I'll need Ben here to help me with the fields and the livestock."

"No. Ben is going to school. You promised me this."

"And who's gonna help me around here?"

"You can work in town. There's plenty of work for carpenters. I hear they're building a new inn. And we'll sell the hens and pigs. Your ginseng crop will get us through the winter."

"I'd make more going into business with Floyd."

"That's out of the question, and you know it."

"I don't want to leave the mountain and go live in town." Pa's voice was rising.

"Shush. You'll wake the children."

"And what about Nellie and Rachel? What's they gonna do without their Ma?"

There was a pause as Ma pondered. "I'll bring them with me." I could tell Ma was thinking hard now, her voice was trailing off, the way it did when she was making lists in her head, seeing the possibilities. "I'll find a place to stay near the sanitarium so I can visit Sam every day."

Mary was sniffling, wiping away tears. I guided her back to bed and got into my own. I stared up at the ceiling, my hands tucked under my head, elbows extended, waiting for sleep. I mulled over the events of the past few weeks, and it all circled back to me: if I hadn't convinced Ma to let me take Sam to town, he wouldn't be sick, and she wouldn't be leaving us.

By morning they must have decided because they told us to prepare for departure. Ma sent a letter to the Fosters inquiring whether they might need an extra hand around the inn, and in return, I could lodge with them when school started in September.

It was July, and our garden had an abundance of crops: okra, squash, beans, potatoes, beets, peppers, and cabbage. Pa's cousins came to help us harvest. What the women didn't jar was put aside for Floyd to take to Stewart's General Store in town to barter for supplies and money.

Pa sent me out to lure in our pigs. I took one of the paths leading up the mountain one bright morning with a bag full of corn kernels and salt. I planned to scatter the bait around the grounds where I knew they rooted around for bulbs in the summer and chestnuts and hickory nuts in the fall. I stopped short when I came upon a spot where there had been a grove of hickory and chestnut trees but was now an empty field on the other side of a stone wall Pa had put up to separate our property from one of his distant relations, the widowed Cousin Belle. The ground was pocked with skid marks where the skidders had dragged the trees down the road. Only remnants of the forest remained. Twisted, gnarled limbs scattered the ground. It was lifeless. As I changed direction, ready to run home and tell Pa what I found, I bumped smack into two men wearing fine wool hats, and those knickers city folk sported when they came to the mountains to 'hike'. They had been surveying the damage as well.

"Well, hello there, young man," one of them said in a serious tone. "Do you live around here?"

"Yes, sir. I'm Ben Taylor. This is Taylor Valley. My cabin is just up the path aways."

The men squinted into the morning glare at the path that led to my cabin. "Is your Pa home?"

"Yes, sir."

They followed me back to the cabin. I wanted to run ahead of them and warn Pa that the lumber company was working its way up the mountain road.

Pa had seen us coming and came out of the cabin to meet us on the road. He shook their hands, offered a seat on our porch, and told me to fetch them some water.

They introduced themselves as government men. One of them wore a brown patch on his shirt pocket that said U.S. Forest Service. "We're surveying. Taking inventory of how much land is being harvested for lumber."

Ma came out on the porch to listen.

"Why's that?" Pa asked.

"Well, sir, we are concerned you see, by the general destruction occurring on such a large scale. Forests are clear cut, destroying habitat, and creating environments ripe for a conflagration."

I didn't want to interrupt but had to remind myself to ask Ma how to spell conflagration and find out what it meant.

"We're following the Beaufort Lumber Company activity in this valley and are pretty sure they will be approaching more of your kin to sell them the rights to cut. They pay one dollar an acre for the right but make much more once those trees are sent to the market."

"So, what brings you here?"

"Pa, cousin Belle must've sold her rights. I just saw it! That whole grove of chestnuts and hickory are gone!" I blurted.

Pa and Ma exchanged glances.

"I don't aim to sell the rights to cut the trees on my land if that's what you're worried about," Pa said to the men.

"Do you have your land marked? Deeds recorded?"

"I do. And I have a structure on every parcel so there'd be no mistakin' someone has claim."

It was true, Pa had built smokehouses and other storage sheds on his parcels and marked off the property lines with stone walls. It was a tradition passed down by his Pa when the land was divided amongst the many Taylors living on the mountain.

"My cousin Belle may have needed the money. But so far, we don't." He said it with such confidence, it made me proud. But Ma wasn't as convinced.

"I hear the government is also looking to purchase land from the farmers to protect it?" she asked the men.

"Why, yes, ma'am. That's right. The government has raised some funds to do just that. So, if you are ever looking to—"

Pa crossed his arms. "Never will sell this land."

The man in the brown hat smiled slightly and tipped his hat. "Well, sir, if you ever change your mind on that..." he said, handing Pa a card, then they tipped their hats again, thanked me for the water, and left.

"Ben, go inside and check on Sam," Ma said.

As I departed, I heard Ma tell Pa: "You should've at least heard them out. Who knows how long it will take Sam to recover? You have plenty of land already."

Pa didn't respond. I heard his chair scrape back as he rose, and when I went to the window, he was heading down the road in the direction of cousin Belle's cabin.

8

We went about our chores as if waiting for something to drop out of the sky and hit us. Sam stayed in bed while Ma packed everything she needed for the trip. She piled up clothes, canned food, her paints, and canvas boards, taking everything with her as if she wasn't returning. It made me weary whenever I passed the sick room and saw the pile grow. Any day now, Cousin Floyd would be stopping by to take her, Sam, and the girls to the train station in town where they'd travel miles and miles to Knoxville.

The day she had to go, Mary clung to me, choking on her tears.

"It's only temporary, Mary," Ma assured her. But Mary wasn't having any of it.

She was hysterical, to the point where Pa had to drag her along when they left for the Aunts' cabin. She kept turning around, stumbling behind Pa, looking back at me beseechingly, with both sorrow and accusation. I slunk back inside the cabin to Sam's room to keep him company while Ma tried to calm the girls who had taken to crying as they watched Mary retreat.

"You feeling any better?" I asked him. His body was so weak and frail I couldn't see how he'd make it to Knoxville.

Sam nodded his head, tried to smile. "I'm going to get better, you'll see," he rasped. I patted his head, sat down, and read from one of the McGuffey readers about a pair of children who got lost on their way to school.

"Ben," he interrupted. "Why'd those boys not like us if they're our cousins?"

"You mean Jimmy Jr. and John?"

He nodded.

"I guess 'cause they don't know us well enough."

"How come Aunt Cornelia don't bring 'em to church and picnics like the rest of the family does?"

I pondered. "Not sure, Sam. Those are questions to ask Pa."

"But he don't ever talk about Aunt Cornelia."

"I know," I said, remembering what the aunts said about Cornelia. A wild thing. Once grandpa died, they lost all control of her. One of the prettiest of the sisters, Pa had told Ma once, she was destined to get into trouble with the boys in town, but no one expected it to be with Jimmy Beaufort Sr.

We must have dozed off. I woke, startled, still sitting in the chair, the shadows crossing the room. The house was quiet. I crept out of Sam's room and went to find Ma and the girls. They were stitching the last pieces of a quilt Ma planned to take with them.

"Are you hungry?" Ma asked.

"No, ma'am."

"There's soup on the stove. I'll fix you some."

I followed her into the kitchen and sat down. As she placed the soup in front of me, I caught a whiff of mint and saw a bulge in her apron pocket. The herbs from Aunt Bertie. I couldn't figure out why she'd be carrying them around now, she hadn't had a sick episode since Sam took ill. Maybe she'd found it somewhere and decided to get rid of it, but why not send it back with Mary and Pa?

"Are you looking forward to school?" she said brightly.

"Yes, ma'am." I didn't want to disappoint her. The Fosters agreed to take me in as a boarder and in return I would help them with chores.

"You'll enjoy it, Ben. Just you wait and see. And then we'll all be together at Christmas. Sam will be better, and we'll all have stories to tell about our adventures."

"Yes, Ma." I wasn't so sure.

That night the moon whitewashed my room and made me restless. I woke with a start to the sound of Ma downstairs working in the kitchen, perhaps preparing more food for their journey. A loud crash and her cry made me jump out of bed. I raced down the steps to see if she was all right, but she wasn't in the kitchen. Not wanting to wake anyone up, I searched for her on the porch without calling her name. Nothing. A shadow crept across the yard—Ma, heading to the outhouse. I waited on the porch for her return. I heard the guttural sound of an owl hooting in the distance. The trees whistled. She'd been gone a while and I didn't know what to do. Finally, she came out of the outhouse, clutching her gut, bent over, retching in the dirt, wobbling.

"Ma!" I ran to her.

She wobbled, half limped, half stumbled toward me. Her white gown had a large stain on the front. As she got closer, I saw what it was: blood. It covered her arms, her bare feet, her hands. I thought she might be dying.

"Ma!" I took hold of her shoulders and led her to the porch. She was shaking. "Sit here." I ran inside for a blanket and wrapped it around her.

"Water." She motioned to the bucket on the porch.

I took the lid off and brought a gourd full of cool spring water to her cracked lips.

"Should I get the Doc?" The thought of traveling on the road in the dead of night, a full moon at my back scared me, but losing her frightened me more.

"No." She pulled herself upright and breathed in deeply, eyes closed. The wind caught a strand of her hair, twirling it around her forehead.

"You gonna be ok?"

"Yes, Ben. I'm going to be all right. I just need to sit here for a few more moments and collect myself."

"But, Ma. The blood."

"It's nothing. Don't tell Pa. I'll clean this mess up in the morning before he gets home. No one must know what you saw tonight. Ok? This is our secret."

Again, why was it the women wanted me to keep everything from Pa? It didn't seem right.

When she saw the confusion in my face, she said, "I don't want him fretting about me before we leave. I just had an accident, that's all. I'll be fine if you just give me a moment."

We sat there together in a fragment of moonlight, and listened to the insects chirring, owls cooing, and the creek rambling in the distance. Hushed, our breathing measured, waiting for—what? A shift in the breeze, light, sound, color in the trees, a signal that a new day was approaching, and we had no choice but to face it with strength and courage.

. . .

When the day came, Floyd brought his truck and we loaded it up with jars of food, a large suitcase, and the few items the girls had to entertain themselves: dolls and books. We carried their things into the passenger car. Although they were at first glum, the girls and Sam perked up, chattering with each other, pointing at people. Ma laughed and fussed with her hair. I envied them going off on a new adventure without me.

"Now, you listen to your Pa." Ma leaned down and kissed my cheek. "And be helpful with the Fosters."

"Yes, ma'am."

"Don't be sad. We'll be back before you know it."

I hated her for being so bright when inside I was feeling miserable. Pa and I stood on the platform and waved as the big train carried them away.

I spent the next few weeks at the cabin with Pa, helping him with the corn harvest, butchering, and smoking the few pigs we were able to round up. He planned to bring some of the meat to town to sell. He left me one day to visit with Floyd on some business. I spent it cleaning and sharpening our butcher knives. At dusk, he came into view over the crest of the knoll, a family of foxes slung over his shoulder on a long piece of hemp, their tails flapping behind him.

He flung them down on the porch in front of me and said: "Found these hiding in a den. Gonna case the hides and pack them up to send to Sears and Roebuck. I'm guessing it'll be worth enough to buy you some new shoes and trousers." He stretched his arms to the sky to loosen his shoulders. "Go fetch me some water."

In the dimming light, the vixen lay there, her black eyes open, vacant, sad, fixed on me. I held back tears. "Yes, sir."

PART TWO
HICKORY RUN
1926-1928

9

The community hall Pa had been working on was finished. It was nicknamed the Hall of Education, Damnation, and Salvation. It served as a school during the day, a movie theater on Saturdays, and a pulpit for traveling preachers on Sundays. The Methodists, Lutherans, and three branches of Baptists shared access to the hall on alternating Sundays.

No longer just a lumber camp, Hickory Run was bustling. People built small portable shacks. When the lumber operations built new rail lines in the forests, they followed with their shacks. They called them set-off houses because they'd drag them up a mountain on the top of a railroad car and set them off beside the tracks in the forest where they were working. By now, railroad tracks were being laid down into the farthest reaches of the mountains. The lumbermen used the lines to climb the mountains with their skidders, cut down, and drag trees to a rail car. They'd stack them like matches and bring them into town to be milled.

Men came to work at the mill and in the woods from the cities up north or down south: Atlanta, Birmingham, Knoxville, even as far as Lexington, Kentucky. They brought their families.

And they brought with them their peculiar habits. The owners of the businesses in Hickory Run did very well catering to the different needs of the workers and their families. Folks like my Pa were not better off. He had to send all of his wages to the sanitarium and the boarding house where Ma was staying.

I worked for the Fosters before and after school, in the morning and well into the evening. The inn was full of guests, tourists from out of town who planned long hikes in the mountains. They were up late every night playing cards in the parlor, laughing, playing the piano, singing. I imagined more than a few had snuck in some of Cousin Floyd's whiskey, which could be easily bought, I found out, at the local pharmacy if you claimed a mild illness.

I figured that out one night when I was fetching water from the spring on the outskirts of town. Although Foster's Inn had a well, the guests didn't like the metallic taste of the water and every night, I made a trip to the spring. It shot out of the side of a hill about a quarter-mile from town. Mr. Foster told me to take his horse and wagon after supper to fill up twenty jugs and bring them back. One evening I was late getting to the spring. Dusk was descending like a purple veil over the mountains, and the roads emptied. The dirt road to the spring passed by the back entrances of the business district. I passed store owners sweeping dust from steps or shaking rugs out onto the road. A few called out to me in greeting. "Howdy, Ben. How's your Ma and sisters doin' in Knoxville?"

Up ahead, I heard the sounds of wheels crunching on the dirt and looked up to see Cousin Floyd's truck with Pa in it. They pulled up alongside, and I asked where they were going so late on a Monday evening.

"We got some business in town," Cousin Floyd replied.

"Best get back to your chores." Pa cut off any opportunity for small talk.

I glanced back at the contents in the flatbed and recognized the jugs. I continued on my way but stopped where I thought they wouldn't notice and tied the reins to a tree limb. Then I scurried down the path in the cover of the shadowy trees to see where they were headed. They stopped at the back of the pharmacy. Mr. Beyer came out to greet them, looking both ways to make sure everything was clear, before gesturing to them to bring in the moonshine.

■　■　■

One of my duties was to clean out the massive stone fireplace in Foster's Inn before the guests woke, and above the mammoth mantel hung Ma's painting of the fox cubs scampering around their den. It haunted me every morning. It made me awful homesick. My only consolation was that

Mrs. Foster admired the painting so much she wouldn't let Mr. Foster sell it. She bought it from Ma right before she departed for $50.00. That was the most money Ma had ever made on a painting before. It paid for four months' rent at their boarding house in Knoxville.

But I had a leaden heart every morning as I scraped and swept away the ashes and lugged them in a tin bucket to the back garden.

"Why the glum face?" Mr. Foster asked me one morning. "Not looking forward to school?"

"No, sir." Although he and Mrs. Foster were very kind to me, they could not replace the warmth and comfort of my cabin and my family.

And while I enjoyed learning, I never fit in with the other students who treated me with a mixture of scorn and envy. I was a hillbilly with more brains than any of 'em. That is, except for Emma Sloane. She was smart, kind, and the reason I managed to drag myself to school every day. Otherwise, I'm not sure I'd have gone to school, mainly because my cousin Jimmy badgered me constantly.

One morning, I went to school with little sleep. I'd been running around all night catering to the needs of the guests: towels, hot baths, clean glasses, more firewood, then had to clean up after them. My head hung low and my eyes were half-closed. I was so darned tired.

Jimmy, who was positioned at the desk next to mine, punched my arm. "Hey, Taylor, wake up. You just missed what the teacher said."

The sound of scraping chairs filled the air as other students turned in place, expecting to find me with my head down on my desk asleep. Emma Sloane shot me a sympathetic look.

Startled, I stared straight ahead at the teacher, Mr. Vorhoss. He frowned at me but scolded Jimmy. "Mr. Beaufort, if you disrupt this class again with one of your outbursts, you will be sent home with a note to your father."

"You're gonna havta learn Ben Taylor how to stay awake, Mr. Vorhoss," Jimmy snickered.

"You mean, he's going to have *to teach me* how to stay awake," I shot back.

I felt a swift kick on my shin. "You're gonna fail out of school. What will your Ma think of you then?" Jimmy Jr. snarled under his breath.

When there was a break in the day and the other students filed outside to go home for lunch or circle in clusters to gossip, I stayed in my seat and tried to catch up with my homework. Mr. Vorhoss was tolerant of me taking up his only free time of the day and encouraged me to work hard.

"I grew up just like you, Ben," he told me. "Working all night, school by day. I had no choice either. My parents were dirt poor. But look at me now. I make thirty-five dollars a month."

He stood before me in a threadbare suit, shoes just past the point where polish could do nothing to improve their appearance, and a white shirt with a frayed collar. Even though he was a good teacher, I also knew he had gotten the job due to Dr. Sloane, who was his distant cousin or some such, and the good doctor was on the town board which hired the teacher. Mr. Vorhoss came from an eastern county, had finished his schooling at a state university, and was a boarder at the Sloane's. He didn't own anything, and I knew he meant well, but the thing was we owned land—lots of it. We had crops of corn, a lush garden. We had ginseng that we could sell. We had honey and whiskey. I knew we weren't well off like some, but I never thought of us as dirt poor. I was thinking about all of this one day when I decided to follow my cousins home.

I hadn't meant to, but one evening after school let out, I saw the two of them loping along ahead of me and figured chores at the inn could wait. I ducked behind some trees so they wouldn't catch me spying. They took the main road into town and then cut down a lane I'd passed several times before but never knew where it led. The dirt road was flanked by gigantic elms with arching limbs forming a tunnel of green that led to the house. It stood two stories high with stately white columns, bay windows as big as my front porch, and a veranda so large it could hold all of the guests from Foster's Inn.

I stood behind one of the sheltering elms holding back a gasp as the twins ascended the steps of the veranda to greet Aunt Cornelia, who was outside waiting for them, her arms outstretched. She wore a light blue dress. Her golden hair reminded me of my sister Rachel, and a wave of homesickness swept over me. She wrapped her arms around her two boys and led them into the house. I waited for a few minutes, debating with myself whether spying on my cousins and aunt was the right thing to do. My curiosity won out. I crept forward, scouting around the house until I found a window open with noise coming from the inside. I climbed up a magnolia tree, reaching a level where I had a bird's eye view into the dining room under the cover of waxy green leaves.

The dining table was more spacious than my bedroom, and the food laid on top of it was a feast my family only experienced at Christmas. Uncle Jimmy was eating with them. They had a roasted turkey, yams, some kind of squash, bread, butter, and on top of the sideboard, pies. Not just one, but several to choose from. The chandelier twinkled; the lace curtains fluttered in the evening breeze. It was a perfect setting for dinner that none of the participants appeared to appreciate. Through the open windows, I could hear Aunt Cornelia coaxing along the conversation.

"How was your day, boys?"

John opened his mouth, but as soon as he did, his father shot a look of utter disgust from across the table, which caused him to clamp it shut. Jimmy Jr. gobbled his food, oblivious to his brother's distress. Aunt Cornelia tssked and patted John's hand, but she didn't speak up for her son.

"I may have a breakthrough on the Gavin deal," Uncle Jimmy's voice boomed. It startled me, and my foot caught up in a branch.

"That's nice, dear," Cornelia said with little conviction.

Jimmy Jr.'s head shot up, and I ducked behind the veil of limbs. "You hear that?" he said.

But my uncle continued, ignoring his son. "It *damn* well is nice. If I can get to him before those *damn* government lawyers do, I can make thousands off his trees. He has prime timber and doesn't even know. Damn fool."

Cornelia's gaze went to the window. I stood as motionless as an owl and caught a flicker of recognition before she turned her attention back to Uncle Jimmy. "You really shouldn't swear in front of the boys, dear."

• • •

I would see Pa every once in a while. He made an effort to come to the inn, and we'd go to a local diner to share a meal and talk about our week. Our conversations would sometimes stray to Ma, but mail was slow in the mountains, and sometimes it would be weeks before we heard from her. When we did get mail, I had to read Ma's letters to Pa because he couldn't.

"Sam is recovering, and the children love being in a big town. We stroll in the park every day, and I take my sketchbook. I will have many paintings to show and sell at Foster's when I get back. I hope all is well. Have you seen or talked with Mary? Her letters to me sound cheerful enough. I hope she likes working with her aunts and the botanist, Dr. Clarence."

One chilly fall morning Pa came to the inn asking if I could take a day off to help him harvest the ginseng.

"It's been a few years since I harvested up there," he told me, "takes that long sometimes for a good crop to mature."

The forest was a fireball of color as we marched, climbed, and shimmied our way up the side of the steep grade that led over the waterfalls and into the magical forest where the ginseng grew.

"Look for the yellowing leaves," he said. "Easy to spot them once you learn to recognize 'em."

He showed me how. We scoured the forest floor for the plant, and when we spotted a cluster, we sat on our haunches, pulling it carefully out of the ground.

"Looks are deceivin'," he said, pointing at one of the gnarled knots of fleshy white roots covered with specks of rich brown earth. "That one you have there will fetch us five dollars."

I wondered why he hadn't included me in his ginseng harvest before. I lost track of time pulling at the plants, and unlike other chores I had to do around the cabin and at the inn, my mind was filled with happy thoughts and stillness. The forest insects sang, blocking out the sound of the whistling trains, the clamor of the wagons and cars that bustled in the town below, and the cackling laughter of the guests at Foster's Inn. Although it was dry that fall—there'd been no rain since August, and it was now October—warm moisture pulsed from the ground. My hands caked with wet soil when I dug into the dirt. The musky scent of rain reached me when my knees crushed the remnants of dead maple leaves lying on the forest floor.

Having gathered two sacks full of the root, we picked ourselves up off the ground, my knees aching from the effort, and batted the dirt and dead leaves off our trousers. Then we headed upwards to a grassy bald where the cattle fed, and we would get a view for miles.

As we climbed higher, we left the dark forest and stepped out onto a ridge that led across the mountaintop until we reached a plateau of land covered with thick grasses that had already turned golden brown from the drought. My hat flew off in the whipping wind. We worked our way to the edge and scanned the horizon. The view before us was waves of mountains blazing gold and crimson. The air felt dry, and I inhaled, catching a whiff of firewood burning. Pa pivoted on his heels to the left and stopped dead.

I turned to where he was staring and saw it too: a plume of black smoke rising above the tree line directly over Taylor Valley. Without saying a word, we both scrambled back to the path and home.

I was out of breath, trying to keep up with Pa's long strides. Our cabin sat on top of a knoll; it was clearly out of danger from the fire raging in the valley floor. But that didn't deter Pa from doing what needed to be done.

"I've seen this before," he said. "The winds will carry sparks into the air, and if they land on the trees, they'll fire 'em up."

We cleared dead brush around the outside of the cabin. He gave me an ax, and the two of us hacked away at the picket fence. We removed the newspaper from the walls, wooden tools, buckets, bowls from the kitchen, piled them up, and dragged them far away from the buildings onto the road. Bess was kicking at the barn door. We let her out, blinded her with a cloth, and led her to the springhouse. The spring, that even in the dry weather had never let us down, ran through the wooden pipes Pa had made out of tree limbs and flowed into the springhouse. And it was our only hope to quell the ash that was raining from the skies. Pa jumped on the roof of the cabin, and I handed him buckets of water, which he dumped on the roof. We returned to the springhouse to gather more and did this over and over until nightfall. My throat was raw, parched, my lips cracked, and my nostrils filled with smoke.

As darkness fell, we sat on the edge of the porch and watched red flames creeping up the road on the edges of the forest. My thoughts filled with dread, hoping our hard work wasn't for nothing as the wind whipped the flames in the air. In the surrounding forest, sparks landed on tree tops and whole trees went up in flames. The heat seared my skin and I pressed a cold cloth to my face. Pa sat stone still, his breathing measured, his eyes never leaving the forest and the flames.

I took a long draw of the spring water from the bucket.

"Shouldn't we leave, Pa?" I said, as the fire licked at the edges of the road.

He didn't answer me. His face was covered in soot, as was mine. I saw the white of his eyes peering into the distance. He wasn't panicked and that soothed me. But still, I was anxious to scurry off before the fire came any closer.

"We ain't goin' anywhere," he said with finality. And he pointed up at the sky.

Over the trees, I saw a crackle of lightning. The air grew thick, a rumble of thunder shook the foundation, a loud clap rang out, and the steely skies emptied.

We jumped off the porch. Pa started to laugh, a big deep laugh. He raised his arms in the air, craned his neck back so that his face met the rain as it smeared his cheeks with black trickles of ash and dirt and sweat. I did the same, the rain washing relief over me.

■   ●   ■

The next day, we took off to determine the source of the fire. The trail of destruction took us out of Taylor Valley and over the crest of a low-elevation mountain into another small valley called McConnell's Cove. We followed the railroad tracks into the interior, and along the way, passed the charred remains of a few of the newer homesteads, vacation homes, now untended, that had sprung up along with the railroad tracks. I wondered if the owners knew that their cabins were burnt to a crisp and steaming in the early morning dew.

We turned a corner and came upon a field of black stumps. The ground was hard, smelled of fire. We kicked up ash with every step, some of it hot and sparking with embers. Skid marks scarred the land where large trees had been cut and dragged over the earth.

A tired group of men ambled our way, including Mr. McConnell and his son, Finn.

They meandered over to where we stood and we shook hands. Their faces were covered in ash.

"What happened, Hank?" Pa said.

"We had this area cut," Hank said. "Beaufort Lumber came, paid us $25 to lease twenty-five acres. I figured they was doin' me a favor, wanted to clear this field for a crop soon anyhow."

"But what started the fire?"

"Theys dragged some logs across the field there," Hank gestured. "And when it rubbed up against the slash, it sparked. Just didn' expect it would get so out of hand so quickly. I've done burned slash before to clear for a field, but I ain't never seen anything like this."

"It just kep' burnin'!" one of the men blurted.

"How'd you put it out?" Pa asked. I wondered if it was still under control or if the rains were just a reprieve, and a spark was smoldering under the earth somewhere beneath our feet waiting to reach out and burn our ankles.

"We had men here working all night. Surprised you didn't hear about it in town. We had some men from the lumber camps come up to assist. The company brought a water tank up by rail. They hosed everything down. Wasn't much we could do but cut a break up there"—he motioned to the edge of the field— "and the fire ran out of fuel at the crick." A small creek acted as the barrier, keeping the flames from crawling across to the waterwheel and mill.

Pa took it all in, nodding his head, clenching his jaw as Hank McConnell filled in the details of the lumber operation, describing the shocked expression of some of the men, *furriners*, who worked for the company. They had never seen a forest fire get out of hand so quickly. Yet they caused it all with their stupidity.

"Any damn fool knows not to drag logs over slash when there hasn't been rain in months. Who the hell was in charge?" Pa said.

Hank's face went blank at Pa's rage, embarrassed he had any part to play in this catastrophe. "Why, I wasn't even here if that's what you's gettin' at, Bob. Me and Finn were in town, deliverin' cornmeal to the store, and pickin' up supplies. We was makin' our way back when we saw it and was the first to set off the alarm back in town. Just turned around and went right to the lumber yard askin' them to send up a train with the water tank."

Pa's cheeks puffed up, and he blew out a gush of air in resignation and disgust. Hank McConnell's head hung low with shame. He was kicking at the ash with the toe of his boot, blackened from the dirty work they had done all night. Finn stared blankly at the field of ash. I tugged at Pa's arm.

"Pa, let's get to town," I said. "Mr. Foster is gonna be wondering why I've been gone so long. He might be worried about me."

"It ain't my fault," Hank said weakly. But I knew he was broken by the devastation and I was embarrassed that Pa was making him feel worse for it.

Pa glanced at the millhouse. The roof had a burnt-out hole in it from the flames. "I've got to git Ben back to town and his job at the inn. I'll send for Floyd and other kin, and we'll help you repair that roof," Pa said.

Hank got teary-eyed. "Thank you, Bob. I'd really appreciate it."

10

I'd never seen Pa so angry before, and it worried me when he left me at the steps of the inn. Mr. and Mrs. Foster came out to greet us.

"You smell like fire. You get caught up in that forest fire too?" Mr. Foster asked.

Pa doffed his hat and stomped off in the direction of the Beaufort Lumber Company building.

I was anxious to follow him and needed an excuse to get out of my chores for the day. I began hacking loudly.

"Why, son, you sound horrible!" Mrs. Foster said. "You poor boy. Why don't you go to your room and lay down for a while? The chores can wait another day."

Mr. Foster glared at her, but she said, "Most of the guests left this morning anyhow. You can catch up with your chores after lunch. Now go and wash up at the spring. And get out of those clothes. I'll burn 'em. You smell like a campfire."

"Yes ma'am," I said and went to the back as if to go to the spring. But instead, I followed Pa.

I used the cover of a large oak in front of the Beaufort Company office building to listen to Pa confronting Jimmy Beaufort Sr. It wasn't hard—they left the door open and Pa was shouting at Jimmy.

"Your men dragged logs across dead limbs in the middle of the day, in this heat, with high winds and no rain for weeks. What the hell were they thinkin'?"

Jimmy Sr. sat at his desk, glaring. Pa paced the floor, throwing his hands in the air, when my uncle slapped his palms on the desk and pushed himself up. He was a couple of inches shorter than Pa, but he made up for that in girth.

"Who the hell do you think you are, Bob Taylor, comin' in here and telling' me how to run my business? You're just a hillbilly moonshiner. And if it weren't for the fact that you are related to my wife, I'd have you run right out of town!"

Pa put his hands down on the desk and leaned over it so that his face was right in Jimmy Sr.'s. "Don't you try to threaten me the way you do my sister."

At this, Jimmy threw his head back and let out a booming laugh. "You Taylors are all the same," he said. "You just don't know when to back down." He scrunched his brows and gestured for Pa to sit.

Pa reluctantly took a seat across from Jimmy, and they both stared like two dogs in a fight. I took the chance they couldn't see me and worked my way closer to the open door, so I could hear what they said next.

"Now, Bob, let's be clear." My uncle used a conciliatory tone. "I don't want to cause no trouble with you or any of the other folks on the mountains. But the days are coming when you'll have to decide. Are you with me or not? The cost of lumber is going up, the economy is booming. Now is the time to sell me that parcel you've been holding out on."

"I ain't never gonna sell you any of my land, and you knows it," Pa said.

Jimmy linked his fingers and laid them to rest on his expansive chest, his mood shifting, and I worried that he might hurt Pa somehow. I wished Ma was there to guide us. She'd know what to tell Pa to do. She'd march in there and break this up before things got out of hand and Pa said things that would cause my uncle to follow-through with his threats.

Instead, Aunt Cornelia showed up, which made me jump out of my skin.

"What are you doin' here, crouched down and spying like that?" she said. She was holding a basket with a checkered cloth draped over it. Her head turned to the open door when she heard Pa shout something and ignoring me, stepped into the office, shutting the door.

I put my ear to the door, but their voices sounded muffled.

"What are you doin' here, son?"

I pivoted to find myself facing the barreled chest of a watchman who had heard the commotion and was checking on his boss.

"Scat!" he said to me, pointing in the air.

I caught a glance of Jimmy Sr. splayed out on the floor of his office, Cornelia cradling his head before I found the nearest tree to hide behind while the watchman entered the office.

Pa swung open the door and scurried away before the watchman could apprehend him. I followed paces behind him—dodging behind trees, all the way to the pharmacy. He knocked three times, and someone opened the door to let him in.

Panting, I sat down at the base of the tree, wondering what to do next. The land Jimmy coveted must be the old forest where Pa grew his ginseng. What else did Pa have of any value? The woods around our cabin had been cleared for fields. I wondered how many acres of old forest Pa owned. The memory of the sight of those railroad tracks leading into McConnell's Cove made me shudder. So out of place, so foreign to the woods, was this how it was to be from now on?

I had to talk to Pa. I wanted to protect him, and I needed to know how. If Ma wasn't here to help, Pa only had me. I had to do it. For the sake of the family. I couldn't let him face my uncle alone.

I ran to the door that led to the back of the pharmacy and hammered on the door. In my panic, I forgot the code Pa used just moments earlier. A peephole slid open and two eyes stared down on me: Cousin Floyd.

"What?" He closed the hatch and called for Pa. I heard chairs scrape against the floor, followed by steps to the door. It swung open. Pa stood before me, his cheekbone red and raw.

"Ben, what are you doin' here?" He reached for my arm and pulled me inside.

Five men huddled around a table playing cards. Swirling cigarette smoke hung above their heads. Pa motioned for me to sit in a corner. He swigged down a tumbler of whiskey, wiped his mouth with the back of his sleeve, propped his elbow on the table, and spoke to Floyd.

"I think he's serious this time," Pa said.

"It's blackmail," one of the other men said. Through the thick fog of smoke, I made out the face. It was Mr. Gifford, whose daughter Amelia was in my class.

"Jimmy Beaufort has nothin' on you," Floyd drawled. "He ain't got no idea where we hiding our still. And if he wanted to send the law after us his own company men would be the ones losing out."

That made the other men at the table chuckle.

"I'd say he's jealous you may be makin' more than I am selling your 'shine than he is cutting them trees," one of them said. This set them all off.

Pa was the only one not laughing. He was stretching his jaw and wincing in pain. "I don't think he's bluffing this time."

Floyd sighed, flung his arms over his head, bent his bony elbows, and placed his hands behind his head to prop it up. "You and I know, Bob, he's made threats before. He wants you to give in and sell 'im that parcel. Hell, he's bin sending men up my ways, surveying the land, seeing where his next crop of trees is gonna come from."

"He's gonna run outta trees soon!"

"He'll just find another mountain."

The chorus of men grumbled in agreement.

"You might be better off selling to the government," someone said. "They's meeting about it at the hall this week."

"I ain't selling anything!" Pa slammed his fist on the table. Everyone turned to him, then me.

"Ben, you best be gettin' back to work," Floyd said, slurring his words.

■   ■   ■

Pa's altercation with my uncle weighed on me, that, and Ma's absence. But I was saved by the movies at the community hall. And Mary Pickford. I fell in love with Mary Pickford. The whole town was packed into the community hall one golden evening to watch her in *My Best Girl*. She was a salesgirl, and Buddy Rogers was the object of her affections. Oh, how I wished I was Buddy Rogers. He had everything: the son of the store owner, charm, looks, and Mary Pickford's adoration.

Mary transfixed me, with her big soft eyes, as she dropped her bag in the street so that Buddy would have to pick it up and return it to her. This went on until he finally kissed her, and the audience gasped with both delight and shock. So, this was how it's done? I just had to wait until a girl indicated her interest in me by dropping a book or something on the way home from school. And then I'd retrieve it for her, and we'd kiss.

I filed out of the hall with the rest of the crowd, everyone excitedly talking about the movie. Preacher Joe was sitting in the back of the hall, arms folded over his chest, gnawing on his lower lip in deep concentration. Why he showed up to watch the movie, I wasn't sure, but I had a feeling he planned to speak about it the next day when the hall was filled with churchgoers. I ducked my head down so he wouldn't see me, but it was too late.

"Is that you, Ben Taylor?" he said.

People sidestepped past me as I stood there, bolted to the floor in shame.

"What are you doing here, son?"

"Why, same as you. Watching Mary Pickford."

He eyed me critically. "I see. And what did you think of the movie?"

"I thought it was…" Something caught in my throat when I tried to explain the crush of emotions I was experiencing. "Beautiful," I said finally.

Preacher Joe's jaw dropped. "I see." He stared behind me to the far wall where ten minutes earlier, the projected image of Mary and Buddy kissing in the wind flickered.

He decided now wasn't the time to lecture me. "How's your mother?"

"She's fine. Sam's getting better. They should be home soon."

"Well, let's hope so, son. Say hi to your Pa for me. Tell him I'm here every other Sunday if he needs to talk."

"I will, sir." I scrambled out as fast as my feet would carry me, not wanting Preacher Joe to ruin a perfect evening. When the hall transformed into the House of Salvation in the morning, everyone but him would forget it was the Hall of Damnation the night prior.

Lying in my bed that night, the curtains billowing from an unusually warm autumn wind, I thought about who might flirt with me the way Mary Pickford did with Buddy. Emma Sloane, maybe. She sat a row over and two up from me, and once in a while she'd drop her pencil and glance my way. I always thought it was for my cousin Jimmy Beaufort who sat behind me, but one day I caught her looking straight at me, and it was then she produced a quick smile before returning her attention to the front of the room.

Other than Emma, most of the girls mooned over the Beaufort boys, especially Jimmy. John, with his stutter, was too shy to talk to any of them, but often on the way home from school Jimmy was talking up some fish he'd caught or a new rifle his father had given him. He was always boasting about something.

One day, weeks after the incident between Pa and Jimmy Sr., I walked past my two cousins in a hurry. It was a Friday; guests would be coming to the inn for dinner and Mr. Foster needed help in the kitchen. I wasn't paying any attention to my cousins because I needed to get to the inn on time. Suddenly I fell hard, my palms broke the fall, scraping against the dirt. I felt bits of stone dig into my palms as my pack flew off. The impact scattered my books, pencils, and slate about five feet in front of me. The boys who'd been gathered around my cousins to listen to their tall tales all guffawed at my expense, and as I rose to gather my things, John stammered, "Aww....nnnnow look what yyyou've gone and done, JJJJimmy."

Jimmy scoffed. "Poor Ben doesn't even have another clean shirt to wear while he's waiting on tables for the tourists."

This set off another round of laughter. Emma Sloane, looking on from the sidelines with a group of girls, came over to help me scoop my things off the ground. I jammed my papers and books into my pack, my face red with fury, thanked her, and stood up. I wasn't going to let Jimmy Beaufort get the best of me; I had planned to just move on. That was until he pressed his face so close to mine, I could smell the mint gum he'd been chewing. "Your Pa's nothin' but a no-good bootlegger."

That's when I hit him. He flew to the ground. "Why'd you dadoo thaaat?" John said. Jimmy rubbed his jaw, got up, and lunged at me. But John stepped in his way to prevent him from reaching me and got caught up in the scuffle. I accidentally hit John in the head while trying to defend myself from Jimmy's blows.

I was eating dust when Mr. Vorhoss came outside and pulled the three of us apart. He berated us for fighting in the yard and threatened to kick us out of school. I brushed the dirt and sweat from my brow and grimaced at my torn trousers. Blood dripped from my nose where Jimmy had hit me, staining my shirt—the only clean shirt I had. But Jimmy came out worse, and I felt good about that. I'd ripped his shirt wide open, and the buttons had scattered. I'd gotten him good with my right fist, which was smarting. His left eye was puffy and red.

"Wait 'til my Pa finds out what you've done," Jimmy Jr. yelled.

"That's enough, boys," Mr. Vorhoss growled in a low voice. "Now git out of here. Go home, wash up. I'll speak to your parents."

He glared at me with disappointment, and I trudged off, but not before thanking Emma Sloane for helping me.

The next morning, I walked in to find Jimmy Sr. standing at the front of the room with Jimmy Jr. and John hidden behind him. My uncle took up so much space in front of the desk we couldn't see half the chalkboard behind him.

Jimmy Sr.'s gaze landed on me. "There he is. Look what you've done to my boy."

Although he'd been looking down, Jimmy Sr. placed his fist under John's chin and made him face the room. His lip was cracked, red, and raw, swollen twice the size so that it took up the lower half of his face like a ghoul. The other students snickered.

"Quiet, all of you!" Mr. Vorhoss commanded. He was visibly stressed to see Mr. Beaufort in his space, and he shot a look at me as if to say, 'why are you putting me and the rest of the class through this utter nonsense, you should've known better.'

"Ben, come here," Mr. Vorhoss said.

I shuffled my way to the front of the room.

"What do you have to say to John?"

If Mr. Vorhoss hadn't been the one to ask, I don't know if I would've admitted any guilt. After all, Jimmy had started the whole thing, and John had gotten in the way. But I knew I'd only cuffed John on the head in the scuffle by accident and didn't inflict that swollen lip. And it just seemed like an injustice to me that the Beauforts, sitting in their glorious home on the edge of town because they cut down all the good trees and set the forests on fire, had any right to tell me that what my Pa did to make money to keep Sam in a sanitarium was wrong.

But I'd have done anything for Mr. Vorhoss, he was so good to me, and I reluctantly mumbled an apology. And then my uncle said to John, "Tell him."

John started to say something, but it came out all jumbled, and a few of the students giggled, and this made my uncle's face turn red, and he shouted, "Say it!" so that we all straightened to attention.

"I accept your apology, Ben. Don't ever touch me again or I'll send the law after you," John blurted with such clarity that the room went silent in awe.

11

That winter we had ice storms in the mountains, and Ma wouldn't leave Sam to come home for Christmas, so Pa and I spent it with Aunt Bertie and the aunts. I was looking forward to seeing my sister Mary again; it had been over six months since we parted, and I only had chance encounters with her when she came to town to bring honey or herbs to Stewart's General Store.

Dr. Clarence, the botanist lodging with them, had left for the season and wasn't coming back until spring. But Mary stayed busy recording the pressed plants she left behind. I watched her one day as she studiously sat down in front of the oil lamp, dipping a brand-new pen into the inkwell, labeling the plants.

"How'd you learn those plant names?" I asked.

She was deep in thought and she pushed a large book at me. It was a botany book, filled with pictures and Latin names. Mary scrawled (*Hydrastis Canadensis)* on the parchment, underneath a flattened sample of goldenseal.

"Good for respiratory ailments: coughs, congestion, colds," she said, jotting it all down in her notebook.

"How do you know?"

Mary pushed air out the side of her mouth to blow a strand of hair out of her eye. "Aunt Bertie is teaching me where to find the plants in the woods and what they are good for, and Dr. Clarence is teaching me how to translate this into scientific language."

I was impressed but confused by her high and mighty attitude. I highly doubted Aunt Bertie even knew what 'scientific language' meant nor cared as long as the plant did what it was supposed to do.

That wasn't all that had changed about Mary in the several months since we'd seen each other. She'd shot up in height and filled out in those places girls do, making her appear even more and more like Ma. But she had little interaction with other folks her age, being cooped up with our aunts and a botanist all summer and fall, so she had no idea.

"Have you been to the movies yet?" I said.

Mary was concentrating on her plants and scowled at me when her pen slipped, causing a blotch of ink to settle on the paper.

"No, Ben. I haven't the time. Now leave me be so I can finish this work."

"You might enjoy Mary Pickford shows," I said.

"Mary Pickford?" She laughed. "When did you get to see a movie with Mary Pickford?"

"At the community hall. You need to come to town more often."

"I'm in town enough," she sniffed. "Delivering herbs to the pharmacist." She leaned in and lowered her voice. "And I know Pa and Uncle Floyd go there often as well to sell their whiskey." She turned her head left and right, making sure nobody would overhear, although there was no one else there.

On this subject, I knew more than her. I puffed up my chest. "*I know that. Ever since Pa sold off the livestock, he's been making money selling whiskey.*"

"But where's the still? Aren't you worried someone's gonna find it, and have Pa arrested?"

I shrugged, trying to convince her I wasn't worried, although inside my gut told me Pa was playing with fire, taking too many risks. And we had so much to lose.

The aunts made us a feast of roasted turkey, potatoes, squash, bread pudding, pies. We exchanged small gifts. I bought my aunts and Mary ribbon from the General Store. Pa bought them new utensils for cooking and a crate of oranges from Florida. Mary gave us all cards with pressed summer flowers, and the aunts gave us honey, jars of herbs, a new shirt, and wool socks for Pa and me they made with their own home-spun thread.

We sat up all night and listened to Pa tell his tales from their childhood growing up in the mountains, often interrupted by Aunt Bertie, correcting him if she thought he had gotten a particular feature of the story wrong. The fire crackled, the winter wind threw bursts of snow and sleet on the glass windows, our faces warm and glowing, a small glass of whiskey for each of us; I was filled with joy.

We stayed a week cutting firewood, patching holes in the roof, and chinking the walls to keep out drafts. Pa took a sack of corn kernels with the promise to bring back meal after he visited McConnell's mill. Then we put on our new socks and shirts and slipped on our boots one morning while the sun was still behind the mountains. Pa wanted to take a detour back to the cabin to check out some activity on the mountain that Bertie had told him about—the Beauforts had cut a new road.

We hiked all morning on narrow paths cut by pigs or deer. It didn't deter Pa one bit that the fresh, wet snow which had fallen overnight was clinging to the mountain laurel. He'd sweep right past it while clumps of snow would drop onto our shoulders. The sweat and melted snow dripped down my clammy back. By the time we reached Raven's Bald, which was our destination, I was soaked and shivering. The bleak sun had turned brighter and the bald radiated heat. We found a dry spot on a huge boulder and took out lunch. Pa gathered some sticks and built a fire. "Take off that shirt," he said.

I did as he asked. He made a tent with some sticks and draped our shirts near the fire. I ate my corn pone as the sun warmed my back. I must have dozed because I woke to grumbling sounds in the distance and thought it was thunder. Pa was biting into an apple, scanning the horizon. He cupped his eyes and pointed. The range ahead of us was riddled with a railroad zigzagging up the mountain.

"How they supposed to get a railroad train way up there?" I said.

"Special engines," Pa said. "They've already got people working."

I followed his line of sight to a spot at the base of the mountain to see a community of people in setoff shacks. The lumbermen took advantage of the break in the weather to cut and haul trees.

"That used to be where Bill Reed's family had a cabin," Pa said.

"You mean the Cherokee family? The ones who bring the ramps and baskets to town to sell?"

Pa licked his lower lip, which was dry and cracked. "Same ones."

"Why'd they sell it?"

"May not have had a choice, son."

"Why's that?"

I had sprouted up and was only about one foot shorter than him but felt years younger. He turned to look down at me with a sad smile. "Cuz Bill got into some trouble with the law."

I opened my mouth to ask more, but my attention was diverted to the loud scream of an engine. Pa took out his spy glasses to view what was happening.

"Can I see?"

He handed me the glasses, and I saw the strangest looking piece of machinery, a coil of cable tethered to a flatbed on the track. The men pulled the cable like an octopus' arm. It slithered up the mountainside to where they had felled a tree. Steam was blowing hard as the engine cranked, dragging the log over the scarred forest floor, scraping up the dead leaves, brush, bushes, anything in its way, to be positioned next to the railroad bed. They piled them up to be loaded on a car with giant tongs. We sat and watched until the car was stacked with the logs, six feet round, all on top of each other, and tethered to the flatbed to be carried to town.

"Holy smokes," I said, impressed.

Pa said nothing, just picked up his sack and started back down the path in the direction of McConnell's Cove.

∙ ∙ ∙

We reached McConnell's corn mill as the clouds streaked with orange. Mr. McConnell met us at the door to his barn.

After greetings, Mr. McConnell said, "Glad to see you, Bob. Bin meanin' to ask ye about somethin'." He nodded at me. "Finn's in the mill. He'll grind that corn for you."

I hoisted the sack of kernels over my shoulder and headed to the mill. When I entered Finn was finishing grinding another sack of kernels. He acknowledged me without saying anything, so I took a seat to watch him. Finn had been in the Great War. Pa said he came back damaged. It wasn't physical, nor in the head. Pa said it was his heart that was injured, where it mattered most.

He was the only McConnell son and word was that since so many of our neighbors' sons hadn't made it back, Mrs. McConnell knew she was blessed. However, she would never gloat about it, but she was overcome with joy and fainted at the sight of him walking up the path home when the war was over. Finn showed little emotion at his homecoming, and it had been that way ever since. He was 19 when he left for the war and was closing in on twenty-eight now, but he still had no interest in girls or marrying or moving away. Working in the mill was all he did, and that was all he wanted to do. Unfortunately for the rest of us, when Finn was running the mill, it put a damper on what was otherwise one of the few social occasions people had in their day. Some said they liked it better when Finn was off doing something else and Mr. McConnell was working because that way, they'd hear some news about their neighbors.

Before Finn went to war, he was known for his marksmanship. He won contests and was legendary for miles around as an expert sharpshooter. He was often seen with his Remington, scouting the woods for squirrels or gobblers. He had a good eye too. Folks said he could spot a gobbler up in a tree hundreds of yards away before anyone else did, and he could bring it down with one shot. He went to the war to be a sniper, and his targets were Krauts.

Everyone said Finn wouldn't talk about what it was like in the war, so they never bothered asking. I tried as much with Finn that day and got nowhere, so instead I filled in the dead space between us with my stories.

"Pa and I saw something interesting up on top of Raven's Bald," I said.

He paused from filling up a sack of ground corn and looked at me like I was some stranger, with no emotion in his eyes. I wasn't deterred. I figured maybe he just needed a little coaxing and became more animated in my storytelling: arms flying as I imitated the skidder with the octopus arms, hands claw-like when I mimicked the logs being lifted onto the flatbed. My face was red, and I was huffing by the time I was done. I sat back down, a little embarrassed. Finn's lip curled into a smile, but he didn't let it linger too long. He held out his arm for me to hand him my sack of corn.

While he did his job, I went out to find Pa and some water. He was on the porch with Mr. McConnell deep in discussion.

"Son, how'd you like a job this summer?" Pa said.

"Why I've got a job, Pa. At the Inn."

"Wouldn't you rather be out in the mountain air all day than cooped up in town?" Mr. McConnell said.

"Why I guess." I imagined the disappointed look in Mr. Foster's eyes if I told him I couldn't work for him at the height of the tourist season. Plus, I didn't want to lose my chance to stay in school.

"Mr. McConnell here has made us a business proposition," Pa said. "He wants us to herd his cattle this summer on our land, and for you to keep track of 'em. Says he'll pay ye one dolla' a head 'til they go to market in the fall."

I did the math in my head. I knew the McConnell's had at least fifty if not seventy head of cattle they took to the market on good years.

"Why aren't you using your pasture land?" I said.

McConnell threw his hands up in the air. "The Beaufort Lumber Company is all over the hills, boy. Just bought up the last grazing pasture for miles around, Bennet's Field. They's puttin' tracks through it to reach up the mountain thar." He pointed to a ridge in the distance. "It's too dangerous. They may wander off and git run over by a train or worse, hit by a falling tree."

Pa stretched his long legs out and lifted himself up. He shook McConnell's hand and said. "Ben'd be glad to help ye out." And that was that.

When we went to retrieve our sack of cornmeal, Finn was scooping some into a big barrel he kept in the corner of the mill; his pay.

"What do you do with all that meal?" I asked him.

He shot Pa a look before returning to me. "We sell or barter it. To the General Store. To your Cousin Floyd." His eyes held mine for a moment claiming a deeper understanding than I had expected. I shuddered. Seemed the moonshining business was a community affair.

12

The mountains opened up to an early spring morning the day Ma came home from Knoxville. Spring has a distinct smell to it, and as I trudged to the cabin that morning, my mind reeling with the news, drowning in sorrow, I had to suppress the urge to run into the woods and let the trees, pulsing with energy, shield me from what lay ahead: my grieving mother and an empty bed where Sam once slept. I passed by McConnell's Cove and the forest marred by the fire. The canopy was black and beheaded. But the cruel irony was the dogwoods and redbud trees that haunted the woods like ghosts—wisps of white and purple flowers that appeared between the charred remains of oaks. And the tangles of ivy and honeysuckle made you realize that even with all the destruction, the place was brimming with life. It only made me bitter because Sam wasn't here to see the hope of new life.

I hadn't seen Pa in weeks. When he got the call from Ma at the pharmacy, pleading for him to come to Knoxville before it was too late, he got on the first train. He arrived just in time to say good-bye. They brought Sam home in a small coffin.

Ma was sitting on the porch, staring into the horizon. When I approached, she greeted me with a wan smile, took my hand in hers, and patted it softly.

"So good to see you, Ben. You've grown up."

"I'm fourteen now." With all the sorrow, no one had acknowledged my birthday.

I bent down and kissed her head, wrapping my arms around her small body. She shivered. "Let me get you a blanket," I said. "Where's Pa?"

"He's digging the—" she choked.

I went inside to find a blanket and found my aunts and cousins. They had brought any food they had along with them: jars of fruit, vegetables, breads, pork, pies, chutneys, and butter. The women bustled about the cabin: cleaning, dusting, sweeping, clearing the cupboards of mice droppings. And in the middle of the room was my brother's small coffin made of pine.

My memory of that day shifts; family trooping up the side of the knoll behind our cabin where Pa and Uncle Stan had dug a grave in the soft spring earth. I carried one end of the coffin while Pa carried the other, our extended family in tow, Ma wailing as Mary half carried her up the hill. Nellie and Rachel moved glumly alongside Ma, not speaking. There was a stiff breeze at the top of the knoll, where a leafless oak bursting with spring buds anchored the family plot. Two small crosses made of tree limbs marked the location of babies Ma lost at birth after Sam was born and before she had Rachel.

Preacher Joe said words I don't remember, the women huddled around Ma. Aunt Bertie held on to her so she wouldn't keel over into the grave as we lowered the coffin into the hole.

.   .   .

After Sam was buried nothing was the same. A pall fell over the cabin, infecting Ma and Pa like a tree fungus. Mary stayed with us instead of going back to work with Dr. Clarence, bristling with pent-up energy and resentment that Ma wouldn't come to her senses and take up her duties. Instead, they fell to Mary: the cleaning, washing, cooking, as Ma sat in her rocker on the porch.

I hoped her mood would shift with the change of seasons. It started in the valleys; trees began to leaf-out, and as weeks went by, the green carpet unfurled up the mountain until it reached us, as if the hand of God laid it himself, willing the forest to breathe new life into our family and forget our grief.

We didn't have preserved food left over from harvest. No ramps hung from the ceiling, no jars of preserves. We had nothing to eat but cornbread and whatever our extended family left us out of pity. Ma insisted I go back to school and she fought about it with Pa. One night their fighting woke us all up. Mary and I jumped out of bed and went to listen at the top of the loft. Pa spoke gently but Ma continued to wail. When she stopped, probably out of exhaustion, they went to bed and in the morning acted like nothing had happened. Ma looked longingly out the windows as the awakening spring taunted her. Pa went to the fields to plant corn. I went back to work in town, bringing with me a few of Ma's sketches. Mr. Foster bought them on the spot, maybe out of pity, I don't know. But I used the money to buy some chicks as we had none, and I brought them home with me when I came back on a Sunday.

Mary met me at the door and pulled me aside the moment I arrived. I dropped the crate of chicks on the porch, and they chirped in protest to be let out.

"I can't put up with this anymore!" she practically spit into my ear.

"What's wrong with you?"

Her arms flailed. "This! Ma is heartbroken and won't do nothin'! The girls are running around like animals. I can't keep track of 'em. And Pa and Ma are constantly fighting."

"Over what?" I said.

She took hold of my collar and dragged me into the cabin. "This." She pointed to a stack of bills on the kitchen table.

I leafed through a few and caught the gist. They were from the sanitarium. Letters threatening Pa with the law if he didn't pay. A past-due notice for Ma's last month of rent. It all amounted to well over $300.00.

"We'll just have to rebuild is all," I said as Mary fumed next to me.

"What good am I if I can't get paid like you?" she said. "I should be going back to work with Dr. Clarence."

"What do we do about the girls then? And Ma?"

"I got it all worked out," Mary said. "I'll take Rachel with me. She's easy to watch over. And Cousin Biddie said she could take in Nellie 'til Ma comes to her senses."

I dreaded the idea of all of us breaking up again. "Nellie won't like that."

"She'll have no choice."

"But I'll be back soon," I said.

Mary scoffed. "You gonna take Nellie with you while you herd cattle?" She had a point.

"And besides," Mary continued. "Someone needs to talk some sense into Pa. Dr. Clarence told me"—and at the mention of her mentor, she straightened and put her nose in the air—"that Pa's old forest is valuable for preservation."

"You been up there?" I said.

"Of course," Mary said. "The aunts all know the way. Dr. Clarence showed me the rare plants that are growing up there. She says the *government* would *pay* Pa for the land if he would just sell it." She folded her arms over her chest with indignation.

"He won't do it," I said forcefully. "He says he can make just as much 'senging."

"Humph," Mary said. "Dr. Clarence said once people find out where it's growing, they'll poach it."

"No one's gonna poach Pa's ginseng, Mary. Why's this doctor putting these fool notions in your head?"

"They're not foolish notions!" She tossed her head and stomped away.

Ma didn't put up much protest when Cousin Biddie came to collect Nellie. Cousin Biddie had a household of kids, and we all knew it would be better for Nellie, at least in the short term to be in a home overflowing with love and joy, since none of these were available in our cabin at the time.

I went home in May to start my job as a herder. Pa built a small shed below Raven's Bald, big enough to sleep two men. "Bin meaning to build somethin' up here anyways," he said. "Make sure people know it belongs to me."

It had one room, a small fireplace with a pipe leading out of the ceiling, some cookware we gathered from home, and two pallet beds. I stayed there during the week while the cattle roamed the mountain range, keeping track of them and keeping them away from places where the snakeroot grew next to streambeds so they wouldn't contract 'milk sickness'. Pa insisted I ride our plow horse Bess to the range and use her to track the cattle. The McConnells put bells on a few lead cows, and we led them to the range, an area that covered several acres of land Pa owned. Bess was a reluctant participant, but together we made a team. I coaxed her along the trail by feeding her cubes of sugar, and she allowed me to ride her without much fuss.

The days were long and lonely. Once in a while, another herder would come along, crossing paths in search of his own cattle. But for the most part, it was just me and the wind and the cattle. I read books Mr. Vorhoss had lent me: *The Great Gatsby*, *Riders of the Purple Sage*, *Tarzan of the Apes*. He'd been reluctant to lend me the *Great Gatsby*, telling me it might be too adult for me when I pulled it off the shelf in his boarding house. This, of course, made me want to read it all the more.

"What's it about?" I asked.

He shrugged as he leafed through some other books on his shelves, determining what might be appropriate for my fourteen-year-old mind. "It's just a dull story about rich people in New York."

I'd sit and read and get lost in another world, imagining myself in the American west, the jungles of Africa, or the great house Gatsby owned. I was enthralled with Gatsby and his everlasting love for Daisy. What was it, I wondered, that made a man so crazy over a girl like her? I'd sit leaning against a large boulder, my face warmed by the sun, daydreaming about Gatsby. And as I watched the puffy clouds skitter across the sky, I thought of Mary Pickford and Emma Sloane, and I'd feel an ache in my gut like I'd never felt before and a longing, which I interpreted to mean I was in love. I made a pact with myself I'd see the world and get away from the mountains when I got old enough. And I'd bring Emma Sloane with me.

I wasn't always alone. Once a week, Finn made the trip on his horse to bring me more salt for the cattle. He'd stay the night, and we'd build a fire and sleep under the stars if the weather was good. Those were good evenings. We'd make a big fire and watch the dark dome above us fill with twinkling starlight.

Finn liked hearing me tell stories, so I obliged him. Some I'd read in the papers, or in the books I was reading, some I made up. While I talked, I'd watch as his face, flickering in the orange glow, broke into a smile, and it made me feel good. He was the best replacement I had for my brother Sam, who had always been eager to listen to stories.

When I had quieted down, and my breath returned, I lay down on my sleeping bag next to him and listened to the night sounds. "Finn?"

"Uh hah."

"What was it like in the war?"

The air went silent, I could hear his measured breathing. Moments ticked by. I figured I'd lost him and he'd just turn over and go to sleep without answering. Instead, he said, "When you shoot a turkey, you gain something from it. You figure I'm gonna eat it or give it away to someone who needs it to feed their family." His hands swiped the air.

"When you go to war and shoot a man, even if he's your enemy, you lose something, and you spend your days searching for it."

"What's that?" I said.

His face swiveled towards me, eyes glinting in the firelight. "A part of your humanity."

The next morning, I woke to the screeching sound of metal grinding against metal. The wind had carried the sound of the distant railroad chugging up the ridge toward the lumber camp. I rubbed my eyes and glanced over at Finn's bag lying next to mine. It was flung open. I felt the inside of the bag, it was cold. "Finn?" I called.

The railroad whistled, sending a plume of white steam into the frigid air. I jumped out of my bag to look around. There he was, standing at the edge of a precipice, gazing at the distant mountainside riddled with tracks, swaths of forest gouged out of the earth.

"Finn?" I called again. But with the breeze, he may not have heard me. I walked toward him so that I was only yards away. His feet moved closer to the edge, like he thought he could walk on air—one more step and he'd be over the side. Panicked, I called out louder, "Finn!"

He swirled around, spooked—aiming his rifle dead at me. His face was long, drawn, aged beyond his twenty-eight years.

I lifted my arms in the air. "It's me! Ben Taylor!"

Life came back to his eyes. "I-I-I. Wh-whe, where?" he said. He stumbled forward, dropping his rifle beside him. When he gathered himself, he said, "I wouldn't've bin able to shoot ye anyways. Can't even shoot a gobbler outta a tree no more. I can't see that far no more." He stated it like a confession.

"You must've been sleep-walking." I was perspiring, and when the breeze hit the back of my neck, I shivered. I picked up his rifle and led him back to the campfire to make breakfast.

■   ■   ■

On weekends I went back to the cabin to see Ma and gather food supplies I'd need for the week. Usually, when I came home, I'd find her sitting on the porch. Sometimes she was drawing, many times she wasn't. Her mood hadn't changed.

One day I came home and found her painting. Entranced. Rachel and Nellie sat next to her, playing with June bugs. They had tied a string around their tiny legs, treating them like they were pets.

Nellie ran to me. "Come see, Bennie. The June bugs make a humming sound." She put her small pudgy hands in mine and dragged me to the porch.

The poor creatures tried to get away from the girls, spreading their wings, hurling into the air just to be brought crashing back down by a string.

"Let 'em loose, girls. That ain't no way to treat a June bug."

Rachel huffed at me, took hold of Nellie, and stalked off the porch, bugs swinging by their hips.

I plunked myself down on the chair next to Ma. Tuckered out from the dusty ride, my mind reeling from reading Gatsby. He'd gone and got killed because he was trying to protect the love of his life.

"Ma. I've been thinking."

"Hmmm?" she said, dabbing her brush in the palette, stroking a tree limb onto the canvas.

"I've been thinking a lot about a girl."

She set her brush down and eyed me with a note of curiosity, as if just now realizing she had a teenaged boy.

"A girl? What girl?"

"No matter," I said. "Just that I was wondering, when do you think it will go away?"

"What will go away?" she said, tilting her head.

"This feeling, Ma!" I could feel the heat rising to my face. "I can't seem to stop the feeling and my mind." I got up from my chair, agitated, taking hold of the sides of my head. "I can't shut my head up! I sometimes feel like it's gonna explode!"

Her face went from curious to merry. It washed away the grief for a brief moment, made her appear ten years younger all of a sudden, and I wanted so badly to just run over and crush her in my arms. But I stopped myself out of pride. She saw me draw back and stiffened herself, coughed, became serious, and said, "Well now, Ben. I'd say you have a crush. It happens at your age. It'll happen again as you grow up. There will be other girls to admire, I'm sure. The important thing is that you stay respectful. Keep your distance. Make sure you always do the right thing."

That was it? Her advice? Do the right thing? What was the right thing? I knew I'd have to address this with Pa. She was no use whatsoever.

She sighed. "Sometimes, I wish I'd never met your Pa."

I watched her sideways, embarrassed she'd say something she'd regret. But she ignored me and kept on talking like I wasn't there, staring off in the distance as if the horizon would provide answers to all of her questions. "Oh, he was a good man. But my mother told me he wasn't right for me. I should've listened. When I met him, I was teaching in town. He was there doing some carpentry work. I went to a church dance one evening, and there he was…He just swept me off my feet with his charm and good looks." She waved her hand in the air in defeat.

"However," she continued looking right at me. "One thing you can do about your mind"—she put her finger on my head—"is do what I do. Something creative. You like to write. Take that journal I gave you back to the range and write down your thoughts." She went back to surveying her painting in progress. "Lord knows one can get mighty lonely in these mountains, but beautiful as it is, you might as well write about it. Chase the demon thoughts away."

Although I took her advice, I still wanted to ask Pa what he thought, but the summer rolled by before I had the chance. The McConnells and I herded the cattle from the rangeland down the mountainside to the cove where their next stop was into town and onto trains heading for the slaughterhouse in Knoxville.

I continued schooling that fall, riding Bess into town when the weather allowed it. I didn't want to go back to the Inn and leave Ma. And I knew Pa was struggling. The extended family pitched in where they could. The cousins would stop in to check on Ma. Cousin Biddie brought Nellie home every weekend and gave Ma seed for the garden, even helped Ma plant it. But without me around to tend to the weeding and watering, it barely survived the summer. The only crop Pa made sure to grow while Ma was gone was corn. And although it was a mainstay of our diet, I knew the real reason he and Floyd tended their corn crops was to make whiskey for moonshining. It was the one sure way to make money and get us out of debt. After they harvested their corn, Pa went into town with Uncle Floyd weekly. My stomach always flipped, filled with dread when I saw him jump into Floyd's truck under cover of darkness, jugs jangling in the back.

13

I knew their luck would run out eventually. It started to deteriorate that evening at the community hall. A few government men came to town to talk-up the National Park in the Smoky Mountains. I begged Pa to take me with him, and he agreed. The whole town showed up to listen. They offered cash for the rights to people's land.

One of them, a man who worked in partnership with the government, named Kephart, took to the podium like a cow to pasture.

"We must save these glorious forests from the onslaught of the saw," he said.

The hall brimmed with people radiating heat and energy which bounced off the walls. I caught sight of Dr. Clarence sitting near the podium, transfixed by everything Kephart said.

"How much?" one man called.

"What are we supposed to do with ourselves once the government takes our land? How are we supposed to grow food?" another shouted.

I sat next to Pa in the back of the room, feeling his body tense up each time the men from the government spoke. Their sugar-coated tongues offered sweet deals, and if a man could prove he had nowhere to go, they offered the right to lease the land back from the government until he could find employment elsewhere.

"But you all are sayin' we can't hunt, we can't cut down trees to clear fields, we can't use it for firewood," someone scoffed. People chortled in agreement.

"What kind of deal is that? Why would anyone stay?"

A bulky figure stepped out of the crowd of men clustered in the back of the room. It was Jimmy Beaufort, Sr. He strolled to the front, turned his back to Kephart and the stage, waving his arms in the air, addressing the crowd. "Don't listen to these government men! They don't have anything good to offer you all. I do, however. Give me the right to cut your timber, and I'll pay you a dollar an acre. Plus, I can give you all a job cutting trees or at the mill here in town." That brought out catcalls and stomping feet. "Now that may not seem like much, but just think, you get to keep your land and farm it."

A man cupped his hands around his mouth and bellowed, "No, you'll just burn everything down while you're at it!"

Laughter tore through the hall. Uncle Jimmy simmered in place; his mouth set in a frown. He scanned the crowd to seek out the heckler.

"The unfortunate event at the McConnell's was not the fault of the Beaufort Lumber Company." His icy blue eyes glowered as they cut into the crowd. "Now, if you'd like, I can go to the courthouse and look up all the deeds in this here county and see which ones are legal and which ones aren't. I got lawyers who can do that for me. And if there's a discrepancy, well then…" He paused, puffed his chest, hitched his thumbs on his red suspenders. "The courts tend to favor those willing to pay off the taxes."

A hushed shock fell on the audience. Husband and wives whispered into each other's ears with worried looks. More boos and hisses followed. The government men stood with their arms across their chests waiting for this intruder to finish so they could continue to press their case, but the mood of the crowd was shifting, and they waited to see where it would go.

Uncle Jimmy raised his hand to shush the crowd. Pa craned his neck, his body taut.

"You all should be more appreciative of what my company has done for this town. If we didn't build these railroads, how do you think the tourists would get here?"

"We don't want 'em!" More guffaws.

Jimmy Sr.'s jowls puffed red, and his eyes bulged. "Tell that to the Fosters then. And what about the General Store? You stop by there any day of the week but Sunday, and they have more customers than you can count on your two hands. Most of 'em my workers. And all of you," he swept the crowd with his arm, "benefit from that. You there, Mr. Davis, you sell them your milk and butter. And you, Mr. Meyer, your wife's homespun yarn. Don't tell me you all don't need the lumber company."

This quieted the crowd. Uncle Jimmy glared round and stalked to the back of the hall. The heat was overwhelming me, so I left Pa to go outside for some fresh air. That's when I saw Aunt Cornelia, standing awkwardly, wringing her hands together, seeking someone out.

I approached her. "Aunt Cornelia." She jumped.

"Oh, it's you, Ben. Where's your Pa?"

I motioned to the hall. Her face was in the shadow, and she avoided my stare. Her hat was angled deeply over one side of her face. "Go git him for me, will ye?"

I ran back inside and tugged at Pa's shirt sleeve, whispered in his ear. He followed me outside and walked up to Cornelia.

"Did he do this to you?" he said. That's when I saw what Cornelia was hiding under the brim of her hat: her left eye, swollen shut, raw and red. She was hanging her head down in shame, and a strangled cry escaped her. Pa took her by the arm, led her to a bench, told me to sit with her and went back inside the hall.

"Maybe we should get the sheriff?" I called after him, but he wasn't listening.

Within minutes the large body of Jimmy Beaufort Sr. flew out the door of the hall, landing with a thud on the street, and Pa was looming over him, kicking. "You son-of-a-bitch. What kind of man beats his wife? My *sister*. You won't get away with it, you bastard!"

"Ben, go get the Sheriff," Aunt Cornelia pleaded as people started pouring out of the hall to watch the spectacle.

As it turned out, the Sheriff was there. He came out like the rest of the crowd when they saw Pa take hold of Uncle Jimmy's collar and haul him out the door. He and a few men pushed their way past the onlookers and held Pa back before he could land a blow on Jimmy Sr.'s head.

"That'll be enough, Bob," the Sheriff said.

Someone helped my uncle stagger to his feet. Blood ran from his nose. He swiped it away, marched up to Pa, clocked him in the jaw, and spat on the ground as Pa staggered back. "You'll regret this," he growled.

Cornelia jumped up from her seat next to me and ran. I watched her retreating figure as it dashed down the street and faded into the distance.

"Git your Pa out of here," Sheriff Parsons said.

I half carried, half dragged Pa to the back door of the pharmacy, hoping someone would be there to let us in. He crumpled to the ground by the door, put his head in his hands, and started to sob. I'd never seen him so broken. I knocked on the door, and he waved at me to stop.

"I just want to sit and think," he said, his eyes watery.

We sat there for I don't know how long before he sighed and stood up. We walked together up the road leading out of town where we had parked Cousin Floyd's truck under a street lamp. Just as we were about to climb into it, out of nowhere comes John Beaufort. He saw me first, ran over, and slammed a note into Pa's hand.

"It's from my Ma," he said, glancing nervously around.

Pa climbed into the truck. "Let's go, Ben."

I turned to John.

"She was t-t-trying to protect me," he said. "From my Pa."

I nodded. Without him saying anything else I understood what had happened.

It turned out the note from Cornelia warned Pa that Jimmy Sr. had plans for Pa's land. He needed it. He needed access to the upper reaches of Hickory Run Creek, which ran right through Pa's land and the old trees in Taylor Grove. Pa had a clear title to the land. It had been passed down to him by his Pa. Cornelia had no rights to it. I wondered if this was the reason Jimmy married her in the first place, thinking by marrying her, he'd be able to harvest the prime timber in all of the Taylor Valley. Pa was stubborn, and Cornelia knew it. But Jimmy Beaufort would stop at nothing to get title to the land.

The seasons passed, and we all believed that things would get better. And for a while, they did. Ma's health improved, and Nellie and Rachel came back to live with us. We had Christmas at home, and the aunts came to stay with us, bringing all kinds of goodies and sweets, plus new dresses they had made for the girls. Mary had matured into a young lady. She sat regally watching the goings-on, pre-occupied at times, listless, like a caged cat, waiting for someone to let her out. She shared in the merriment when possible, but I'd often find her up in the loft, scribbling something in the big notebook she dragged everywhere, some new important piece of information she had thought of that day about an herbal remedy.

"Ma's making gingerbread with the girls," I said. "She told me to come get you."

Mary flapped her hand in the air. "I'll be down in a moment."

Too old now to sleep with the girls, I stayed in what was once the sick room where Sam slept. It was next to my parents' bedroom, and that Christmas Eve, I heard them after we had all gone to sleep, giggling like children. Ma said something that made Pa laugh. Then it went quiet until I heard their bed creaking. I fell asleep to the sound of their soft moans.

By the time spring came, Ma was humming again, going about her chores, her face aglow. I'd catch her on the porch, attention on the distant mountain range, a small smile on her face, her free hand on her expanding belly. My sister was born that fall. They named her Sarah, and she breathed new life into our home.

Our lives began to get better as Pa paid off debts, and Ma fussed over the baby. I studied and stuck to my goal: to get off the mountain and see the world. Go to New York, visit the places Gatsby did. I still had a crush on Emma Sloane. She was the prettiest girl in high school. That fall I asked her if she'd like to go picking chestnuts with me.

"That's very kind of you to ask, Ben," she said. "But we're fifteen years old. Too young to court. I don't think my father would allow it."

"What if I brought my sisters? Or you brought a friend?"

She slapped my arm playfully. "Maybe."

I went with my sisters instead. We had a ritual every fall. There was a trail that led into a grove of enormous chestnut trees where the Taylor family would gather to collect chestnuts. Some we kept to roast for ourselves, others we brought into town to sell at the store. That was the first fall we began to take notice of the blight that was infecting the chestnut trees. We'd hear about it from neighbors but hadn't seen the devastation ourselves, thinking Taylor Valley was immune to the problems of the rest of the forest. And as it had been a dry season that summer, their leaves were curled and brown, which was unusual for October. Even so, we gathered baskets full of nuts.

I loaded Bess with a basket of chestnuts and one sack full for Emma and went to town. I planned to take the sack to the Sloane house after visiting the store. I pulled up with Bess in front of the store to find Jimmy Jr. and Emma at the front entrance. Jimmy had his hand planted against the wall above her head. He was gaping down at her while she shrank away, embarrassed by the attention.

I dismounted, grabbed the basket, and headed for the door, brushing right past them, my ears aflame.

"Why if it isn't Ben Taylor." Jimmy sneered.

Emma took the opportunity to duck under his arm and escape his bulky presence. She got in step with me as I headed into the store. "Hello, Ben," she said. "I see you brought some chestnuts."

"Yes," I said. "I have some for you too."

She blushed and pretended to be interested in some fabric as I made my way to the counter.

"These are getting rare to find around here, Ben," Mr. Stewart said. "I'll pay you five dollars for the basket."

I swelled with pride until he leaned in closer to tell me, "I'll deduct it from what your Pa owes me."

I felt the heat creep up to my face when right next to me, Jimmy hissed, "Figures the hillbilly doesn't pay his bills."

I turned around to face him, my fists clenched.

"Now, boys, take it outside. I don't want no trouble in here," Mr. Stewart warned.

People's heads turned in our direction. Emma was biting her lower lip. She slipped outside before I could say something in retort. I stormed out of the store, jumped up on Bess, and kicked her too hard. She jolted, then trotted down the road. When I got to Emma's house, she was waiting on the porch. I slid off Bess and handed her the sack.

"I'm sorry about that, Ben. Jimmy Beaufort is a bully."

I plunked down next to her. "I know. But I can handle him. I wanted to right then and there, but Mr. Stewart is good to my family. I didn't want to cause no trouble."

She peeked into the sack. "My, you sure got a lot of chestnuts!" She glowed like sunshine.

"You're the prettiest girl I've ever known." I had no idea how that came out of my mouth, but it did, and as I watched her startled expression, I wished I had a way to take it back.

Then a funny thing happened. She reached over and kissed me on the cheek, so light, so soft, it was like being touched by a feather.

The look on my face must have alarmed her.

She pulled back. "Oh, no. Did I do something wrong? I'm sorry, I—"

"No! No! Not at all. I was just—"

"Emma!" a voice called from inside the house, and a large woman came to the door and peered out at us through the screen. "Your Pa's on the phone. He wants to talk with you. And you need to wash up for supper." Her attention turned to me with knit brows. "Who's this young man?"

"I'm Ben Taylor, ma'am. Pleased to meet you."

"Ben Taylor? You Bob's son? My, you've grown. You don't remember me, do you? I'm a cousin once removed. Lila Chapin's the name. You go ask your Aunt Bertie. Me and her used to play when we was youngins. We was best friends 'til I had to come to town an' work. Oh, how I miss livin' in the mountains. I met you when you was just a little tyke," she gestured at her hip to indicate my height when I was five, "runnin' aroun' the yard chasin' chickens. Yes indeed, came to your house after Sunday services."

She went on and on, as was the custom of our kin, while Emma and I stood awkwardly, sneaking glances at each other, trying to suppress a giggle. I couldn't wait for her to finish so I could say goodbye to Emma properly. But Lila Chapin—distant cousin—never gave me a chance. Emma side-stepped her into the house, throwing me a smile while I had to stand there and listen to old Lila yammer on about all the mischief her and Aunt Bertie used to get into when they were young girls: chasing chickens, sleuthing for salamanders, trolling for trout. She even worked her big body out from behind the screen door to continue, as if it had been years since anyone had paid any attention to her. After what seemed like an hour with no sign of her mouth letting up or Emma coming back, I interrupted. "I've gotta go. It was nice meeting you."

I jumped up on Bess and gave her a gentle kick, my mind reeling from Emma's kiss and what it meant.

14

I was enjoying a quiet autumn evening on the porch. The sun was setting, leaving behind streaks of cherry-colored clouds. I was with Ma and the girls. Pa was at Cousin Floyd's. The gurgling sound of an automobile engine and a cloud of dust brought our attention to the road where the sheriff braked his car in front of our cabin and got out.

"Mrs. Taylor." He doffed his hat. "I'm looking for your husband."

"He isn't here," Ma said with as much composure as she could muster.

I gulped down bile and stood up, scooped up baby Sarah and took Nellie by the hand, leading her into the house. I listened to what they said from the kitchen window.

"I have a warrant to search the premises." He held out a piece of paper. "Here and up yonder at your cousin's place."

"Whatever for?" Ma's voice cracked.

"There's been a complaint they's running a still up here."

"Go ahead," Ma waved her hand in the air, "take a look around. You won't find anything."

The sheriff and two of the men he brought with him spread out. I watched them from the window as they walked up the path leading to the spring house and up the hill. Then I came outside.

"Take Bess and warn Pa," Ma said, motioning to the barn.

I crept to the barn and let Bess out as quietly as possible, led her up a path in the opposite direction of the sheriff and his men, and jumped on her to take the back route to Cousin Floyd's. I didn't know where Pa kept his still. But I had a feeling where it might be. I had learned a few things about making whiskey from listening to Pa talk about it with Floyd and reading about it in the newspaper whenever someone was caught. The operation needs to be near a spring as water, like corn, was a crucial ingredient in the manufacture of whiskey. I followed the small creek that empties into Hickory Run by the bridge. The creek cut through Floyd's property, and there was no path, so Bess walked in the stream. She wasn't too happy about that, and I had to urge her on with both threats and encouragement. Up and up the creek we went, I scanned the woods for signs of a fire, also needed to make whiskey.

I smelled smoke after about a half-hour of riding. By now, the forest was gloomy. It made it easier to find the flames. I slid off Bess and tied her to a tree limb then followed the scent. Before long, I heard my Pa's laugh and Floyd's voice. They stood over a copper vessel, propped up with stones, a small fire lit under it, coils leading into jugs, filling up with a clear liquid. I stood in the shadows for a moment, watching Pa and Floyd laugh about something before I leaped out from behind a bush.

"Pa!" I ran straight to him.

He jumped back, reaching for his gun.

"Pa, it's me." I waved my arms in the air.

"Ben? What are you doin' here?"

"Pa, the sheriff is after you. He's on his way up the road to Floyd's cabin."

Floyd picked up a bucket sloshing with water to douse the fire.

"Leave it," Pa said. "They'll see the smoke."

Pa took hold of my shoulders.

"You git outta here, now. Git back to the creek. Go home to Ma and the girls."

His face was contorted by the flickering flames, but his eyes wide with fear. I ran back to get Bess but turned when I heard shouting from the woods, flashing lights from lanterns, and the baying of a hound dog. Odd, I thought, I hadn't seen a dog with the sheriff. But it wasn't the sheriff who found Pa and Floyd trying to hide the evidence of their moonshining—it was two Prohibition Agents. The barking dog pinned Floyd against a tree. An agent held a gun to Pa, who had since dropped his to the ground. None of them saw me there at the edge of the forest. I wanted to scream, but I fell to the ground in terror.

"Now, boys," I heard the leader say. "Let's not do anything you'll regret." He was aiming his comments at Pa and Floyd.

"Git your dog offa me," Floyd said.

The agent commanded them to simmer down while pointing a gun at Floyd. In that instant, the sheriff came into view. "What the hell are ye'all doin' here?" he said to the agents.

I couldn't see the faces of the agents, but I could see their silhouettes in the darkness. Their shadows danced in the flames. In an instant, they turned their heads to respond to the sheriff and his men, and Floyd reached for his gun. The agent let go of his dog, and it lunged at Floyd. I heard him cry out as the hound tore into his leg. Floyd shot at the dog, and it pitched back, squealing in pain. In the confusion that ensued, both Pa and Floyd took off running. An agent shot Floyd in the back, and he cried out before buckling.

I yelled out, "Pa!" He swung around, stopped in place, and put his arms in the air.

. . .

They arrested Pa and put him in the town jail. The bond was set at $500.00. Court day wasn't for another six months. If he couldn't come up with the bond, the sheriff told Ma, he'd have to stay in jail and work on the road crew through winter until he had a trial.

Ma and I went to see him in jail the next morning. He was sitting in the corner of the cell, his head in his hands when we walked in. They let us sit in the same room with him while we talked. The sheriff felt awfully bad about the whole thing.

"Mrs. Taylor, if your husband weren't so danged stubborn, none of this would have ever happened. But I had no choice but to do what I did. I got a complaint from Jimmy Beaufort, but I didn't know your brother-in-law had informed the Bureau as well."

Cornelia came to visit while we were there. She strolled in, picnic basket in her gloved hands, blue dress swishing in her wake. Her gaunt elegance was out of place in the jail cell.

"I warned you, Bob," Cornelia said.

"Where are we going to get $500?" Ma said, her hair unkempt, face pinched in worry. She was wearing a house dress with breast milk stains across the chest.

"You're not," Pa said. "We don't have any money. It's all gone to the sanitarium. I've got nothing."

Cornelia's face twitched. "What about Floyd?"

"He's dead," Pa said.

She gasped. "How—"

"Cornelia, didn't you hear what happened last night?" Ma croaked.

Cornelia flinched. "No, I uh. I heard the agents found Bob's still was all. Jimmy told me this morning." She leaned in towards Pa. "I told you he'd find it!" she hissed.

Pa shot up off his bunk. "I'll figure a way out of it."

Cornelia stood up to face him. "There's no other way, Bob. And ye know it. Jimmy won't stop 'til he gits what he wants."

"Yeah," Pa said. "That's what you think, sister. That's why he got you!"

Cornelia faltered, speechless. Ma started pacing, wringing her raw, cracked hands. "You Taylors never know when to quit!"

"Your best option is to sell to Jimmy. He told me while I was walking out the door. He'll strike a deal with ye. He'll pay your bond, get the Bureau to drop any charges against ye if you agree. He needs to run a rail line across those falls to git to his last patch of trees in the upper reaches of Hickory Run. And he'll even give you a job with the lumber company."

Pa squinted in disbelief.

Ma gripped his shirt, her knuckles turning white. "You have to take the deal, Bob."

"Pa ain't gonna sell Taylor Grove!" I said.

Ma rounded on me. "You shush!"

"Bob, it's the only way out of this," Cornelia pleaded.

Pa sat back down at the end of his bunk. "Git outta here, Cornelia. Go back to your cowardly husband and tell 'em he can go to hell."

It was a dreary November day when they took Pa away on a railroad car with bars on it. He was standing amongst a group of men, mostly strangers, and a few negro men who lived outside town and had been accused of stealing at the general store. As the train pulled away, Pa came to the bars and waved. I ran after the train until it was out of sight. When it rounded a corner I stopped, doubled over in pain. My heart raced and I had a gnawing pain in my gut—panic setting in because now I was in charge of the family.

Jimmy Beaufort Sr. wasted no time in getting legal rights to Cousin Floyd's land. Floyd left no will, and he never recorded the deed. And once Beaufort had control of the land, he started building track up the road that passed our cabin.

Ma heard all kinds of terrible tales about how the men on the road crews were treated. The word was they were made to work in ditches filled with swamp water, digging, and breaking up rocks. They were fed one meal a day consisting of cornmeal and not much else, and if they complained, they were beaten.

This tore her up. She bit her nails down to stubs. I'd find her staring out the window each morning with her brows creased in worry and grief. She neglected baby Sarah. The winter months dragged on. We'd get mail sporadically from Pa who told us how much he missed us but left out anything unpleasant.

When Sarah started coughing, Doc Sloane wanted us to move out of the drafty cabin for the winter, or he told Ma, she'd get consumption. Ma contemplated going back home to Pennsylvania to live with her sister's family, taking me and the girls with her. But we didn't have any money for the trip, and the roads in winter were tricky. It would be hard to travel with all of us. The aunts offered to take us in, but there wasn't enough room for everyone. One night I sat with Ma while she tore at her fingernails. She'd long since given up trying to groom herself, and she hadn't touched a pencil or paintbrush in weeks.

"Ma, maybe we should ask Aunt Cornelia if we could stay with her? She's got that big ol' house in town. I've seen it."

Uncertainty passed over her. Even I hated the idea of living under the roof with that son-of-a-bitch Beaufort, but I'd sacrifice anything to save my little sister and Ma from burying another child.

"I'll go to town and call her for you."

I took Bess to the General Store and made the call. Aunt Cornelia picked up the phone by the third ring. I wasn't sure what I was going to say, I hadn't practiced, so I just blurted out the first thing that came to mind. "The baby's sick. We need help."

Aunt Cornelia drove to our cabin the following morning in her black Chevrolet. She bustled in with a basket full of food, took one look around the cabin, and cringed. I gave her a rag to wipe off one of the wooden chairs, caked with dust, and she cautiously sat down on the edge, facing Ma.

"Stella, it's time to take matters into your own hands. This is no way to live. This is no way to bring up a family. Just look at poor Sarah over there." She pointed in the direction of Sarah, her mouth drooling, her hair a disheveled mop, her cheeks swollen from coughing. Cornelia pressed toward Ma. "Ye can't lit her die like Sam."

Ma shuddered and gasped. "I'd never let that happen!"

Cornelia straightened. "Well, then. I've got a message for ye. From Jimmy. He says to tell ye that his lawyer can fix it so ye can sell over that deed of land to the lumber company."

Cornelia put her hand in the air to stop her from speaking.

"Now I know what yer gonna say. But it's for the best. If ye don't sign it over, Jimmy might try to take it from ye when Bob gits his day in court. They don't lit ye keep yer land if yer can't pay yer taxes on it. And what do ye have to pay with?" She gestured in the air at our surroundings. "With this money you can fix up the cabin and buy medicine for baby Sarah. Don't let Bob's stubbornness drive ye and the family into abject poverty."

I was impressed she even knew what abject meant.

"Why don't you just help us out instead of trying to take Pa's land away from him? You know how much it means to him," I said. "And everyone knows it was your husband who told the Bureau about Pa and Floyd because he wanted to steal their land. Now Cousin Floyd's dead, we're in this mess and he's still trying to take our land."

"You just keep quiet, Ben!" Cornelia snapped at me.

I was too angry to keep quiet. "Your husband beats up you and John. He's a bully and a thief. It's not even as if he needs the money. He's got more than all the rest of us put together. And—"

Ma interrupted me. "Ben!" She paused before continuing weakly. "Take Sarah to the kitchen and wash her up."

"But, Ma—"

"Now!"

I picked up Sarah and took her into the back of the cabin, where the pitcher of water stood by the sink. Quickly I swiped a rag over her face and hurried back to the main room before Cornelia talked Ma into something she'd regret. When I got back into the room, Cornelia was standing over Ma while she signed a piece of paper deeding Taylor Grove and the acreage around it to the Beaufort Lumber Company for two thousand dollars. "Don't worry about it." Cornelia patted Ma's hand. "I promise ye, Jimmy won't cut down those old trees. He just needs to be able to git his tracks over that ridge."

I was horrified. My stomach lurched so hard, I thought I was going to be sick. "No, Ma. Don't do it!" I yelled. Why would Ma believe a word of what Cornelia and Jimmy Beaufort said?

Ma finished signing the paper, then looked at me. Her eyes were haunted, hooded, and her expression so drawn she seemed to have aged decades, with desperation in every line.

"I've got no choice, Ben." Her voice cracked and she started to cry.

Cornelia rested her hand on Ma's shoulder. "It's for the best. You'll see."

I wanted to hug Ma and tell her we'd be okay, but I couldn't bear it. I walked out, fighting back tears.

We paid the bond to get Pa back before Christmas. All of us came to greet him when he got off the train from Knoxville. But our joy turned to disbelief at the sight of him. He stepped off the train a broken man. I didn't even recognize him. He'd lost a lot of weight and his hair had thinned. And he had a cough.

On court day, the whole Taylor family showed up to lend their support. The Judge was a distant cousin on Pa's mother's side of the family. Judge Becket took one look at Pa, half standing, half leaning on a cane, coughing, all of us standing behind him and threw the case against him out. The Bureau agent mumbled something about a miscarriage of justice, and everyone in the audience hissed and booed at him. Judge Becket gaveled us to keep quiet. The agent was escorted from the courtroom by the sheriff, who warned him to get in his car and get out of town.

"Or you might not make it through the night alive. These people don't like their supply of whiskey being taken from 'em," he told the agent.

Pa was let go with no more time in jail. He was free, but he was never the same.

PART THREE
THE GREAT DEPRESSION
1929-1933

15

When I was sixteen, the stock market crashed. October 1929. I learned all about this from reading the papers. They showed pictures of people in New York City standing in line outside churches waiting for a free meal; men sitting on crates at crosswalks trying to feed their families by selling apples; factories closed; people out of work, loitering in the streets, making everyone nervous. While the rest of the world was falling apart and unemployment rose to 30%, Hickory Run just continued about its business. The mountain people knew how to feed themselves; they'd been doing it for generations. Need meat? Go hunt down a gobbler or lure in your pigs. Vegetables? Grow them. Meal for bread? Grind your corn. Although my family wasn't rich, we weren't desperate. Somehow that made us feel a little bit better about losing our land.

Tourists still came to Foster's Inn, oblivious to the economic crisis. The government was still buying up people's land for the park, and most of our neighbors on the mountain sold out and went to work for the Beaufort Lumber Company.

But not Pa.

We went back to our way of life in the cabin using what land we had left to raise chickens, pigs, and crops. Ma wanted to move to town with the money we had made from the sale of the land, but Pa refused. He tried to keep to his old ways, even if he limped and coughed his way through, never really recovering from his weeks working the roads. He wouldn't talk about it either.

One day while I was helping him turn the field to plant corn, I asked him, "Did they treat you poorly on the road crew?"

He draped his hands on top of the hoe and stared off, then shuddered like he remembered something. "Nothin' I couldn' handle," he said and went back to hoeing. He didn't last long at the effort though. By noon he was limping back to the cabin to rest awhile on the porch. I'd catch up with him later. He'd be asleep in his chair, his breathing heavy, wheezy.

The rest of us continued with our lives as well. We had Cousin Floyd's truck, which made it possible for me to get back and forth to school and finish my high school degree. I listened to my friends chatter about their plans when they graduated. Emma Sloane was heading to a teachers' college. Most of the boys went to work for the lumber company. By the spring of my last year, many students stopped coming to class. I'd walk in, and it would be half empty. Mr. Vorhoss always gave me an appreciative smile and encouraged me to take the exams for college. But events transpired that put all of those plans on hold.

Jimmy Beaufort Sr. shot himself in the head. It happened on a soft summer night right after the family had finished eating their supper. Aunt Cornelia had taken the boys to town to get ice cream at the store. As they walked home, they heard a gunshot coming from their house. Cornelia screamed. The neighbors came out on their porches to see what the commotion was about and saw her and the boys running down the lane. They found him sitting in his rocker, his head half blown off, brains splattered on the wall behind him, his lifeless hand still clinging to a pistol. It took a few weeks for the story to trickle out onto Main Street. Like many people, Uncle Jimmy believed the market crash was only temporary.

Soon after buying up Pa's acreage in Taylor Valley, Uncle Jimmy entered into negotiations with the government to sell his land holdings for the new park. As part of the deal, the government gave the Beaufort Lumber Company the right to continue cutting until there weren't any big trees left to harvest.

What did my uncle do with this money? Like everyone else, he thought the stock market crash in 1929 was just a quirk. He didn't think the economy would continue on a downward spiral. That wasn't what the politicians told everybody. He took all his money and invested in a company out in the mid-west that constructed kits for mail-order houses, thinking he'd move his family there just as soon as he was done taking all the trees out of the Tennessee side of the Smoky Mountains.

Unfortunately, the company he invested all his money in went bankrupt a year after the markets crashed. The Beauforts were broke. He'd even mortgaged his big house to help pay for an expansion of the rail lines. The only way out for Aunt Cornelia was to sell the company, along with the land. And that's when the big trees in Taylor Grove came into the hands of the Lavery Lumber Company.

■   ■   ■

Lavery Lumber took aggressive measures to harvest the last trees in the west branch of Hickory Run Creek. Their path of destruction cut through the heart of Taylor Valley. The train tracks led right past our cabin, to Cousin Floyd's land, to the distant ridge. As Pa predicted would happen, they laid tracks to the waterfalls. It was only a matter of time before they got to Taylor Grove and the big trees. Pa kept watch. My herding job was over since we lost our good pasture land, so I spent the summer of 1931 helping Pa with the upkeep of the cabin. We fixed the roof, repaired some fencing, and planted where we could, while the trains rumbled by, shaking the foundations. Every day Pa took his rifle and hiked up the trail that led to Taylor Grove, and I followed him, worried he'd kill somebody if he found a lumberman trying to cut one of his big trees.

We'd follow the tracks which wound their way past the waterfalls to the patch of trees in the upper reaches, and to my great relief, there was no sign that the company was going to cut in Taylor Grove. Pa considered the owners 'furriners', and sent letters telling them about the pact he had with the Beaufort Lumber Company. But his letters went unanswered. He was suspicious they wouldn't respect the agreement. I sat with him many days just staring up at the big trees, his rifle perched by his side. In the background, we could hear trees being cut and dragged; the train whistling as it toted stacks of lumber down the mountain. We even hiked up there at night to sleep in tents and watch the fireflies mating. They hovered over the forest floor, twinkling like fairies in the inky night.

Even though Pa's health was failing, and his spirits dampened, it was a good time for Ma. She had recovered from her grief and returned to her painting. She was now a celebrity of sorts in town amongst the tourists. Ladies invited her to their teas to discuss her art. She displayed her paintings in the community hall, as well as Foster's Inn and thrived on the attention. She sympathized with Pa, but I think deep down, she was also resentful that the man she had married was getting carried away with paranoia and his stubborn refusal to accept the change coming to the mountain people. The government was buying up land all around the Smoky Mountains. My aunts and the people of McConnell's Cove were some of the last hold-outs. The agreement was if the government bought your land, you could stay until you found a new place to live, but you couldn't do anything: no cutting the trees, no clearing land for pasture, no harvesting ginseng. I felt some of Pa's sorrow. We were losing our way of life along with our neighbors. But whenever I raised my concerns about it, Ma took on a distant look as if our troubles were part of a past she didn't care to remember.

Aunt Cornelia had no choice but to sell her house in town and move back in with her sisters. The Beaufort twins took up jobs with the Lavery Lumber Company. I'd see them once in a while in town buying supplies.

"Howdy, John, Jimmy," I said one day when I saw them at the store.

Jimmy Jr. grunted a hello, while John returned a 'Howdy'.

"Where y'all living now?" I said.

"We're staying in the setoffs just like the rest," John said.

Jimmy took off to the back of the store, looking for something.

"How's your Ma?" I said.

"She's doing just fine," John said. He smiled. "She's happy to be back with hhher sisters for now."

"You go to visit much?"

John shook his head, wistfully. "Wish we had the time. Been working."

"Well, I'll look in on her for y'all."

When she turned seventeen, Mary was accepted to the university, and we went to the aunts' cabin to say goodbye. I was so proud of her. She had all of her worldly belongings packed in one trunk that Ma had bought her. Dr. Clarence had a car to drive them to Knoxville. We all carried on about her leaving the mountain. The aunts had assembled a basketful of goodies to take along for the trip: jars of honey and apple butter, bread, sandwiches, satchels of herbs. We pressed in on her, the girls hugging, crying intermingled with light laughter. Wiping away tears, we waved as Dr. Clarence drove down the road and away from us and the mountain.

Cornelia, who had never really gotten to know Mary before moving in with the aunts, turned to us, her eyes red from crying. "It feels like it's all falling apart somehow." Then she took off into the woods.

"She's just missin' her boys is all," Aunt Peg said.

"That and the visit from the government folks rattled her good," Aunt Ophelia said.

"What government folks?" Pa said.

"Might as well tell ye," Aunt Bertie sighed and walked back into the cabin.

Ma and the girls went with Aunt Ophelia to check on the hives while Pa and I sat with Aunt Bertie to hear the news.

"Government men come by here and telled us we have to git. Theys gonna take everybody's land aways." She swept her arms in the air with emphasis. "They call it eminent domain."

"What the hell is that?" Pa said.

"It's the law is what it is."

"Well, we gotta git a lawyer then. They can't take this cabin. It belonged to Pa, and now ye'all." Pa said.

"That's what we tol' 'em. They ain't gonna listen to a bunch of old wimmin."

"Dr. Clarence spoke up for us," Aunt Peg said, looking up from the quilt she was stitching. "She said the government is allowin' some folks to stay if theys too old to leave. We's gotta get permission. If we stay, we can't do things like we used to though. No cutting down trees unless theys already dead, for instance. But theys let us keep our sheep for pasture and chickens."

"And we's can grow food," Aunt Bertie said.

Pa rubbed his lower jaw, deep in thought.

"They'll be comin' round to you too, Bob," Bertie said.

"They already have," Pa said. "I don't have much land left anyways. I sold most of it to Beaufort. Now it's in the hands of the government, and theys lettin' the Lavery Lumber Company cut everything down!"

Bertie shook her head in disgust. "Don't seem right, does it? Theys tellin' us we can't cut any more trees yet they lettin' these companies come in here and cut 'em all down anyways. Theys gonna have a park full of empty forest!"

"What's the point of it?" Aunt Peg chimed. "The tourists won't have any trees to look at."

Ma came back with the girls and said she had errands to do in town. Pa frowned at her. He'd been hoping they'd stay the night.

Just as Pa said would happen, the government folks came by one morning to speak to him about moving out and on. He wasn't budging.

"Ye'all can go to hell," he said. "What I've got left here is mine. And I ain't moving."

The three men, dressed in suits with matching hats, shuffled their feet uncomfortably, their eyes darting back and forth from Pa to each other, wondering who might speak up first.

One of the braver ones cleared his throat. "Well, uh, sir, Mr. Taylor. We've been instructed to tell you that you have no choice in the matter. By next summer, all of this land here—" he gestured—"will belong to the government of the United States. Now we can pay you what it's worth, and you can move on peacefully. Or you can try to stop it in court. That is your right."

"Yes, but," another man interrupted, "that would not be wise, sir. Many have tried, but they've lost every time."

They stood solidly in place, sweat trickling down their brows. A couple of them reached for a handkerchief to wipe it away.

Pa stood, arms crossed over his chest, squinted at them. "Git off my land," he said in a low voice.

"What's that, sir?" they leaned in closer to hear.

"I said," Pa's voice rose a register, "git off my land." He picked up his rifle which had been propped against the oak we stood under and slung it over his shoulder.

"I think it best if you leave now," I said, trying to prevent Pa from doing anything foolish. I beckoned the men to follow me to their car.

"He hasn't been feeling well since he was put on a road crew," I said once out of Pa's earshot. "I'll have my Ma talk to him about it. We will want our lawyer to see any paperwork and know we are getting a fair price." I threw back my shoulders to try and appear taller than I was. I was bluffing, of course. We didn't have a lawyer unless you counted the distant cousin Judge Becket. But I was pretty sure that if Dr. Clarence was going to help the aunts, she'd be willing to help us too.

The night was thick and steamy. Clouds choked with rain hung heavy over the mountains, preventing the breeze from cooling things off. I tossed and turned that night until I realized it was a waste of time trying to sleep. I went out on the porch, and there was Pa.

"Let's go up to the Grove," Pa said. "It'll be cooler up there for sleeping."

We set out with flashlights into the darkness, set up our tents, and built a small fire to ward off the biting insects. Neither of us said anything as we waited for the clouds to break up or break open. Sitting in the grove felt like a steam bath. The trees sucked the water right out of the air. And then it rained—spitting at first, then a clap of thunder before the sky opened up and shed its moisture. I ran straight into the tent for cover, but Pa stayed outside for quite a while longer. He put his face toward the rain and just let it soak into him.

We were lulled to sleep by the plinks and plunks of the rain dripping off the leaves, only to be woken up by the sound of axes chopping and men shouting. Pa reached for his rifle. The nape of my neck prickled. I followed him out of the tent. We didn't have to walk far to find the source of the noise; a crew of three men, including my cousins Jimmy and John, took turns using axes and a two-handled saw to cut down a giant poplar. They had already cut a deep notch shaped like a wedge of pie into one side of the tree. Wood chips flew in the air around them, their shirts soaked with sweat, they puffed and huffed as they wacked at the tree.

Pa shot into the sky with his rifle. They stopped work and swiveled in our direction. "What the hell y'all doin' up here?" Pa yelled.

Jimmy came up to us with his hands held high. "Now Uncle Bob," he said calmly. "You don't want to cause no trouble up here. The foreman told us to start cutting down trees in the Grove. We's just doin' what he told us to do. If you've got trouble with that, yous best take it up with 'im."

"I'll do that," Pa said and stormed off.

I wanted to follow, but he told me to wait. "You stay here, 'til I git back. I don't want these boys cutting down no more trees while I'm gone."

It was a long, awkward wait. My cousins and me, along with this stranger, leaned up against fallen logs while the sun starting climbing past the canopy and flickering the forest floor with light. Various insects pecked at our ears, and we swatted them away with our hats.

"You boys know each other?" the stranger asked. He had red hair and freckles. His face was sunburned, and his ears stuck out of his head at an odd angle.

"Could say that," Jimmy snickered. "We're cousins."

"Ho boy."

Jimmy stood up. "We ain't getting' paid 'til this here tree is cut. Now I don't know what your Pa was thinking, but the Lavery Lumber Company has every right to cut these trees."

John threw me a sympathetic glance. "Wwe can wait."

"Wwwhat'd you say?" the redhead mocked John.

John frowned. "I said we can wait!"

The young man shut his mouth. Jimmy spat on the ground and looked me dead on. He picked up one handle of the large ax and motioned to the redhead. "Come on, I ain't waitin'."

Panicked, I scanned the forest for Pa. I had nothing to stop them with, no gun, no weapon of any sort. I pleaded with John. "Tell your brother to stop!"

"Jimmy, let's at least wait 'til Ben gets his Pa," John said.

Jimmy scowled and dropped the handle.

"Well, I ain't waitin'!" the redhead said and picked up the handle again.

John tore it out of his hand. "I said, wait!"

The redhead shoved John in the chest, and he fell backward. "I ain't listenin' to nobody but the foreman. And he said to start cutting down these trees. They'll be sending more men up before long and we'd better look like we've done something." He motioned to me. "Now git out of our way. This tree's gonna fall, and it ain't safe to be here."

He and Jimmy took up the saw and started grinding their way through the other side of the trunk. John took hold of my arm and led me away.

They struggled with the saw, sweating, grunting, pulling. I kept my view toward the horizon, waiting for Pa. After what seemed like hours, he came striding over the horizon, panting, wincing in pain from his bad leg, his rifle aimed at the boys. Jimmy saw him too.

"What the hell?" he said.

"Pa," I yelled and ran to get the gun out of his hands before it was too late, and he did something he'd regret. "Pa!"

Jimmy ignored him, because, at that moment, there was a loud crack as the saw cut through the vast trunk, and the tulip poplar started to topple to the ground.

"Pa!" I screamed again. But it was too late.

The poplar groaned and teetered. Its large limbs crashed onto the smaller trees, cracking them in half. One of these came crashing down on Pa's head.

It was like watching a picture show in slow motion. One second Pa was standing his ground, the next he was pinned under a large limb. And in between these two moments in time, I screamed, but nothing came out. Like in a dream, when you sense danger, and try to ward it off, and your mouth is open, but no one can hear you. Perhaps the dreamlike quality of my father's death was due to the sounds of the falling tree and crackling forest, or maybe the fact that we all saw what was about to happen and were aware of our helplessness to do anything about it. I don't know. What I do know is that after Pa collapsed, I ran to him, and so did John. I held his gashed head and his blood stained the ground. I pleaded with him to stay alive, keep breathing. His breath went shallow until it stopped. His eyes never opened for me to say good-bye.

Jimmy just stood over me while I watched my father take his last breath, his eyes cold and calculating, holding the handle of the saw, without the slightest appearance of remorse or guilt.

16

We buried Pa next to Sam. Ma moved us to a rental house in town after selling the last parcels of our land. Rachel took a job at Foster's Inn. She liked it there because the ladies who came to town left behind bonnets, scarves, and half-empty bottles of perfume for her to take.

The Lavery Lumber Company leased our cabin from the government to turn it into a store for the lumbermen that settled in Taylor Valley to cut down the last of the trees. It would be a few years they said, then they'd clear out and let the cabin rot. I got a job running supplies from the General Store to our old cabin for the lumbermen and their families. Each time I brought supplies, my pace slowed, and I lost any spring to my step. Our road was now leveled, the big rocks removed and graveled. Uncle Floyd's old truck made the route in the same gurgling way it always did, but this time instead of jugs in the bed, it held nails, tools, pieces of lumber, flour, lard, sugar, coffee, salt. The front room had been turned into a quasi-meeting space shelved with supplies. In the evenings, lumbermen sat around spitting tobacco juice at the sides of a pot-belly stove inserted into the fireplace, complaining about company wages. I recognized distant cousins. The kitchen was blasphemed with nails, bolts, screws, and oil cans, which sat on the shelves where Ma had kept jars of apple butter and honey.

The proprietor of our cabin-turned-store told me to put my load in the back room. It was the room where Ma used to keep her art supplies, the sick room when Sam was ill. The bed frame Pa had made was still intact; the proprietor had put planks on top and piled it with rubber tires. The room had sacks of flour, salt, sugar. A barrel of pickles. I dropped my load on the floor and scurried out of there. One of my distant cousins, Steve Taylor, one of Cousin Biddie's sons, caught up with me outside.

"How's your Ma and the girls doing?" Steve asked.

"About as well as can be expected," I replied. "How's your ma and pa?"

"Oh, theys gone now," he said. "They sold out the farm and took off to Knoxville looking for work. I plan to meet up with 'em jus' as soon as I'm done workin' for Lavery."

"Humph," I said, wanting to leave. His story was becoming an all too familiar sad refrain.

"Remember those days when we'd go up yonder and pick chestnuts to bring to town?"

"Sure do."

He shook his head sadly. "Well, those old trees are dead now. We was up thar the other day, scouting for chestnuts to cut. Theys all got the rot. Hollow'd out."

■ ■ ■

One day the proprietor, a Lavery Company man, asked me to collect some meal from McConnell's mill. Along the way, I saw the abandoned cabins of the families who had sold their land and moved. On Sundays, Ma attended the new church in Hickory Run, but some families came from town to attend services and try to hang on to the last remnants of their lives at their Baptist Church. I went once by myself, but I found it depressing, the old voices crackling as they sang the familiar hymns, Preacher Joe staring out at a congregation with the pews half empty, frowning. I never went back.

I pulled up to the mill and went to find Finn, hoping he'd offer a piece of advice, inspiration. I figured if he was able to carry on with life even after what he'd been through, then so could I. Finn was working the mill with his Pa. But instead of uplifting my spirits, he told me some sad news. The McConnells had sold out. Everything. They were moving. Mr. McConnell bought a piece of land on the south end of town and was going to start over.

"I hate to leave here, Ben," Mr. McConnell said. "But the government ain't given us all much choice. I can't make a living if there ain't nobody livin' here no more and they's offerin' forty dollars an acre if we leave, less if we stay and lease."

I did the math in my head and realized Ma had sold out for half that price.

"But the new company store and the lumber camp is right down the road," I said.

Mr. McConnell shook his head. "Won't be for much longer. They's clearing out the trees 'round here quicker than we all thought it would happen. Hell, there won't be none left for the park!"

That's what my aunts had said. They had worked out a deal with the park, thanks to Dr. Clarence's intervention. They sold their property at a reduced cost to the state, and in return were given a life's lease to stay. The state allowed them to keep their sheep, garden, and bee hives. But they couldn't go into the woods and collect herbs anymore (although I know Aunt Bertie did quite often), and they had to use wood from fallen trees. The state would not allow them to girdle any live trees to clear a pasture, and they couldn't set any fires to the brush. Once they all died, the cabin would be either demolished or left to rot.

Finn followed me to the truck and loaded it with sacks of meal. "Sorry about your Pa. He was a good man."

"I miss him so," I said, choking back tears. "What are you going to do, Finn? You leaving with your Pa?"

"I don't favor livin' in town," he said.

I waited for him to explain, but he clenched his jaw, sighed, and walked away.

■   ■   ■

Aunt Cornelia didn't last long living with her sisters. The work was too hard. They tried to put her to work: milking the cow, weeding the garden, all the things they had been brought up to do living on a mountain farm. She demurred whenever possible. I guess the last straw was when Aunt Peg asked her to help pluck a chicken, and Cornelia told her she couldn't because she had just painted her nails.

I had to drive the truck to their cabin, lug her suitcase filled with dresses—none of which she had been able to wear over the past year—onto the flatbed to bring her to our apartment in town. As we pulled away, she shouted out her goodbyes and I couldn't help noticing the wave of relief that passed over Aunt Bertie's brow. Ma welcomed her as she was in desperate need of companionship. And she helped pay the rent with money the boys sent from their earnings at the lumber camp.

She and Ma had a good time going through the suitcase full of dresses—remnants of a past Aunt Cornelia hoped to reconstruct by returning to town. Ma clapped her hands with glee when Cornelia offered a dress to Ma for an upcoming tea party with the ladies in town. Ma was invited to give a painting lesson.

"That lavender is stunning with your eyes," Cornelia gushed.

She was looking for an invite to the party. Ma obliged by asking the host if Cornelia could accompany her.

"Of course," said the lady host, even though I had heard rumors that the Beauforts had fallen down a few notches on the social scale since Uncle Jimmy had shot himself.

Still, he wasn't the only one who fell victim to the Great Depression. As time went by, others followed suit. The tea party Ma was attending was being given by a woman whose own husband had recently hung himself in Knoxville. She had to sell her mansion and bought a small colonial at the end of our lane.

Cornelia infected Ma with delusions of high society. But I knew a frilly dress didn't put us in that league. I watched in disgust as Ma and Cornelia's friendship blossomed. They started dressing the girls in clothes that Rachel and Mary had never worn while growing up on the mountain.

"That is just downright ridiculous," I said to Ma one day as she dressed Nellie up for her first day of school in a dress made of satin with a large sash. "How's she going to play in that during recess?"

Ma ignored me as she tied the sash, stepping back to admire Nellie.

"Can I have a sash too?" Sarah squealed. I rolled my eyes. She was only six years old.

"Walk me to school, will you, Ben?" Nellie pleaded with me.

I took her hand and led her down the street. The school had expanded and now had four classrooms, three more teachers, and Mr. Vorhoss as the principal. He met us at the door.

"My, my Miss Nellie, don't you look pretty today," he said. "Ben, could you stop by and see me in my office after you drop Nellie at her classroom?"

Nellie pulled self-consciously at her hem and thanked him. I walked her to her classroom. The other students turned to gawk, a few tittered. One nice girl took mercy and patted the chair next to her for Nellie to sit.

Mr. Vorhoss stood up to greet me with a warm smile. "Ben, so good to see you. I'm so sorry to hear about your Pa."

And then he got to the point. He beseeched me to consider taking the exams for college. I adamantly refused, telling him how much I appreciated his belief in my abilities.

"I just can't leave Ma and the girls right now."

Truth was, I had no ambition since Pa died. And Ma's new companionship with Cornelia was troubling me. I'd stay home with Rachel, Nellie, and Sarah while the two went out to dine, tea, and meet up with their lady friends. While Ma's familial instincts waned, mine sharpened. I knew I had been right about Nellie and the dress. She came home that day, tear-stained cheeks, scarred knees, from being teased and tripped in the playground during recess.

One day I pulled Ma aside to talk some sense into her.

"Why are you spending so much time with Aunt Cornelia? And why doesn't she get a job?" I said.

Ma was baking cookies for an event at the community hall. A group of government men was coming to talk about the new economy that was going to spring up from the park.

"What's wrong with you? You know she doesn't have any skills. She can't even read or write. Besides, Jimmy and John send her money."

I struggled with my words, not sure what to say. I felt it was blood money and hated taking it. How do you tell your mother about the death of her husband? What I had seen? The look in Jimmy Jr.'s eyes when that tree fell on top of Pa. It was murder. And now Ma was taking up with the murderer's mother like a long-lost girlfriend. I hated to put a damper on her fun. For once she was light, free of the burdens of life as a housewife in the mountains, able to create her art, share friendships with other womenfolk more like her than our mountain family.

"She's lazy, is all," I said.

"She's lazy, that's all," Ma corrected.

"Who is?" Aunt Cornelia breezed into the room with a dress slung over her arm. "Oh, hello, Ben."

I mumbled a hello, stepped out, and overheard Cornelia say, "Stella, be a doll, will ya and iron this dress for me? I don't know my way around an iron. Always burnin' myself."

Things came to a head when the two of them went out to the picture show at the community hall one Saturday evening. I was sleeping in my bed when I heard loud voices outside my window. Rachel, Nellie, and little Sarah came running into my room, calling my name.

"We heard Ma screaming!" Rachel said.

My mind cleared, and I reached for Pa's rifle under my bed. When I got to the porch, the light was shining on a man sitting down, holding his bloody head. Ma was standing over him, a rock in her hand, her dress half torn off. Her hair was undone, half out of its bun, her eyes wild. Blood was trickling from a cut in her lip. "Ben!" she said.

Before I could ask what happened, I heard Aunt Cornelia screech and a man yelling. I turned to where the noise was coming from—a car in the dark driveway. I ran to the car and saw through the back windshield a man raising his hand in the air and then a loud slap. I swung open the back door to find the white ass of a man staring back at me. Aunt Cornelia's stocking legs bent at the knee, her legs kicking the air. The swoosh of air alerted the man to my presence. He twisted his head, and as he did, Aunt Cornelia kicked him in the crotch.

He screamed and clutched his privates. "Christ woman!"

"Serves you right, you bastard!" Cornelia shouted.

I aimed my rifle at him.

"Ma, call the sheriff," I yelled.

Ma was in a daze. "Ma!" I yelled at her. "Call the sheriff!"

Cornelia put herself back together, got out of the car, and pulled at my arm. "No, Ben." She ran to Ma. "Go inside, Stella. We'll take care of this. Go make sure the girls are ok."

The man who had assaulted Ma was up by now, groaning, dabbing at the gash on his head. He lurched toward me, and I swung the rifle back and forth between the two men.

"You git outta here, now!" Cornelia said in a ragged voice. "Go now, or he might shoot ye!"

The men straggled to their car. The one who'd been kicked in the groin spit at Cornelia's feet. "Bitch," he said. The tires squealed and gravel spewed as they peeled out.

I lowered my rifle, arms trembling.

"Oh, Ben. Thank you. I don't know what would have happened if you hadn't come along when you did." She crushed her mouth with her fist.

I walked away from her. I didn't have anything left in me to say. I went inside to find Ma and the girls huddled and crying. I got a rag to clean Ma's lip and led her and the girls to their beds. Within an hour, Nellie and Sarah stood in the doorway of my room, shaking with fear that the 'bad men' would come back. I was sitting by the window, rifle in hand, thinking the same thing. I let them sleep on my bed while I stood watch. We never saw or heard from those men again. Ma told me they worked for the Lavery Lumber Company and had used their charm to entice her and Aunt Cornelia into their car after the movies.

• • •

It wasn't long before the financial collapse trickled down to our small town as well. Mountain people went without luxuries, but now the staples became a luxury too. As the government bought up homes in the mountains, people came into town to find work. And as the timber depleted, so did the jobs with the Lavery Lumber Company. The General Store extended credit where they could, but usually, with the understanding it would be paid with cash or goods. If people had nothing to barter, there was no credit.

We had gone through most of the money from the sale of the land. Some of it went to assist Mary at the university, some of it went to paying off old debts, most of it went to paying rent and keeping up the lavish lifestyle Cornelia pushed on us. When it was gone, we had to rely on my job transporting goods up the mountain to the lumber camp store and Ma's paintings. Soon income from this work dried up. Not many new tourists came into town and the ones who did already owned Ma's paintings. The Lavery Lumber camp in Taylor Valley pulled out the last of the big trees in the winter of 1932. The Fosters had to let Rachel go. "We just don't have that many people coming in off-season," Mr. Foster said.

I gave up dinners so that little Sarah could eat. We ran out of fuel. Aunt Cornelia's dresses hung in a closet, outdated and frivolous. That Christmas Ma couldn't afford any treats or presents. Mary came home to visit and brought a box of chocolates. But Nellie got it in her head that we all deserved a gift. So, when she caught of glimpse of a shiny red package tied with a bow left behind in the community hall after church services one morning, she figured she'd take it. She presented it to us all after a dinner of chicken and biscuits that Ma managed to scrounge up.

"Where'd ye git that?" Aunt Cornelia said as she fingered the bow.

"At church!" Nellie exclaimed with pride.

"Someone at church gave you a present?" Ma said.

"That's charity," I said. "You shouldn't have taken it."

Nellie's lip trembled as if she might cry. Mary ran to comfort her.

"It's ok, Nellie. Let's open it and see what you got."

Desperate for a glimmer of joy, Nellie and Mary carefully unwrapped it, making sure to save the paper. There was a long velvet scarf with tassels on the ends inside.

Ma held it up. "What could this be for?" she said.

Mary recognized it for what it was. "That's a piano bench cover."

We examined it more closely, and all agreed it would fit perfectly on a bench.

"Where'd you git this?" Rachel laughed.

Nellie pouted. "I found it sitting on the floor by the back of the hall, and since we were the last to leave, I figured Santa had left it for us."

We all got a good laugh at her expense, and Ma made her put it back in the box and deliver it to the community hall the next morning.

· · ·

Aunt Bertie took her mule to town and stopped in to visit with us. One look around, and she sensed things weren't right.

"Ben, you look like you've lost weight. Your pants are falling down."

I pulled at my trousers. It was true, my belt was the only thing holding them in place. I had lost weight, and my ribs stuck out.

Aunt Bertie pulled out a sack from her bag. "This is for Sarah's cough."

Ma took it gratefully and immediately made some tea. Poor Sarah's cough had returned with a vengeance. Doc Sloane said there was nothing to be done about it but rest and clean air. She rasped and wheezed her way through the days cheerfully enough, not knowing any other life. Doc Sloane said it wasn't consumption, it was asthma.

Aunt Bertie bustled about the kitchen preparing a meal. She'd brought a hock of ham, beans, onions, and garlic. My mouth watered as the ingredients stewed, and the aroma filled our tiny kitchen with memories of the mountain and our cabin.

"You can't let the children starve," she scolded. "You two must find some work. And if ye can't, then come and work with us, and we'll give ye some of the bounty. Thars plenty to go 'round if ye are jus' willin' enuf to work for it."

Ma thanked Bertie profusely for helping us as Cornelia sat stone-faced in the corner with a hot cup of coffee in her hand.

"Why don't you send Ben to live with us and he can bring back food once in a while? We could always use the help of a man. Lord knows we've lost most of our kin. Theys all moved away."

"I don't think that would be wise, Aunt Bertie," I said. I had no intention of leaving Ma and Aunt Cornelia in charge of the girls. Not after the latest incident with those men.

Bertie put her hand on her hips. "Well, why not?" Her brows arched. Ma and Cornelia avoided her stare.

"I'll come up once a week," I said to avoid having to explain. "Help you when I can in exchange for some fresh vegetables and meat."

Bertie clucked. "Why you want to spend your time here in town where the water is dirty, and the air reeks of smoke I just can't figure."

Mary wanted to come home, but Ma insisted she stay in school. However, we couldn't send her money to help pay her tuition or board, so she took a job as a teacher assistant at the university and continued her studies part-time. I agreed with Ma on this. There was nothing in Hickory Run for her, no jobs, no prospects. Even Doc Sloane gave his services without pay. I had no prospects either. Soon Jimmy and John Beaufort stopped sending money. They had lost their jobs and were searching for work in Asheville. One morning I found Cornelia digging through the garbage for coffee grounds from the previous evening.

"What are you doing?"

She swirled around as if being caught stealing, a handful of grounds in her hand. Then she burst out crying and slumped in a chair, the grounds oozing through her fingers and staining her blouse.

"We can't even afford coffee!" she cried.

Ma came into the kitchen. "What is all the commotion about?"

Cornelia was blubbering, and Ma went to comfort her. In between sobs she said, "I tried to buy us some coffee this mornin' and was tol' at the store we had no more credit! When is someone around here gonna find a job?"

"What about your boys?" I yelled. Ma put her hand on my arm to calm me. I was seething with rage. "If it hadn't been for your son Jimmy, we wouldn't…" I stopped.

Cornelia eyed me suspiciously.

"Wouldn't what, Ben?" Ma said.

The air was charged with tension. Something passed over Cornelia's face—recognition? Fear? I never knew. But I couldn't continue. I couldn't tell her that her son caused her brother's death. I didn't have the heart.

"Well, enough of this nonsense, anyhow," Ma said, handing Cornelia a towel to clean her coffee-stained hands. "Ben, I got some news for you.

There's a meeting tonight at the hall. The National Park Service is holding it, and they're recruiting young men like you for jobs in the new park."

I was skeptical. "Doing what? There ain't no trees left worth cutting."

"Aren't any," Ma said pointedly. "And that's the reason they're hiring young men like you. To build roads, plant trees, and set it all up for the tourists."

"Where'd you hear this?" Cornelia said.

Ma waved a flyer in our faces. "I got it at the store. If you were looking for an opportunity instead of coffee this morning, Cornelia, you might've too."

Cornelia took the flyer. "Maybe my boys can git some work. They's still lookin'."

The thought of working with either of the twins made me cringe, but I went to the meeting anyway. It was our last hope.

PART FOUR
CIVILIAN CONSERVATION CORPS 1934-1938

17

That spring, I applied for and was accepted into Camp 46 of the U.S. Civilian Conservation Corps. Two hundred young men enrolled, and I was lucky to get a spot, or so the man at the National Parks office told me when I went to retrieve my paperwork.

I'd get paid twenty dollars a month—more than our family had seen in quite some time—and be allowed to keep five dollars of it for myself, the rest I was to send home. I joined up and took my place amongst other men my age aboard a truck caravan, which carted us up the winding mountain roads. We passed familiar places such as Taylor Valley and Raven's Bald until we reached a level field known as Fullers Gap. This was to be my new home. Our camp consisted of several army surplus tents. Each held rows of cots, enough to sleep forty men per tent.

The first day, the camp doctor instructed us to line up for physical exams and pick out a uniform. I stood in line with some sorry-looking boys. They came from all over the east coast—New York, New Jersey, Massachusetts, Pennsylvania, the coal-mining towns of West Virginia, the slums of the inner cities. They had foreign-sounding names like Diaz, D'Ambrosio, Hershkowitz, and Lisowski. They, like me, were underweight and malnourished. The staff handed out old war uniforms that fell past our bony hips and floated around our torsos. We looked like young boys trying on their Pa's shirt. The commanders in charge told us not to worry, we'd fit into them eventually.

We had to get our hair cut and go to the doctor's tent for a physical. One of the young men came out of the doctor's tent shaking his head and flapping the paper. "I don't know what this says, but the Doc told me I have hookworm."

Others mentioned being treated for tuberculosis, scurvy, and lice. Those infected with some type of disease were placed in quarantine so they could be treated before being put to work. I went into the doctor's tent and waited to be seen. To my surprise and joy, when I got to the table, there was Doc Sloane.

"Ben Taylor," he said. "Good to see you. I figured you'd be stationed at one of these camps in the mountains."

He did a physical on me, listening to my heart, my lungs.

"How is Emma doing?"

"Oh, she's fine. She is almost done with teaching college."

He gave me a vaccination shot for typhoid and smallpox. "Now Ben, as I understand it, they'll be looking for young men like you to lead the others."

"How do you mean?"

"Men like you who can read and write, follow directions, know how to do some carpentry, and know their way around these parts. They'll need all the help they can get. You'd be a natural leader."

"Thanks, Doc."

And then came lunch and men in uniforms shouting orders for us to line up for chow. I sat next to a young fellow who looked emaciated. His eyes were red and crusty from some type of infection, and he had a terrible tick. When the food came, he never said a word. His manners were deplorable. He gobbled the food up so fast the rest of us watched in awe, thinking he may get sick.

"You ain't eaten in a while, huh?" said a dark young man from across the table.

The red-eyed fellow wiped his mouth with the sleeve of his olive-green uniform.

"Show some manners, will ya?" another fellow called.

I handed him a napkin. His bloodshot eyes darted around the table, looking for more food. I was about to offer him some of mine when a server came along with another platter of turkey and gravy. We gasped and quickly reached for seconds.

On the way out of the dining tent, the dark-skinned fellow grabbed my arm.

"Hiya," he said. "Been meaning to introduce myself since we sat together in the truck."

I'd hardly noticed, I'd been so overwhelmed and tired from the journey.

"Tony. Tony Delaney." His smile was explosive.

"Ben. Ben Taylor."

"Nice to meet ya, Ben. You from 'round here?"

"Yeah, I know these mountains pretty well. Grew up over yonder. I used to herd cattle around here. They'd come down off that there ridge," I pointed to Raven's Bald, "and cool off in this glen."

"Well, I'm glad to know ya then. Cause this here," he flung his arms wide, "is just a big old wilderness to me. Full of bears, big cats, and wolves."

I laughed. "We haven't had wolves around here in decades. And as for big cats, I've been walking in these woods as long as I can remember and never come across a mountain lion. And I'm going on twenty-two years old."

"Well, that's good to hear."

"What about snakes?" a tall bean pole of a man overheard us talking and strode up and introduced himself as Stan Lisowski.

"Snakes, yes. All kinds. Rattlers, copperheads. You gotta watch out for those."

They clucked nervously, eyeing the ground.

Tony followed me to the barracks where the staff instructed us to find a place to sleep, unpack any belongings and place them in the army trunks stationed at the end of each cot. Tony and Stan found the cots next to mine. They gave us a half-hour break to acclimate ourselves to our new living arrangements. Within minutes it was clear some men didn't have the slightest sense of good hygiene. The tent reeked with body odor the likes of which I'd never confronted. I unpacked my meager belongings, a few books, a tin of cookies Ma had made, my journal and writing implements, and ran for the open air.

Our first task for the day was to dig latrines. They put us in groups of four, handed us shovels, and told us to dig holes twice the length of our body and half as wide. I was paired with Stan and Tony and another fellow named Matt from Philadelphia who appeared jaundiced. We took turns, two at a time, digging inside the hole. Matt spent the majority of the time complaining.

He was in the hole with Tony, dirt flying in the air above their heads as Stan and I leaned on our shovel handles, wiping sweat off our brow.

"What kind of place is this anyway? How come they don't have latrines already set up for us? They knew we were coming," Matt said.

The man in charge, Captain Blake, passed by and overheard.

"You complaining, young man?" he barked. Blake was a burly man, stout in the chest, with bushy eyebrows and wiry gray hairs that stuck out in all directions.

Matt jumped. "No, sir."

"That's good. Because we can't have you men using the woods as your personal toilet." He marched away.

Matt pulled himself out of the hole to take a break, even though it seemed he'd hardly dug four inches. "Hey, anyone of yous guys got a cig?"

Tony started rooting in his shirt pocket.

Captain Blake had eyes in the back of his head, he was looming over Matt as he tried to light his cigarette. "Did I say you could take a cigarette break?"

Matt flicked the match he had in his hand and dropped the cigarette in his front pocket.

"Get back to work!" Captain Blake shouted at us as we stood there gaping.

"Christ, what a wet blanket he is. It's like they think we enlisted in the army or something. Only without the guns," Matt said.

"He sure is hard-boiled," Stan said.

Tony took hold of the handle of his shovel and jumped down into the hole. "I'm going to have to go soon boys, and I don't want to run into any rattlesnakes. Let's get this thing dug."

It quickly became apparent to Captain Blake that quite a few young men in Camp 46 had none of the skills necessary to build the infrastructure we needed around the barracks. As Doc Sloane predicted, the carpentry skills I acquired from Pa set me apart from the majority of the fellas. I was made a platoon leader and put in charge of teaching the men how to handle a hammer and nail. They also recruited some locals, and it was good to see them after weeks in the woods with a bunch of jumpy young men. Some of my own kin came to work at the camp, setting us up in a real shelter made of milled wood they trucked in from Hickory Run. We constructed outhouses to cover the latrines and built showers even though the water supply was a dug well and limited. And we transformed the dining tent into a wooden hall.

The local men from Hickory Run appreciated the work. Many of them were too old to be in the Corps (unless you were a veteran of the war, you had to be between the ages of 17 and 25), but they had families to feed. By that fall, we had the place shipshape, more like a permanent residence for two hundred men than a temporary tent city.

Captain Blake sent a crew of men and me to clear the fallen limbs and other debris that was clogging the opening to the spring at the base of the waterfalls so that we could have a regular supply of water. We hiked our way up the glen following the sound of the falls until our path was obstructed by a dam the size of a house.

"Holy Jesus, how the hell do they think we're gonna be able to clear all of this?" Matt said. In the few months we had been at camp, his complexion had tanned, and he had gained some weight. All of us had actually. All but Tony. For some odd reason I didn't understand, Tony could eat twice as much as any of us and still not gain weight. He was slight of build and smaller than the rest of us. What he lacked in stature he made up for in enthusiasm.

And although he was inept at first with an ax or any sort of tool that a man of the woods would be familiar with, he had an innate curiosity that made him a quick study. He was good at following my cues too. If I told the fellas to do something and they slacked off, he picked up the pace and barked at them to do the same. "Come on, fellas," he'd say in his tenor voice, "see how it's done?"

I broke the ten men up into groups, gave them each an ax, and told them to start cutting up the wood into manageable sizes for hauling out of the creek bed. We needed to have access to the base of the falls to run a water pipe. As we hacked away at the vegetation, Tommy screamed and jumped around, slapping at his back. I ran over to see what the matter was.

"A snake fell out of that tree and landed on him!" someone pointed to an overhanging limb.

I rushed at him and ripped his shirt off. A black snake thumped to the ground and slithered under a rock.

"My gawd! I'm gonna die. It bit me!" he screamed.

"You aren't gonna die," I said calmly. "That was a rat snake. They don't even bite unless they sense danger. Here let me take a look."

Sure enough, the fella was right; there were two puncture wounds on his back. The men grumbled, searching the sky for falling snakes.

"All right now," I said. "There's no reason to panic. The rat snake isn't poisonous. But just to be safe, Freddy, why don't you and Tommy head back to camp and get him a ride to Doc Sloane in town."

"I don't know my way back," Freddy said.

I rolled my eyes. How long had we been in the woods? Months now and some fellas just couldn't find their way out of their own sleeping bags. Before I even had to ask, Tony volunteered.

We cleared the glen, stacked the wood, and hauled it to camp for burning in the wood stoves in the barracks. When we got back, I was surprised to learn that Tony and Tommy were still in town. They didn't arrive until late in the evening, after Taps.

"How'd it go?" I asked Tony as he got ready for bed.

"Great. I got to meet the prettiest girl I've ever seen in my whole life."

"Oh yeah. Who's that?"

"Her name is Emma. The Doc's daughter."

I bolted upright in my cot. "You mean she's back?"

By the light of the small lantern, I could see Tony's surprised expression. "How do you know her?"

I slumped back. "We went to school together."

"Well, she sure is pretty."

I turned on my side and pretended not to hear him. My mind was reeling. Emma was back. I wondered how long she'd be in town. It was five days until we had a day off. Emma was back.

• • •

It was a very long wait until Saturday when Sergeant MacDougall drove a truckload of guys into town for their weekly recreation or to purchase items like soap or cigarettes with their monthly allowance of five dollars.

"If you're not back here at 10 pm, I'm leaving without you," Sergeant MacDougall said as he dropped us off in town that Saturday.

"I'm staying overnight, Sarge," I said.

Tony looked at me funny. I hadn't told him my plans.

"How you gonna get back?" MacDougall asked.

I shrugged. "I'll walk."

"I'm staying too, Sarge," Tony said.

"What?" I said.

He leaned in and whispered in my ear. "Just cover for me, will ya? I'll sleep on the floor of your kitchen if I have to. I just want to make sure I get to see that pretty girl again."

What a disaster, I thought; he was following me around like a puppy. Any other time I would have loved to show Tony around Hickory Run, but he was getting in the way of my plans to see Emma.

We piled out of the truck. As we passed some of the girls in town the guys catcalled and whistled. The girls giggled, a few smirked.

"We gonna see you lovely ladies at the movies tonight? It's King Kong!" Stan shouted at a group of girls as they passed by, thumping his chest. Matt shoved him in the back, and he went tumbling onto the sidewalk. He picked himself up and flew at Stan. I jumped in between them.

"Knock it off, fellas."

Mr. Stewart was standing outside the door to his store, eyeing us with a grim expression. We split in two, some of us heading to the soda jerk to order an ice cream soda, others to the Pharmacy. I knew the ones heading to the Pharmacy would be hungover in the morning. Tony, Lou, and I went into the General Store. I wanted to buy some gum, and the fellas wanted to buy cigarettes. I didn't like cigarettes. I'd tried it once outside of school, but then Emma told me she could smell it on me and turned her nose up at it. I'd rather smell like mint when I saw her.

As I glanced at a stack of magazines, I heard a commotion and Mr. Stewart, who was getting on in years, yell at Lou and Tony. The two of them were like twins, both with olive skin, under six feet tall with a mop of black hair so thick they could barely get a comb through it. The only difference was that Lou was an alto and Tony a tenor. Tony's voice hadn't caught up with him yet. I came upon the goofballs wrestling each other in the corner over a baseball card.

"You either buy something or you get out!" Mr. Stewart said.

"Listen daddy-o," Lou said. "We're thinking of buying up the store with all the money we're making building the roads in the mountains up there." He thumbed toward the window.

Mr. Stewart clenched his jaw.

I walked over to them, cuffed Lou on the side of the head. "What's gotten into you two?"

Tony took hold of Lou's arm and pulled him outside.

They laughed as they exited, and I went to buy my gum and noticed my aunt's honey lining the wall. It made me glad to know they were still keeping their bees. I bought a jar for Ma and the girls.

Mr. Stewart leaned over the counter and grumbled, "You tell those dagos I don't want any trouble in my store. Here me? They scare the other customers off."

I gulped. "Yes, sir."

At the movies, I kept looking at the entrance, hoping to see Emma, but she never showed. A bunch of other town girls did, however, and seated themselves within arm's reach of a gang of the guys. Who knows what went on when the lights went out in the community Hall of Education, Damnation, and Salvation on those restless nights, but the guys came back in a better mood.

I reluctantly brought Tony home with me after the movie let out. Ma was ecstatic to see me. She clapped her hands and shouted in the air. Guiltily, I realized it'd been a long while since I had stopped home on my monthly excursions to town. I didn't always have as much time. When she found out we were staying overnight, she sent the girls to the neighbors to borrow sugar for a cake and then set about making one. Tony immediately turned his charms on my sisters and by the end of the night, they fawned all over him. I had to drag him up to my small bedroom and lock the door so they wouldn't follow us in.

The next morning, I woke to the sound of him chatting it up with Ma in the kitchen below. The smell of coffee and biscuits permeated the air. I waited for the fog to lift and scrambled into the shower. It was good to feel hot water again. I plotted my next move: get rid of Tony long enough to see Emma without him tagging along.

"Ben!" Ma called. "Come get your breakfast."

I went to the kitchen to find the girls dressed in their Sunday best, hands cupped under their chins, listening to every word coming out of Tony's mouth in between bites of biscuits and eggs.

"Ben, Tony here tells me you haven't been going to church up at the camp."

"No, Ma, they haven't set us up with a chapel yet. I'd head up to the old church in Taylor Valley, but not sure it's even there still."

"Well, Preacher Joe tells me there aren't many people still living up there. Apart from a few squatters."

I took a break from eating. "Squatters?"

Ma flapped her hands. "You know, people who are staying illegally."

"Where?"

"In their homes! The same homes the government bought off them. Or, if they've been caught, they scatter deeper into the woods and find abandoned places and stay until they're caught and sent packing."

"That doesn't sound like a good way to live," Tony said. "Flitting from one place to another, hoping not to get caught. Why would anyone want to stay in the woods by themselves anyway?"

We all stared at him. He just wouldn't understand.

"Where's Aunt Cornelia?" It was the first time I noticed her empty seat at the table.

"She left us."

"Shacked up with a man," Rachel said.

Tony guffawed.

"Hush, Rachel. You know I don't like that kind of talk," Ma said.

Rachel's face went bright red. "Well, it's true!"

Ma turned to me. "She has a beau. He owns a house on the other side of town." She glared at Rachel. "Away from the busybodies."

"Why don't they get married?" I said.

"She doesn't want to upset the boys."

"The twins? Who cares?"

"I heard it's because if she gets married, she can't collect help anymore," Rachel said.

"Rachel, that's enough!"

"What's she talking about, Ma?"

"Aunt Cornelia gets money just like we do. The twins are working at a camp up in the Smoky Mountains somewhere. Surprised you haven't run into them yet."

Ma reached for Tony's plate. "You two coming with us to church?"

"Sure will, Mrs. Taylor."

"I have a few things to get done in town, Ma. But take Tony with you. He'd enjoy it, I think."

Rachel's face lit up. I was glad of the chance to shake him because I knew what church Emma went to—the Presbyterian—and it was nowhere near Ma's church in town.

I waited outside the Presbyterian Church for her. When she stepped out, she was linked to Doc Sloane's arm and laughing at something he said.

"Emma," I called and waved.

She squinted in the morning light, cupped her hands over her brows to see who was calling, recognized me, and waved. She left Doc Sloane to walk in my direction.

"Ben Taylor. Just look at you! You must've grown six inches since I last saw you."

"Oh gosh, I don't think I've grown all that much."

"Can you come by the house and have coffee with Pa and me? I made some apple fritters this morning."

"I sure would like that," I said.

I spent that glorious morning on the front porch of Doc Sloane's house, learning all about Emma's plans to be a teacher. The National Park Service asked her to work in schools they planned to set up at the Corps camps to teach the men to read and write.

"The fact that some of these young men can't read or write is astounding!" she said. Her face was animated as she discussed her plans to conquer the illiteracy rates of the men in the Conservation Corps.

Having Emma around to teach the fellas to read something decent wasn't such a bad idea. "I'm so glad to hear about your plans, Emma. I hope you end up at our camp."

When the fellas started getting antsy from being cooped up in the woods for too long, all hell broke loose. Local moonshiners who roamed the hills and kept illegal stills in tucked-away spots too hard to find, would drop by the camp at night and sell the restless ones whiskey. Drunken fights would break out because these fellas hadn't been exposed to moonshine before.

Sergeant MacDougall thought a reading library would keep us all busy. He sent a request to a library in New York to send any discarded books. I watched as the men ripped open the boxes of books and greedily pulled them out. Then they sat on their cots and opened books. I only spotted a few actually scanning the pages—reading—most of them just stared at the books, dumbfounded. I caught one fella with the book upside down.

I took it from him. "You want me to read this to you?"

He snatched it out of my hand, ashamed to admit he couldn't read. "I don't need no help."

I read the cover. "Let me see that will ya?"

"I tole ya, I don't need no help readin'!" he said.

I looked around. A few men greedily gripped their books. Almost too attached. "Hey Tony, let me see that."

Tony ran over with his book. "Um, I can read a little. Got to grade six. But not sure what some of these words mean. What's this one?"

I read where he pointed: the word erotic and a precise description of a woman's most intimate body part. I flipped the book over and read the cover. It was porn.

"Hey, look at this, will ya fellas!" Tommy yelled from his bunk.

A group of us crowded around him as he opened up his book to pictures of women posing in nothing but stockings and feather hats.

"Take a look at those bubs!"

All of a sudden, everyone was asking me to read aloud. We got a good week's worth of reading done before Sarge MacDougall discovered one of the books under someone's cot during an inspection, open to a centerfold of a naked woman sprawled over a bed. He made us give them all back.

Emma interrupted my thoughts about our wayward reading material. "I'm sorry, Ben. Here I am prattling on and on, and I haven't even asked you about camp life. Do you enjoy the work?"

"Mostly. Sometimes I get lonely for home."

"And how is your Ma?"

"She and the girls are doing fine now." I puffed up, feeling proud to be able to say this. If Emma had seen how we lived before I got the job with the Corps, I would have been ashamed. I was glad she had been away at school.

"I've seen your Pa at the camp," I said.

Emma became animated. "Oh yes, these camps have been a godsend to the people in town. He's busier than ever." She inched closer to me on the bench. "Not many people know this, but my father had his own challenges, paying my tuition and keeping Lila on. People couldn't pay him, and you know how he is, he wouldn't ask for money. So, we just managed. But *now*, he's being called to one camp or another every day! Why he can barely keep up! And he tells me the people in town are happy as well to be employed. The mill almost closed until they started getting orders from the camps for milled lumber. Don't pay any attention to the naysayers."

"Naysayers?"

She laughed lightly. "Yes, you know."

"Know what?"

She looked away. "What they say about the young men who come to town on Saturdays."

"The fellas from the camps?"

"Yes." In a hushed voice, she said, "Some of the people in town are, you know, uncomfortable. But you know how they don't like foreigners. Some people around here call them ugly names. Like that one who came here last week looking for my father."

"Tony?"

"Yes, him. Lila says they loiter."

I chuckled.

"Don't laugh. I've heard worse coming out of the General Store."

"Oh." I scratched my chin thinking about what happened the day before. I've seen worse in the barracks, of course. The fellas scratching themselves in private places, burping at the table, passing gas at all times of the day in front of anyone, anywhere. They didn't think much about their manners. But my memory was seared with the image of my cousin Jimmy calling me a hillbilly.

"The people around here are just snobs is all. Don't you pay any attention. And Mr. Stewart might complain about the fellas coming into his store, but I'm sure he appreciates their hard-earned cash. Besides, if one of the guys gets out of line, you can tell me about it. I'm a platoon leader."

She was impressed. "Really?"

"I've got to go," I said. "Before it gets dark."

Her lips puckered. "So soon?"

My mind went to the pictures in the books we had been reading, and I quickly shook the thought of reaching for her mouth with my own and kissing it. I put my hand out. "So good to see you again, Emma."

I squeezed her hand. Then she pulled me slightly toward her so that I could feel the warmth of her breath near my ear, and she kissed me on the cheek.

18

Emma was right about one thing: it's hard to change people's attitudes. Just like the rest of society, the Corps was segregated into camps by race. A large contingent of black men got off the train in town to be transported to our camp. They stayed with us while they waited for their final destination at a base in Pennsylvania. As they descended the train steps and looked about for the buses taking them into the mountains, they were met with long stares by the locals. But that was nothing compared to how some of the men at Camp 46 reacted when the buses rolled into the barracks after dinner one night, and the black men got off and immediately began pitching tents on the perimeter of our barracks. The men stayed with us for a few weeks to help build roads. Some of the Hickory Run boys grumbled about them being too close. It wasn't as if they had never interacted with colored people, it was never that many in one place, at one time. And forget about sharing the bathrooms. The men in charge made them dig their own latrine and drag water in buckets to boil for showers.

One evening, we played cards in our barracks with Sergeant Brett Phillips, the commander in charge of the safety patrol.

"It ain't right," he said.

Matt slapped his cards down on the table in disgust. "I fold."

The laughter from the negro camp got louder, and we all shot a glance toward the door.

Sarge scowled and bit down on his cigar. He was designated the Local Experience Man (LEM). All the camps had men from town who had experience in something and in a position to train the rest of us.

I never liked Brett Phillips. He was a few years older than me but in the same grade in school. Phillips was dumber than a doorknob. Even in school he spent most of his time teasing the girls and goofing off. His father was a big wig who owned the local bank. We all figured that's how he ended up in his cushy position as the LEM—his connections, because he was assigned to safety patrol and knew nothing about safety. He was supposed to train the fellas on how to use the tools safely. The city boys took their lives into their own hands every time they picked up an ax or learned how to use a new tool. The man had no idea how to run a machine, much less repair one. He was an idiot.

"What difference does it make, Sarge?" I said.

His eyebrows shot up. "Difference? They're taking away your jobs."

There was uneasy laughter. I knew he wasn't joking around. He was a well-known mean drunk who picked fights with people over the slightest thing.

"No one's told me I lost my job with the Corps since they arrived," I said.

He took the cigar out of his mouth and poked it in the air at me. "Just you wait. They will."

The next day we filed out of the mess hall after breakfast. The black men stood outside, in a line waiting to get in. Sergeant Phillips walked past them, purposely bumping into a skinny fella towards the end of the line.

"Watch where you're standing, boy," he said.

We held our collective breath, waiting for the young man to say something back that would set Phillips off. He had a temper. Luckily, nothing happened. That time.

But a few days went by, and things started to simmer when the men worked side by side with us building the road. Most of us appreciated the help. But not Phillips. Phillips paced in our barracks in the evenings, ranting, trying to stir up animosity between the races. "Damn negroes shouldn't be here. Why haven't they left yet?"

Phillips had his own office—a small space where he kept records of any safety violations or accidents and sent reports to the government. He was always complaining about that as well. First, because he hated the government, second because he hated the small space and the heat.

One day we walked past his office when I heard him yelling. "Faster, boy. I can't even feel the breeze!"

I was with Tony. We peeked in the doorway to find Phillips sitting, his legs crossed, slung up on his desk, reading a report, and the black man he'd harassed in the mess hall line, fanning him with a big piece of cardboard.

Tony pulled me aside. "Can you believe that character?" he said.

"What a lout," I said.

The man, named Jess, looked mighty distressed. He saw us looking in out of the corner of his eye.

I gestured to him to put the fan down. He saw me and stopped fanning.

"What are you doing, boy?" Sarge said.

"Nothin', sir. I gotta get back to work."

"This is work, boy."

I cleared my throat and stepped inside. "Sarge?"

"What do you want, Taylor?" he barked.

"The Captain told me to tell you he needs to see you as soon as possible."

"Captain? What about?"

I shrugged.

He eyed Jess. "Stay put."

As soon as Sarge left, we said, "Get out of here. We'll tell him you were called to duty by your own commander."

"He's a son-of-a-bitch, ain't he?" Jess said. "I didn't take a job with the Corps to be treated like a slave."

"You just stay clear of him," I said.

From then on, we kept our eye on Jess and tried to steer Sarge away from any interaction with him. But one day, when we got back to the barracks, we heard they had an altercation. Phillips had cornered Jess coming out of the mess hall, struck, and cussed at him. Jess hit Phillips back and broke his nose.

I went right to Captain Blake's office when I heard about it. "Captain Blake, sir?"

He was hunched over his desk, scribbling something in a notebook. His head shot up, and he didn't look too pleased to see me.

"What is it?"

"Sir. I want to tell you something about Sergeant Phillips." I then went on to tell him everything I'd witnessed, the purposeful pushing, making Jess wave a fan on a hot day as if he were some servant, the way he tried to force Jess into a fight.

"That's all well and good, Ben. But I can't have a negro causing trouble with a prominent local man."

I bit my lower lip. "What are you going to do then?"

"Jess Smith is getting discharged."

"But Captain, that isn't fair."

He held his hand in the air. "Life isn't fair, Ben."

I was steaming mad when I got out of there. Someone had to make Captain Blake realize what a bastard Phillips was.

"Don't get involved, Ben," Tony warned me.

When the day came for the men to leave, Tony and I watched the trucks pull up to bring them to the train station in town. Jess wasn't with them. He'd been sent home already.

One of the men, a leader of the platoon named Carter, came up to Tony and me.

"Mind if I bum a cig?" he asked Tony.

Tony took his pack out of his pocket and held it out to the man.

We watched as he lit the cigarette and took a long drag.

"I know you tried to help Jess. He told me to tell you thanks," he said.

"What happened to him?" I said.

He squinted his eyes in the afternoon glare. "Had to go back to his home in Georgia. Lives as a sharecropper. His daddy is dying, and he has five brothers and sisters. It's a mighty shame is what it is. Jess didn't deserve it." He stamped out his cigarette and put his hand out to me. I shook it.

They climbed into their trucks, and Sarge Phillips came up beside us. He stood with his arms crossed over his broad chest, smirking.

"Good riddance," he said and spat on the ground as the last truck pulled out. His venom shook me to my core. As time went by, he grew more unhinged. He'd blow up if a fella made the slightest mistake, particularly if he was from New York or New Jersey. He called the men all kinds of nasty names that came to mind: bohunk, fag, hoodlum. He spat at them, cuffed them on the head, cussed. We'd all had enough.

Tony and I got an idea. When Phillips went into town one evening to get drunk, we jimmied the door to his office open. While Tony kept a lookout, I rifled through his desk. I had a hard time finding what I was after—his accident reports to the government. His desk was littered with half-smoked cigarettes, pencils riddled with teeth marks from his chomping on them while he probably tried to figure out how to spell the word jackhammer. It smelled awful: a mixture of old ashtrays and body odor. I opened a window to keep from gagging.

"How's it going in there?" Tony whispered through the crack in the door.

"Nothing yet," I said. I tossed some papers aside. Phillips wouldn't notice the change of scenery around his desk. And then I spotted something: Camp 46 letterhead, a typewritten report addressed to the U.S. National Park Service signed by Phillips. It was buried under a stack of file folders. It was a carbon copy of a report sent a month prior.

Just as we suspected, he wasn't reporting the accidents that happened regularly at camp, partly because he was to blame. He didn't instruct the men how to hold a tool correctly, he never checked to make sure the tools were put away properly and not sitting around on the ground for men to trip over or worse, fall on top of. And he was responsible for making sure the blades were sharpened, which never happened and made our work more arduous. On top of that, we all knew from almost losing an eye when a chain came undone from a saw, that he hadn't instructed anyone on how to oil and clean the machinery. He was a wreck of a man, terrible at his job. I just needed proof.

There it was in front of me. We'd had five accidents that month in the field, and he hadn't reported any of them. I folded the paper and put it inside my jacket pocket.

As I was exiting, Phillips came round the bend.

"What the hell are you two doing in my office?"

I had to think fast. What would we want from his office?

"Captain asked me to find him some cigarettes, and the commissary is closed. When I told him, he gave me the keys to your office and told me to get some. He figured you'd have some he could borrow, pay you back later," I said.

His face went from incredulous to concern. If Captain Blake wanted something, he was bound to provide. "OK. But I don't want to see you two snooping around my office again, ya hear me?"

"Sure thing," Tony blurted.

I clutched the papers in my chest pocket and ran to Captain Blake's office before he could notice they were missing.

I stopped at the entrance to his office, panting, and asked permission to talk. "Look at this, sir," I said, my hands trembling.

Captain Blake was clearing up for the night and stopped what he was doing to take the papers.

"What is this?"

"It's Sergeant Phillips' report to the government, sir."

"So? And why do you have it?"

I stumbled for a moment, then came up with an excuse for the purloined document. "He gave it to me to edit for him."

"And?"

"He isn't reporting the facts, sir. We had five accidents this week alone. Matt stepped on a rake that was left out, and the handle struck him in the face. He got three stitches in the infirmary. And Phillips was right there when it happened. He even laughed at Matt. Called him a fool."

Blake scowled, swiped the document out of my hands and sat down. He flipped through the papers and then set them on his desk. "You may leave, Ben."

I scrambled out of there as fast as I could. Tony was waiting for me outside.

"What did he say?"

"Nothing," I said.

"What's he gonna do?"

"I don't know, Tony."

We walked back to the barracks, cicadas whirring, birds tittering, a slight breeze. I let the smell of pines fill my lungs, and the forest calm my mind. I knew I had done the right thing.

The next day, Phillips was sent home. And from what I learned; his Pa wasn't too happy about him coming back. Sent him packing to work at his cousin's farm somewhere in North Carolina.

19

Some men deserted because they couldn't take the Corps regiment, the relentless biting insects, or the back-breaking work. Others got injured and the Corps sent them home. But as time passed, our barracks transformed into a small village made up of those men who stayed put. We had showers with hot water, a library with books, an infirmary, a boxing ring, a recreation center with ping pong tables, checker and chess boards, and decks of cards for downtime. We even set up baseball teams and competed against other camps. I was the third baseman, and I almost broke my leg, thanks to my cousin Jimmy.

We took our games seriously. A little too seriously. The baseball league was a matter of pride for the camps. On our days off, we met up with another camp to compete, and the townspeople would come and watch. Local vendors would sell food, people brought picnics. With all the spectators, it was hard not to show off. When the day came that we played Camp 76, I was nervous. I had heard my cousins had enrolled in the Corps and figured I'd be meeting up with them at one time or another on a road crew, but word reached me they were both on the team. Jimmy had a reputation for stealing bases.

It was a sunny spring day, the air was fresh, that time before the bugs hatch. People started arriving an hour before the game commenced. We had built spectator benches. It was one of our first games of the season. The girls poured out of the cars dressed in light cotton dresses, their laughter echoing around the camp. We tossed balls around, showing off for them and then the truck from Camp 76 pulled up and their team climbed off the back.

A couple of blondes walked briskly to meet the fellas as they walked toward our baseball diamond. I saw Jimmy swing his arm around one of them and pull her close. John was behind him, talking to a brunette. I wondered how he managed with his stutter. It had been years since I'd seen my cousins—since Pa died. My stomach turned queasy when I thought about his death.

After the initial excitement of welcoming newcomers to camp, we settled down to play. Matt was our pitcher. He said his years of playing whiffle ball in the alleys of Brooklyn gave him a good eye for it, and he had been lifting weights all winter getting ready. By the top of the ninth, we were ahead by two runs. It was Camp 76's last chance to catch up, or else they'd lose the game. They had two men on base, one on second, and one on third.

Jimmy was at bat and there was only one out. He was a mediocre hitter, but if he made it to base, he was fast. He'd stolen third base twice, and I wasn't planning on letting that happen again.

He hit the ball to right field. It was a grounder. Tony was in right field. He chased after the ball, scooped it up as Jimmy was heading toward second, threw it with all his might to second base, but Jimmy made it safely to base. Two of his teammates had rounded third and scored. It was now a tied game.

Then John came up to bat. He gestured toward Jimmy in some kind of secret sign language the two of them had, and when the pitch came in, John bunted it but it was a pop up, and the catcher caught it. Now there were two outs.

The next batter came up to the plate, and while Matt was in his wind-up, I saw Jimmy coming straight at me out of the corner of my eye, tearing up the dirt. The batter swung and missed, and the catcher rocketed the ball at me. I extended my arm to reach it, and as I did so, Jimmy plowed right into my left leg. The force of his weight threw me in the air, and I landed on top of him, to a collective sigh of "Oh no!" from the crowd of onlookers. My ankle took the brunt of the force. I felt a searing pain. Tony ran over to help me off the field. Jimmy was safe on third.

I was carried to the infirmary and one of the newly hired medics examined my ankle. My only consolation was Emma Sloane was right behind the medic, having seen it all.

She stayed with me while he bandaged my ankle, and we sat and talked awhile.

"I've got good news, Ben," she said. "They'll be starting up a school for the camps, and I've been selected to teach at one near here."

I reached for her hand and took it in mine. "That'll be real fine, Emma. I gotta admit I miss the sight of you."

She blushed, looked both ways, and kissed me on the lips. It was a warm, smooth kiss that filled me from my feet to the tip of my skull and made the hairs on my head tingle. We both came up for air just as my cousin John entered the infirmary.

"Ben, there you are." He approached us, and took his baseball cap off in deference to Emma.

"Miss Emma," he said. "Pleased to ssseee you."

"You too, John." She got up off the cot I was lying on, flushed in the face. "I must be going now. I hope you heal well, Ben."

John stood, meek and unsure what to say. After a long pause, I said, "You lost John?"

This startled him. "No. Just thought I'd check on you is all. He break your leg?"

"No. Just a sprain. Medic said I'll have to get around on crutches for a few weeks." Emma turned at the door and blew me a kiss.

"He's done it before. That's why I ask."

"Done what, John?"

"He's broken someone's leg stealing a base."

I scowled. "That bastard."

"Ben." John's tone was pleading. "I wanted to tell you. I'm sorry about your Pa. I really am."

"It's ok, John. I know it wasn't your fault."

. . .

Having a sprained ankle was fine by me because it meant I didn't have to work on the road crew. For weeks we'd been digging up trees, hacking away and dynamiting stumps, widening dirt paths, using mules and rollers to flatten the dirt to build a road that would cut across the Smoky Mountains connecting North Carolina and Tennessee. It's not that I minded working, it was building a road that bothered me. Anytime I laid down gravel, I thought of Pa. When Captain Blake found out I wasn't able to do road crew, he came to see me.

"Ben, I've got another job for you and it is just as important."

"What's that, Captain?"

"You're one of the few men around here who know how to use a typewriter."

"Yes. Why?"

"Meet me in my office at 0700."

When I arrived, Captain Blake was in a heated discussion behind closed doors with one of the Sergeants.

"I don't understand why we have to take him. Have you seen that sorry specimen? You'd never know he was in the war," Captain Blake blustered.

"Cap, he's a decorated war hero. We need to replace Phillips."

"And his age. He's practically middle-aged."

"The feds are opening up the Corps to vets. They raised the age limit. Besides, this fella is well connected in the community. Everyone knows him and his family, and they've hit hard times. This comes from the top. We need the local support."

"Christ. Have you read his report? They're giving me a sniper who has lost his sight and has shell shock. Tell me that at least he's a Democrat."

"As far as I can tell, sir, he's not a registered anything."

"But these jobs are supposed to be given to Democrats," Blake said. "And that's not me telling you; it comes from the top brass."

"Sir, does it really matter? This guy has a Medal of Honor and Distinguished Service Cross. He picked off twenty German gunners when his troop came under intense enemy fire. He saved his men."

"I know he's a war hero, godammit. Don't tell me what matters around here." Blake let out a long tirade of curse words I won't repeat. I heard something slam on his desk, and then Sergeant MacDougall swung the door open.

"Taylor," he said, surprised at my presence.

I jumped up. "Here to see the Captain."

He cleared his throat. "Yes. Of course. Go right on in."

"Sit down, Ben," Captain said, motioning to a chair. "This is what I need. I need you to write some editorials for the Hickory Run Press."

"Editorials, sir?"

He returned a stare like I was an imbecile. "Yes. *Editorials*. You're going to write some pieces that explain what we're doing here. The progress we're making in this vast wilderness." His arms swept the room.

"You mean like the road we're building through Newfound Gap."

"Exactly!" He rounded on me. It was seven a.m. and his breath, even with the distance between us, smelled like coffee and tobacco.

"And the men," he continued, strutting around the office with his arms flailing. "They came here as boys and just look at them now. Men."

"Yes," I said. "Lou D'Angelo has finally rid himself of a plague of lice. And the fellas insist everyone take a shower at least once a week."

Captain Blake scowled. "Not sure that will do it, Ben. We need something with more drama. And no mention of lice. We don't want to scare people." He scanned the mountains outside the window, searching for something.

"Well, there's the new school," I suggested.

His face lit up as he swung back to face me. "Yes! That's exactly the kind of thing I mean. We can start there. Emma Sloane will be the new teacher. She'll be here every Wednesday evening. You can interview her. She's a local. The townspeople will eat that up."

I was processing the news that Emma would be at our camp school every Wednesday, thinking about our next kiss.

"What else have you got?" Captain Blake shook me out of my daydreaming.

"Well. I um—"

"The road, yes, the road. We are building a road that will allow tourists to drive across the mountain tops. People will come from miles around just to get a glimpse of these spectacular views!" He saluted the mountains in the background.

"Uh. I guess."

"You guess?"

"Well, sir, it sounds a bit like propaganda."

"If it is, Ben, then so be it. Some politicians want to cut off our funding! My boss wants to see our side of the story in the daily news." He leaned over his desk and stared me down. "This is war, Son. We need to beat Old Man Depression."

I was so shaken up and excited about my new assignment, mind racing, that I fumbled with my crutches as I made my way out of Captain's office. There in front of me stood Finn. He had been waiting to enter. His face was gray and gaunt. He was twirling the brim of his hat in his hand.

"Finn."

"Ben," he said, his eyes flickering with recognition.

"What are you doing here?" And before he could answer, I already knew. Finn was the man they were talking about.

"Ben." Captain Blake stepped out of his office. "Do you know Finn McConnell?"

"Yes, sir. I do."

"Good. He's going to be our new Local Experience Man."

"You two will be working closely together. Ben here is a platoon leader." Captain Blake landed his hand on my shoulder and almost made me lose my grip on my crutches.

"Good to hear," Finn said, emotionless.

Blake eyed Finn up and down in disapproval. "Well, come in then." He waved Finn inside his office, and they closed the door.

■ ■ ■

When it came time to write up my 'editorials' for the local press, I had a lot of statistics to work with. The Captain obtained them from the National Park Service and other higher-ups in the government agencies overseeing the Corps and gave them to me to use for the news. I guess he was right about one thing. It was war and journalists dubbed the Civilian Conservation Corps the Tree Army. By 1933 there were over 1400 camps nationwide. Men who had previously been unemployed worked fighting soil erosion, deforestation, and forest fires.

The men of Camp 46 planted a thousand seedlings in the mountains. In just two years, we had retrofitted over two hundred miles of logging roads into paved roads for motor cars. Tourism had grown exponentially.

Local resorts like Foster's Inn set no vacancy records. The mill in town was kept open thanks to our endless need for lumber to build the fire look-out towers, the resting stations, and park structures. We built a legacy that would outlive us all. I wrote all of this and sent copies to the press in Hickory Run, and my articles made it to Knoxville and Nashville, where it mattered most because men of influence in the U.S. Congress read what I wrote. The Captain was so pleased with my writing he asked me to be the editor of the camp newsletter. He named it '*Happy Times*', and I was to fill it with stories for the men and about the men because it would be distributed locally as well. It was about making an impression. They paid me five dollars more per week for my work.

"I think you should interview the men and ask them what they like about being in the Corps," Blake said.

"You mean besides the food?" I was half-joking. The week before Blake had to put down a riot in the dining hall when the men complained about the meat tasting like leather.

His bushy brows furrowed into a V. "Not that. I think it is the duty of every man who has received benefits from the Corps to express their appreciation to the authorities who made it possible for them to receive this training." He recited it like he had memorized it from a government memo.

"Yes, sir."

Back at the barracks the fellas gathered their things for the day's work and watched me with envy as I wrote notes in my journal.

"What's the Cap got ya doin'?" Tony asked.

"I'm going to be writing stories about us. I need to interview a few of the fellas. Any volunteers?"

"Stories?" Stan called to me as he tied on his boots. "What kind of stories?"

Matt laughed. "Like how you play with your pecker all night long, Stan, and the squeaking bunk keeps us up."

Stan threw a boot at his head.

"Or how Sam over there is homesick for his sweetheart, and she's jilting him for the boy next door," someone said.

"Or how about how we all got chiggers while cutting up the slash leftover from the Lavery Lumber Company." That remark set everyone off.

"How about how we almost gave Charlie a concussion throwing our boots at him at night because he snores so loud?" The place roared with laughter.

"Come on, fellas," I said. "I'm supposed to come up with stories about the positive aspects of our work."

They all stopped what they were doing and gawked, then threw their pillows at me. Finally, Tony took pity and stopped it.

"Hey, guys. We can come up with some ideas, can't we? Let's help a fella out." He jumped about the barrack, slapping one guy after another on the back. "Now Fred here has two little brothers at home, and they were starving before Fred took up his position in the Corps, right Fred?" Fred nodded. The men went silent. Tony kept going. "And Lou here, he never knew how to drive a truck until he came here, and they taught him, right, Lou?"

The men started looking down at their feet, ashamed they hadn't thought of these things. "And can't we all say we have some skills we never had before?"

"Yeah, I guess you're right. I know carpentry," a man called.

"And I can identify five trees," another said.

"I know what blister rust is that's killing them," someone else added. Everyone mumbled in agreement. We'd spent weeks pruning white pine to control the blister rust that was sweeping through the forest.

"Ya see, fellas?" Tony was lit up like a Christmas tree. "Now, you got some stories to tell, Ben."

I wrote these things down, but once Captain Blake got his itchy editing fingers on my work some of the language shifted. It seemed as soon as I broke out the typewriter he was at my side, chomping down on a half-smoked cigar.

"Insert here," he said, planting his finger over the page sticking out of the typewriter, "I extend my appreciation to the President and the government for the fine things they are doing for the people of this nation."

"You mean after Lou's quote about learning how to drive a truck?" I said.

"Don't be impertinent, Ben. Just do it."

I gulped, backtracked the page, made some space, and while he hovered over me, typed what he said word for word.

Although I understood why Captain Blake asked me to glamorize the stories and make them more palatable for the general reading public, I was still torn about it. That night after dinner I wasn't much fun with the guys, and Tony noticed.

"What's eatin' you?" he said.

I told him about my day.

"Hey, the Cap'n is right."

"He is?"

"Oh yeah. You don't want the public knowing the real stories about the guys. You know Fred's father is an alcoholic? Fred thinks he takes his money every month and spends it at the bars. His mother writes him that they're still broke and hungry. And me? Well, you wouldn't believe my story even if I told you. So, you're better off writing just good, positive stuff, ya know?"

"What's your story?"

He looked at me sideways. "Like I said, you don' wanna know." He lit a cigarette and the glow of the match flickered on his face.

■ ■ ■

While I recovered from my ankle injury, Blake let me help Emma Sloane set up the library in the schoolhouse, and at times, help her teach the fellas to read and write. Mr. Vorhoss and the local churches raised the money to buy us new books. Emma and I both agreed to get the men to take tests to assess their reading level. Once we had that figured out, we set them up in groups. If others could read, we recruited them as tutors.

One fella named Pablo Diaz had worked in a Cuban Cigar factory in Miami. He told Emma and me he used to get paid fifty cents a week to read to the men while they worked. "I'd stand on a platform and read aloud from the papers to keep them informed of the world and also entertained." He even acted some of it out. "Then they put a stop to it when they found me reading The Daily Worker. Said I can't read no commie papers."

We placed Pablo with the guys reading at the eighth-grade level, figuring his reading material wouldn't stray into politics.

Emma had always been my true love, but I was never sure if I was hers. As we worked side by side, our relationship blossomed. I woke early each morning in anticipation of her arrival at the library.

"Good morning, Ben," she said each day with a bright smile, and we went to work.

One morning I brought her a bouquet of Lady's Tresses I picked from the forest.

"Oh, Ben, these are my favorite." She glanced around for something to put them in.

"Wait," I said and went to the kitchen to find an old coffee can. You'dve thought I had given her a china vase from England the way she fussed over it.

She liked to order me around, and I was used to it. "That book shelf belongs over there," she pointed to the corner of the room one day while we set up the shelving for the books that were coming in every day.

I dragged the shelving to the corner. She put her pointer finger to her lips examining the placement. "Well, actually, maybe over there."

I ignored my throbbing ankle as I moved things around the room for her.

"Oh, Ben, are you ok?" she said when she noticed my limp. "I shouldn't be working you so hard."

I swiped at my brow. "Believe me, this beats whacking away at the underbrush in the forest or pouring gravel for a new road. I'd much rather be here." I stacked a few more books in the shelf.

"With you," I added.

This made her blush and she turned away with a smile on her face to open another box filled with books.

I was sorry when my ankle healed, and I was put back to work in the crews every day. But at least I had Wednesday nights to look forward to when she would arrive at our camp to teach the advanced readers and I would mentor the tutors.

After two years, the enlistees had to decide whether to continue in the Corps or go back home. For most of us, the decision was an easy one. The nation was still in the grips of the Great Depression and nobody's fortunes had taken a turn for the better. A few men decided the Corps wasn't for them and left to try their luck back home in the cities or the coal mine towns they came from. We settled into our barracks like a real home. Some of the fellas made signs and posted them on the entrances to the barracks: Hotel Savoy, Ritz Carlton. Our dining hall became the Tavern on the Green, a tribute to the new restaurant in Central Park.

Another thing happened in 1936 that changed the direction of my life: Camp 46 downsized and merged with Camp 76. My life once again collided with cousins Jimmy and John.

20

The Corps invited us to attend a holiday party in honor of our work in the establishment of the Great Smoky Mountains National Park. Most of us didn't own dress clothes. I asked Emma what we should do about it after school let out one crisp November evening.

"They have to wear ties, of course. And pressed pants and a collared shirt."

"But not many of us have those things, Emma. And we don't have the money to buy them."

"Hmmm. How about I ask my father what he thinks? Maybe some of the men in town can donate clothes they don't need anymore."

Within a week, Emma returned with a truckload of clothes, mostly outdated styles from the early 1900s, packed neatly in boxes. The guys tore through the boxes like children at Christmas. We all thought we looked so dapper as we headed into town for the party.

While growing up, my experience with dancing was limited to family parties that erupted into dance when a fiddler or dulcimer player showed up. And even then, the dances consisted of square dancing and tossing the ladies around the floor. At school they tried to teach us a few ballroom dance steps like the foxtrot and waltz, but I never took to it. My jaw dropped when we arrived at the Hall of Education, Damnation, and Salvation to see the girls all dolled up in dresses, twirling around with local men who came back from college for the holiday. I recognized a few from my school days who had been fortunate enough to go to college. I started to perspire and went to find a place by the wall where I wouldn't be seen by Emma or any other girl who might mistakenly think I'd like to dance.

Tony found me. "What are you doing over here? Get out there." He pointed in the direction of Emma, who was dancing with Tyler

Blackwater while Glenn Miller's *In The Mood* crooned in the background. Tyler flung her around like a yoyo on a string.

"I don't know how to dance like that."

"Are you kidding me? It's not that hard."

"Where'd you learn?"

Tony shrugged. "Me and my mom used to dance around the apartment. She taught me. Come on, follow me."

We went outside and he led me to an alley behind the hall. "The easiest dance is the swing. You just have to count. One, two, three. And you have to lead. Then swing her like this...pull her back in..."

"Yeah, it's coming back to me," I said.

He put his hand in mine and showed me how to position myself as if he were the girl. "Now the key thing to remember is not to step on her feet. If you step on her feet, she's not gonna like it, and she's gonna stop dancing with you." He sounded like he knew what he was talking about from experience.

We waltzed for a few minutes until I started to relax and feel more confident.

Back inside I put a piece of gum in my mouth, ready to conquer my fears. When *Moonlight Serenade* came on, I headed toward Emma. She was chatting with a group of girls on the other side of the hall. Out of the corner of my eye, I saw my cousin Jimmy heading in her direction, and I quickened my pace to head him off at the pass.

"Emma," I called a little out of breath. She swung around to face me. "Wanna dance?"

"I was waiting for you to ask!"

I took hold of her the way Tony had shown me and tentatively led her out to the dance floor. Her hair smelled like peach trees in spring. I began to relax. We floated across the floor as I counted in my head one, two, three, four so as not to step on her foot. I became distracted when I saw Jimmy standing in the middle of a group of girls. Most of them chatted it up with him. One of the girls slapped him in jest on the arm, laughing at something he said.

He asked her to dance and led her to the floor. He leaned into her real close so that he was breathing down her neck. He wasn't holding her like

I was holding Emma, at a distance. A chaperone came over and tapped him on the shoulder, shaking her head. Jimmy started talking back.

Emma glanced over at Jimmy while I was jawing on my gum, thinking what I should do. The gum fell out of my mouth and into her hair. I gasped. She pulled away.

"Ben, do something," she said, canting her head in the direction of Jimmy.

I wanted to tell her a wad of gum was stuck on the back of her head, but I was too afraid. I just dropped her hands and went over to Jimmy and the girl.

"Why don't you two go make out somewhere else?" I said to Jimmy and the girl.

Embarrassed, the girl dashed off. Jimmy shoved me. "Mind your own damn business."

A few of the women from the Auxiliary came over to us.

"Is there a problem?" one of the ladies asked.

We shook our heads. "No, ma'am," Jimmy said.

She raised a brow at Jimmy and me. I recognized her as the owner of the millinery shop in town.

"Good. Let's keep it that way. I'd hate to spoil a wonderful evening."

Jimmy stomped off. Emma and a few of her friends came up behind me. "Thank you, Ben," she whispered in my ear.

I felt the heat rise to my cheeks.

"Oooh, Emma! You've got gum in your hair!" her friend squealed.

Tony saved me. He dragged me away to help break up a brawl that was happening outside while Emma and her girlfriends headed to the ladies' room to get the gum out of her hair.

■　■　■

That winter Captain Blake recruited a group to hike into the mountains and inspect abandoned cabins. It was a thankless task. The Park Service had a list of people still allowed to stay in the park, my aunts included, and a list of places that should be vacated. We left on a cold, bleak February morning to determine if any of the cabins on our list were a hazard and needed to be demolished.

I hated the job, but because Finn and I knew the territory, the Captain told us to lead the group. A small band gathered after breakfast: Me, Finn, Tony, Matt, a new enrollee named Ted who came from the Adirondacks in NY and claimed the weather was balmy compared to his hometown. Tony told him to shut the hell up. Jimmy and John approached as we packed our things.

"We're coming along too," Jimmy said. "Beats cleaning the bathrooms."

We followed the old railroad tracks through Taylor Valley. I saw my family cabin still standing on the knoll.

"I'll check it out," I told the crew. Tony started to follow, but Finn held him back with his outstretched arm.

I went inside. It was an empty shell now. The Lavery Company had left behind a few nails, the potbelly stove stood still in the corner, but otherwise, it was dead. The floor was sound, no water was leaking through the roof. Pa had built this cabin to last. A shutter clapped in the wind. I went to shut it tight. My eyes wandered to the sick room and visions of my younger brother Sam, his raspy breathing reverberating throughout the cabin. Ma making him tea. For a moment, I heard him laughing as he used to after I told him a joke or a story about one of the aunts. But it was just the wind blowing through the chinks in the walls. The newspaper that lined the cabin was now torn and tattered, flapping restlessly in the wind.

From there, we followed the railroad tracks as they wound their way up the ridge leading to Taylor Grove. I barely recognized the abandoned tracks in the riot of overgrown laurel. We had on our newly ordered rubber boots with grips on the bottom so we wouldn't slide as we climbed the slope. I tried to look away as we passed Taylor Grove, but I couldn't. It was a vast, empty, open space. A wasteland of slash and stumps covered in rime, appearing like lost souls wandering an arctic landscape. We trudged over the ridge and descended into McConnell's Cove.

Along the way, we passed a few abandoned buildings that once belonged to Finn's neighbors. I pulled out my list. The men stamped their feet, rubbed their arms, and complained of the cold, waiting for our instructions, their breath forming vaporous clouds in the air.

"This one's on the list," I said, gesturing in the direction of the Leonards' homestead. The corn crib had collapsed, the springhouse was falling into the creek, the barn was intact, and so was the cabin, but I could tell that the roof was damaged from the recent storm, and shingles flapped in the brisk wind.

"No need to check on it," Finn said.

I raised a brow.

"You sure, Finn?"

"It'll stand through the winter. No need to go inside. We'll come back another time to see if it's still standing."

I scratched my head. Tony came up, blowing air into his fists to keep them warm. "Hey, what's up fellas? The guys are getting cold standing around."

"We're moving on," Finn said.

Jimmy pulled up alongside Tony. "Aren't we going inside? It's colder than a witch's tit out here."

Finn wheeled around and stared right through Jimmy. "Keep moving," he said.

Tony pulled me aside as Finn started up the path. "Hey, ain't we supposed to report whether these places are at risk of falling down? I mean, take a look at that porch."

The porch steps were broken, and the floor was sinking under the weight of snow and ice. Before I could answer, I saw a curtain ripple in one of the windows. I told myself it was the wind and followed in Finn's wake.

We passed by three more cabins with the same result. Finn wouldn't let us go in any of them to check on their safety. Finally, Jimmy protested.

"Hey, now. This doesn't make any sense to me. Why are we here if we ain't gonna check these places out?"

"Shut your trap, Jimmy," Tony said. "Finn knows what he's doing."

"You'd hardly think so. He's walking around like he's seen a ghost."

Indeed, that is what we witnessed: the ghosts of Finn's past life. The lives of his neighbors who had milked their cows, raised their chickens, built their barns here in the Cove. Their homesteads abandoned, vulnerable to the elements, vestiges of a lifestyle no longer allowed or wanted in the government's plan for the National Park.

"The park may want to keep a few of these buildings standing as a monument to what it was like around here," I said.

Jimmy scoffed. "A monument to the hillbillies you mean?"

I frowned at him.

"I don't know. I kinda think these places hold a certain charm. Don't you agree fellas?" Tony said.

The other fellas grumbled a reply, not really interested in my cultural heritage.

"It's cold out here. Can't we go into that cabin to warm up?" one of the guys said.

"We gotta keep movin'" Finn replied.

We passed Cooper's Cabin and blacksmith shop. Mr. Cooper had three sons, and they all worked for the Corps in various camps around the Park. One of them, Coop, was in our barracks. He trained other Corps members in the art of blacksmithing. Mr. Cooper was in his late seventies, and the Park allowed him to stay until he either died or his lease ran out. He traveled the park in his horse and wagon with the tools of his trade to mend tools, shoe horses, and do any other odd job that the camps needed on site. We gazed longingly at the smoke trailing out of his chimney.

"Coop's cabin," I said to Tony.

He appeared incredulous. "So that's where Coop grew up? Here in the middle of nowhere. He must've had to hike for hours just to get a sack of flour."

"No different from how I grew up," I said.

We passed the lane that led to the McConnell's homestead.

"No need to stop," Finn said. "I already know it's abandoned."

"Yeah, but aren't we supposed to stop and check it out?" Jimmy said.

I tugged at Finn's arm. "Uh, Finn, I think we better at least stop to eat."

He finally acquiesced when we reached a large barn at the far end of the Cove. It had been owned by one of Finn's cousins, Francis McConnell. Jimmy knew him.

"The fella moved to Knoxville. I know because he used to work for my Pa's lumber company when we were cutting around here."

The men opened up their sacks and bit into their sandwiches. By now, they were used to Jimmy's bragging about the way things used to be with his family. How he grew up in a big house in town that had central heat and plumbing, his own bedroom, a porch that wrapped around the whole house, blabbing away. It was easy to ignore him because none of them had the same experience, and there was no way they could show him up if they tried.

"Bbbblogna again?" John said.

Ted laughed. "Hey, bud, your lips numb or something?"

"Stifle it," I said.

Ted looked hurt. He didn't understand what he'd done wrong because he didn't know about John's stutter.

We munched on bologna, thinking about the warmth of the stoves in our barracks, when the door to the barn swung open. At first, I thought it was the wind, but then a little girl entered. She had on a threadbare dress made of cotton and a bright yellow sweater with holes in it. She had no stockings on but was wearing old work boots that looked three sizes too big. Her cheeks were red and raw from the cold, and her eyes were shallow discs in her face. At the sight of us, she jumped, then bolted out the door.

"Hey! Hey, you!" Jimmy jumped out of his seat, chasing after her. Finn quickly followed.

I got to the door of the barn in time to see Jimmy grabbing the girl as she tried to run from him in her too-large boots. She struggled from his grip, and he slapped her. Finn, who had chased after both of them, took hold of Jimmy's shoulders and shoved him to the ground. He landed on his butt in a puddle of frozen mud.

"Get back to the barn!" Finn growled.

Jimmy stood up; fists clenched. He eyed Finn and me like he saw a conspiracy.

Tony was right behind me, as usual. "Come on," he said to Jimmy. "Let's get back to the barn." Finally, he let Tony drag him away.

I stood by Finn while he interviewed the girl.

"Where's your family?"

"They's inside. It's jus' me and my sister." She was shivering as she gestured toward the cabin where a woman who looked to be about the age of my sister Rachel was staring out the window. We followed the little girl inside.

"Ma'am," Finn said in that soft voice of his that set her at ease.

The older girl said nothing, just stared at us with an open mouth, her hands shaking.

"We've been walking a long ways. Can we sit down?" Finn said. I knew he was seeking a way to appear less tall and foreboding to both of them.

She nodded her head. The little girl jumped into action, pulling up two wobbly chairs for us.

"You gonna make us leave?" the older one said.

"Where y'all from?" I asked.

"We's come from the other side of that thar mountain." The older one pointed in the direction of the Reeds' place.

"You the Reed girls?" Finn said.

The girls nodded. Our Cherokee neighbors.

"I remember you," I said. "You used to bring ramps to the General Store in town with your ma. What happened to your ma?"

"She's dead," said the little girl.

"And your pa?"

"They killed 'im?"

"Who killed him?" I said.

"The jailers."

Then I remembered. Pa told me they'd been kicked off their land because Mr. Reed had gotten into trouble with the law. I wondered if he had ended up on the same road crew as Pa, where cruel and brutal treatment was frequent for every prisoner in the crew, but even worse for blacks and Cherokee.

They both nodded.

"We's jus' stayin' here 'til spring then we's gonna find our kin in Smokemont," the older one said between sobs.

"Smokemont?" I said. "That's a ghost town now. Park bought it up."

"When you girls git to Smokemont, you just keep walking 'til you git to Bird Town. You know your way?" Finn said.

"Yes, sir," she said. "Pa showed us the trails, and we ain't forgotten."

I glanced around the cabin. The Leonards didn't leave anything behind. No blankets, quilts, or clothes. The girls' beds consisted of boards in the corner of the room. There was no firewood stacked at the hearth. They were using fence posts to heat the place, and the end of one was poking out of the fire. I saw no kitchen tools or pots to cook with and wondered how they'd been surviving. Then I saw strung up on the beams strings of cabbage leaves, peas, beans, garlic. They'd been gardening. They'd probably found seed in the garden or barn. A bag of nuts sat on the table, their handmade straw baskets. They'd been harvesting nuts all fall.

"You girls have any meat in a while?" Finn said.

"No, sir."

Finn opened his sack. "Take this." He handed them his rations for the day. "We'll get you more."

The girls clung to each other, afraid to take it from him.

"Go ahead. I won't hurt you," he said.

The older one grabbed the food out of his hand.

We watched them devour the sandwiches. "I'll be right back," I said.

I went to the barn and found Tony. "Tell the fellas we need all the food they've got in their sacks. No questions asked. It's an order from Finn."

We left the girls with a crate full of food: nuts, bread, bologna, fruit. Me, Tony, and Matt found some wood and cut it into cords for the fireplace. We left them a supply of wooden matches. Finn told the fellas he would report the girls' status to his higher-ups and not to worry about them. But we all knew he wasn't going to report anything.

21

The articles I wrote for the 'Happy Times' newsletter offered tips for the new recruits about hygiene, behavior when visiting town, and sports. One of the favorite weekly pastimes at camp was watching boxing matches. Boxing matches gave the guys a way to vent out their frustrations in a controlled environment. Better in the ring than out in the field while working around heavy machinery or tools.

When a truckload of new recruits from New York City came to Camp 46 that summer we turned their welcoming party into a boxing match. The enrollees lumbered into camp to collect their uniforms, and we gawked at them, forgetting how we once looked—scrawny, smelly, and young.

We put them in the ring after the first week to break them in. These matches were not about showing off, but about toughening each other up, letting off steam. The fellas placed bets and let out catcalls, boos, and hisses all in the name of fun. That is until Jimmy got into the ring. He took it too seriously. I don't think I've ever met a man who enjoyed knocking people down the way Jimmy did. Since he was the champion, he got first round with the new enrollees.

A few cocky guys from the Bronx were eager to out play Jimmy. In their neighborhoods, they had been the guys in charge. We called them street-wise fools. The first young fella named Rocco D'Ambrosio was half the size of Jimmy but more agile. He got into the ring and had some sharp moves. He ducked, punched, ducked punched until he had Jimmy huffing and puffing. We started hooting and hollering for the underdog because none of us could stand Jimmy's arrogance. This riled Jimmy up even more. His face went red with rage, and when Rocco got too close, he landed a punch in the head that sent him flying. The referee called the match in Jimmy's favor, and only a few people whistled or cheered.

The next fella to take on Jimmy was another young Italian named Luca Bianchi. He was no match for Jimmy. Round one was called in Jimmy's favor. As Luca exited, Jimmy remarked, "Dago in, Dago out."

Luca pounced on Jimmy, tackling him to the ground, pummeling his face and chest. John jumped into the ring to tear the two apart. Luca lay on the floor, panting, spittle dripping from his mouth, and hatred spewing from his eyes.

Jimmy stood up, wiped the blood off his lip, and spit on him. "Don't ever touch me again, asshole."

I didn't write up that part of the boxing match in the monthly newsletter. But I did have to write a note of encouragement as well as an admonishment for the new recruits, under Captain Blake's direction.

He blew into my office like a November gust. "Ben, we're losing men. Just today, two more recruits deserted. My men found them in town trying to catch the train out."

"What did they do?"

"Brought 'em back, of course! And they took off the next morning." His hand flew in the air. "We need to make sure the men understand the consequences of their actions. How about you writing something like: two of the new recruits, evidently pansies, decided camp life was too hard. They just traded three square meals a day and support for their families for the opportunity to loiter on a street corner, trying to look important."

"Well, sir, I don't know, maybe pansy is too harsh."

Blake rounded on me. "Harsh! For God's sake, Ben." He pounded his fist on the desk, and my typewriter jumped. "When will you realize this is a campaign, son? And you are on the front line."

"Yes, sir." I put paper in the typewriter and followed his orders, adding at the end: it is hoped that no more fellas will follow the deserters' example.

Under the direction of the Corps, we had installed telephone and electrical lines and a favorite pastime was listening to the radio. Growing up I never heard the radio in our cabin. These advances brought the world to us and made the day-to-day routine of our work more palatable.

Then the event of October 30, 1938, happened and the world got a little too close for comfort.

One of the guys' favorite radio shows was *The Mercury Theater on Air*, narrated by Orson Welles. Some of the guys who learned to read got hooked when Welles read *Dracula* and *Treasure Island* over the radio. They'd follow along to improve their reading. You might say Welles was with us in the recreation hall while we listened to his voice boom over the radio, and the sound effects which he recreated— the stabbing of a heart, the sound of the ocean waves—put us right in the story.

That's why the October 30, 1938 dramatization of the *War of the Worlds* came across as so real. And to the men who had grown up in the east coast cities in New York and New Jersey and had family still there, it was a nightmare.

It started off jovially enough. We sat around, making jokes, drinking root beer, waiting for Welles. None of us had heard of or read *War of the Worlds*. He started off reading the introduction to the story and then the show changed over to big band music. We all stared at each other, wondering what was going on. Maybe a break. Men broke into groups, playing cards, chatting. We lost interest. And then a radio announcer comes on to say that scientists have discovered some odd explosions coming from the planet Mars. Our ears perked up because he made it sound like this was some big news. And then, nothing. The music returned, and we returned to whatever it was we were doing. A few men left to head to bed. Suddenly the radio crackled, and another reporter broke up the music. "I'm interrupting this radio broadcast to tell everyone that an unidentified object has landed on a farm in New Jersey." The fellas from New Jersey bolted out of their chairs, pressing their ears to the radio. The reporter spoke with the farmer who told us he saw "*something in the air, and then it landed on his farm.*" A crowd of people soon showed up to gaze at the large cylindrical object, unsure what it was at first. But the experts on the scene believed it to be an alien from space. The end of it flaked off, and people started shouting over the radio, and all of a sudden, the reporter was telling us he was "*terrified.*" As he tried to explain what he saw, "*creatures with tentacles,*" he was cut off, just like that!

He came back on briefly. By now, the state police were at the scene. A strange siren sound came over the radio, screaming, and then shouts of agony, and again, he was cut off.

"*Ladies and Gentlemen, due to circumstances beyond our control, we have lost transmission from the field. We continue now with our piano interlude.*"

"What?" someone yelled. Within minutes they came back on to tell us at least forty people and eight troopers were dead, their bodies burned beyond recognition. A Brigadier General came on air to place the counties of New Jersey under Martial Law from Trenton to Grover's Mill. Military operations were underway.

The next thing we hear is a series of "*We are interrupting this radio show to announce that…*" It went on and on and on. Strange sightings all over the world. A ship landing in New York City, spewing dark, poisonous gas. New York City was evacuated due to the invasion of Martians. The fellas became jittery. The announcer said the army was wiped out in its efforts to defend the city from the attack.

A few began to cry. Tony reached out to me. "You don't think this is really happening, do ya?"

Looking around at the panic-stricken men, I didn't know what to think.

Suddenly, Lou jumped out of his chair, flipping it over. "I gotta get home, right away!" he yelled. "The Martians are taking over the city! My whole family lives there!" He rushed out of the recreation center to the barracks.

I followed the stream of men fleeing the recreation hall. It was chaos in the barracks.

Tony's eyes grew wide with terror. "You gotta do something!" he said. "My mom and my aunt and all my cousins are in New York. I gotta get back home!" He pulled his duffel out from under his bunk and started packing.

"How do you think you're going to get home at this time of night?" I yelled at him and the rest of the men. They didn't listen.

I ran to Captain Blake's quarters and woke him up.

"What is it, Taylor?" he said.

"Captain, the men are in a panic. They think Martians have landed in New York City and New Jersey, and they are trying to get to town to go home."

"What the hell are you talking about!"

I was about to explain when Sergeant MacDougall came rushing up to us. "Captain, we have a situation here that needs your attention."

Blake fumbled into his uniform and followed us to the barracks. The place was a scene of madness. Men had their bags strapped to their backs, shouting at each other, heading toward the trucks.

Blake put his pistol in the air and let off three shots.

The whole camp turned their attention to him.

He put a megaphone to his mouth and shouted orders. "All men stop what you are doing. We are in communication with the U.S. Army and they have told us no one is to leave this camp until they have everything under control. There have been no reported fatalities in the cities. Do you understand?"

The only sound was of dead leaves fluttering in the wind and scraping against the road.

The men started to grumble. A few reluctantly went back into the barracks, others headed to the recreation hall to listen to the latest news bulletins on the radio. There was nothing to report. It was as if it never happened. So, we went to bed. Images of Martians landing on the mountain tops with ray guns pointed at our barracks plagued me all night long. I tossed and turned with the rest of the fellas. It wasn't until the morning that we learned it was all a show, a hoax. The guys who panicked took a ribbing, but I have to admit, I almost ran to town with them.

22

Mary had a job with the Park Service and was able to send money home. Rachel, who was now fifteen, had gotten her job back at the Foster's Inn. Ma and the girls did as well as could be given the economy. Now that I made more money, I could save some. My dream was to save enough to ask Emma to marry me. We had been courting for a year, and each encounter became more and more frustrating. I'd come to town to visit with her at her house. If Doc Sloane was home, we stayed on the porch or in the parlor and held hands. Even if Doc wasn't home, there was Lila, the maid. She watched us like a hawk.

You'd never know we were both twenty-three. They never left us alone. When the time came for Doc Sloane to visit a camp overnight, Emma would send Lila to visit her family, telling her she wasn't needed for the evening. Those evenings we had to ourselves. But our heavy petting always ended abruptly when Emma sat up and told me, "No. Not until we're married."

If we married, we would lose our jobs with the Corps. She was the head schoolmistress at the camp, and they would not allow her to stay if she married. I took college classes for free on the weekends from university professors who came once a week to teach. I would lose my job as well, my income, and my chance at a college degree.

On a hot August night, we both sat on her porch after a particularly steamy encounter that ended with both of us half-dressed. I sat with my shirt open to the fresh night air, she was fanning herself with a handkerchief. We both sipped lemonade in a glass loaded with ice cubes.

"I can't stand it anymore," I said.

"Me neither."

"Emma, let's get married."

"How?"

"We won't tell anybody."

"My father would be heartbroken if we eloped."

"I understand." I got up to leave. "I best be getting back home then."

She reached for me. "Wait."

We went back inside to her bedroom. I watched her undress. A soft breeze fluttered through the window, sending a shiver up my spine. "What are you waiting for, Ben? Take the rest of your clothes off."

．　．　．

Mary came to work at our camp the following spring to train the men on botany. When she drove up to camp in her government-appointed truck, got out of the cab in her National Park uniform, she caused quite a stir. The guys all stood around gaping. Not many had seen a girl in uniform, and not one so beautiful as Mary. She had grown into a fine-looking woman, tall, sun-tanned, with flowing dark hair, and those dark eyelashes. I cringed when I saw Jimmy's jaw drop at the sight of her.

Tony was the first to say something. "What a looker!"

I cuffed him on the head. "She's my sister, you idiot."

Soon enough, Tony tagged after Mary like he had clung to me. He signed up for all of her training sessions. She taught the men how to identify rare and sensitive flowering plants native to the Smoky Mountains and mapped locations for the park officials to plan future trails to avoid those areas. Mary also trained the men on how to find what they called mother trees for the dying chestnuts; those seedlings not infected with the blight. The Park had a nursery, and the men dug up the seedlings to transplant them to the Park nursery in Pisgah. The men also assisted in controlling the blight.

I sat in the back of the classroom while she showed them her pictures of plants, explained what they'd be doing in the field, and making them identify samples from plant pressings.

"Now remember, do not touch the plants unless instructed!" she said in her smooth-as-velvet voice, which made the men moon over her even more. "Your job is to identify and mark them down on your charts. I'll separate all of you into groups. Some will be on the chestnut patrol, some on the wildflower patrol."

"Which patrol will you be on?" Tony said.

The guys all guffawed and launched pencils at his head.

She clucked. "Wildflowers. Ben is in charge of the chestnut blight control and restoration."

.   .   .

The Park Service was optimistic about controlling the chestnut blight and rejuvenating the forest with seedlings. They kept seedlings in their nursery until they were big enough to withstand browsing deer, roaming wild pigs, and other forest creatures. I brought the men into the stands of chestnut groves and identified which ones were worth salvaging, and which ones were dead and could be cut for wood to build structures. We cut down the dead chestnuts and hauled them to the new mill at our campsite. We used the lumber for making bridges, cabins, and signs throughout the park.

The Park Service (and Mary) thought that as long as the blight canker hadn't reached the top, the tree could be saved. We took large tin cans that once held tomatoes, cut through the seam, and wrapped them around the trunk, stacking one on top of the other. Then we filled them with soil and moistened it with water. The theory was the moisture would control the blight. The key was the soil had to remain wet. If it didn't rain, we had to carry jugs of water on packs and hose them down.

The lumber companies left large swathes of open spaces after they cut the healthy trees. This allowed the sunbeams to reach the forest floor and give tree seedlings a fighting chance. The old chestnut trees flung off their seeds as a last-ditch effort to save the species. If the seedling was too big to dig up, we surrounded it with a tarp for protection against browsing. Otherwise, we dug it up to be reared in the safety of the nursery. As I stood in the devastation of what was once a well-shadowed grove of chestnuts, one of the many places we used to go as kids to collect nuts, I wasn't sad, I was filled with hope that maybe our arduous work would someday pay off.

One day at camp Mary sought me out to talk about Tony.

"What is with that guy Tony?"

"He's harmless."

She took off her cap and shook her hair loose from its bun. I was stabbed with pain because she looked so much like Pa and Sam.

"Well, he followed me around like a puppy all day. A nuisance!"

I laughed. "He did the same to me at first. You'll get used to him. How's Ma? And the girls?"

"See for yourself. Drop by when you're in town. She complains you spend too much time with Emma."

"We're courting," I said. "I plan to marry her."

"Be careful, Ben." She lifted herself into the seat of the truck, put it into gear, and waved. "I'll see you tomorrow." I watched the truck kick up dust as it rumbled down the road.

"Where's she going?" Tony appeared out of nowhere and made me jump.

"Christ, Tony! You startled me. And if you must know, she's staying with my Ma in town."

"Oh good!" he darted away before I could say anything.

I went to the school building to check on Emma. It was a sweltering hot day. Emma left the windows open to try and catch any little breeze that passed by. As I approached, I heard her talking to someone. Her voice raised as if scolding a pupil. I peered inside and saw Jimmy leaning over her desk, his broad shoulders blocking my view of Emma.

"You flatter me, Jimmy. But I'm not interested."

"Come on now, Emma. Give some of it up for me, will ya? We all know you're giving it up for my loser cousin."

I saw her fists planted firmly on the desk; her brows furrowed. "He's not a loser."

Jimmy took his hands off the desk, towering over her. "His father was arrested for bootlegging, and his Ma lost her mind when his brother died. The family's cursed."

177

She pushed back her chair and stood up to face him. "And whose fault is it that his pa was arrested?" She jabbed her pointer finger into his chest. "I wouldn't go around talking about Ben's pa that way when your own father beat his wife. Then when things went sour for him financially, he took his own life. Like the coward that he was."

"You bitch!" Jimmy said. "Take that back."

Emma's steely gaze never faltered, even when he lifted his hand in the air to strike her.

I flew across the room.

"Ben!" Emma yelled.

Jimmy swung around to face me. I lunged at him, tackling him to the ground. Emma screamed.

I was on top of him, striking his face with my fists. He grabbed my shirt collar and yanked hard, twisting me sideways and off of him. I stood up quickly and went at him, but he was ready and landed his fist in my gut. I doubled back in pain, the breath taken out of me, gasping for air.

"Ben!" Emma came to my side. Jimmy was standing over us, he pushed her away and lifted me off my feet.

I got my breath back and punched him again. I felt his teeth rip into my knuckles. He fell over the desk and Emma's pencil holder landed on the ground, shattering into pieces.

I was about to go after him again when someone grabbed me from behind and pulled me away. It was Finn.

"What the hell is going on in here?" Captain Blake was standing in the doorway, his fists planted on his hips.

I wiped at my mouth. Jimmy stood up. Blood was dripping from his split lips, staining his shirt.

"Ain't nothing," Jimmy said.

"Just a little disagreement," I said.

We both looked at Emma.

"Miss Sloane, are you all right?" Captain Blake said.

Emma looked at me. By now, she was standing, straightening her blouse and skirt. Composure slowly coming back. I nodded. If she said anything, we took the risk that Jimmy would tell Captain Blake about our affair, which he obviously knew about. And that would end Emma's career here as a teacher, and mine possibly.

"It was nothing, Captain. The fellas were arguing over the latest baseball game results, and well, you know…." She lifted a shoulder in the air. "Boys will be boys."

Captain Blake appeared to be mulling this over, deciding whether to believe her or not when Finn spoke up. "I saw it, Captain. It ain't nothing. They like to brawl is all. That's how it is with cousins."

I silently thanked Finn with my eyes.

Captain Blake jerked his thumb at the broken porcelain, papers, chalk, and books strewn on the floor. "Pick it up."

When Mary's work with the crew was done, she was assigned to another camp. We gave her a farewell celebration and invited the townspeople.

We spiffed up the barracks, cleaned the dining hall until it sparkled, and decorated the tables with summer wildflowers. Captain Blake recruited a local band to play square dance music. We removed the ping pong table, card tables, chairs, and cleared the recreation hall floor for dancing.

One of my cousins, Jake, a well-known fiddler, was hired along with his sidekick, a banjo player named Roy. Jake stood on a makeshift stage we made out of pallets, resting his fiddle on his chest in the odd way of the mountain fiddlers. His bow didn't strum the way the big band violinists strummed, with long strokes. No, he more like jerked it over the strings in a frenzy of motion that made you tap your feet. Roy joined in and the girls from town showed the men the methods of square dancing. The girls set us up in an eight-handed set. Two couples in a square, facing each other. I made sure I was next to Emma, although it wouldn't matter as the dance went along; we exchanged partners each time we did a whirl around the squares, arms hooked, bodies flailing. Cousin Jake was the caller, instructing us what to do and when. The fellas made a lot of mistakes, but that didn't matter. Between calls, Jake would put his bow to the fiddle and sing. One ballad brought a lump to my throat.

I'll buy my own whiskey and make my own stew; If it does make me drunk it is nothing to you; I'll eat when I'm hungry and drink when I'm dry; If a tree don't fall on me, I'll live till I die.

Captain Blake was enjoying himself, taking it all in from the corner of the room, chomping on his cigar, and sipping on some type of amber-colored concoction in the corner. His eyebrows shot up when he heard the lyrics. This wasn't necessarily what he had in mind when he hired my cousin to play. Cousin Jake was oblivious to Captain Blake's grimaces as he just kept on going with ballads I recalled from my youth when we'd all get together in someone's cabin, and there was always a fiddle lying around for someone to play. How peculiar. When I was young, I'd never really paid attention to the lyrics. I was too caught up in the heat of the moment, sitting in a corner of the room, awed as the old folks changed into something else entirely, young, and carefree: worry lines melting from their faces, replaced with merriment. Even Ma used to be transfixed by it. I remembered fondly how she and Pa would swirl around the cabin to songs like this, never knowing the deeper meaning might ring true someday.

Last night as I lay sleeping, I dreamt a pleasant dream; I was resting by the roadside, way down by a pearly stream; The prettiest girl beside me had come to go pay my bail; I woke up broken-hearted in a Knoxville County jail.

The fellas caught on to the dance sequence quickly and swept the girls off their feet. The last song of the night was *The Fox Chase*. We stood in two rows and clapped and stomped along with the beat and pirouetted down the row taking turns with each other. The fiddle and the banjo mimicked the sounds of a fox chase with a pack of hounds. The banjo yelped; the fiddle carried a rapid beat like hounds treading. And it had an effect on the dancers.

The mixture of sweltering heat left over from the summer sun beating down on the building all day, and people sweating, made the temperature in the rec hall almost unbearable.

Finally, the band tuckered out, and we poured out of the hall to cool off in the crisp air that descends on the mountains at night. I squinted at the light from the millions of stars plastering the sky.

Emma and I sat down by a big rock, leaning against each other. I could feel her heart beating.

"Emma," I said.

"Hmm?"

I took her hand, cool against my warm palm. "Will you marry me?"

"Oh, Ben, I'd be so happy to marry you. But what do we do about our jobs?"

"My stint here is going to end soon anyway. And I've been saving money. I've applied for a couple of newspaper jobs. I know we could make it work."

"But what about your mother and the girls?"

"Mary has a good job, and Rachel too. Once Nellie's done with school, she can get a job and help support the family."

"All right, Ben. We'll figure it out soon enough."

That was all I could ask for because our future was so uncertain. The economy hadn't changed. Unemployment was still fifteen percent in the cities. The communities around the Corps camps fared well enough, including Hickory Run, but the press was too small to take on another reporter. Besides, I was sending them my material for nothing. I sent employment queries out to papers in Knoxville, Maryville, even Asheville and hadn't heard back. The most promising lead I'd had so far was from the Corps administration. They wanted me to write for them.

I got back to the barracks, my mind reeling. I wanted to tell Tony I'd asked Emma to marry me, but he wasn't in his bunk. The last time I'd seen him, he'd been dancing with my sister Mary. Come to think of it, I'd lost track of both of them well before the dance ended. But at the time, I'd had other things on my mind.

He stumbled into bed, waking me up at dawn.

"Where've you been?" I hissed.

"I went to town."

"With who?"

"Mary."

"My sister?"

"Yes. She asked me to go with her to town."

"Now, why would she do that?"

The others told us to shush and I lowered my voice.

Tony whispered from across the aisle. "Cause, after all that dancing Mary and I went outside to catch some air, and some of the fellas were catcalling. I think they'd got into that moonshine. Mary was rattled and asked me to come with her while she drove back to town. I walked back to camp."

"What time did you leave camp?"

"Ten o'clock."

"But it's only five miles. It doesn't take eight hours to walk back."

He flopped back down in his cot. "I stayed in town a bit. Now leave me alone, I need some rest."

Within minutes he was snoring.

Although I knew Mary had grown fond of him, I found his story implausible. He could've easily gotten back to the barracks much earlier than dawn. Then I began to wonder whether what I mistook for his loyalty was really love? He was always by her side. Anytime she needed something, a swig of water from the spring, a shovel, or her notebook, he would happily go fetch it for her. She was right, he could be a nuisance, but he did grow on you. He was always eager to please the people he cared about. And over the course of a few months, the two of them grew attached. It was all the guys talked about. How Tony had caught the attention of the pretty science lady. Jealous. I didn't have a chance to ask Tony for more details because a chain reaction of events occurred that continues to haunt me still.

23

It started with the fire. Dark plumes of smoke rose out of the hills. I'd seen it before, with Pa. Alarm sirens went off in camp. We had done practice drills to prepare for this, but even so, the men panicked. They fled in all directions. Captain Blake put me, Finn, Jimmy, and John in charge because we had fought forest fires before. We broke into regiments. Each had a task to be done in shifts. The goal was to control the burn.

Like so many, this forest fire started in the slash left behind from a timber harvest not too far from camp. A bolt of lightning struck a dead stump, brittle with age, and poof, it went up like a match. The job of the first crew was to set up a fire break around the perimeter. They cut and cleared vegetation all day. My crew filled tanks of water attached to hoses and put them on our backs. We followed the first crew out and soaked the perimeter of the blaze. When we got there, we saw other Corps members from camps throughout the park who came to help.

Smoke got in our nostrils, our lungs, our hair. Ash clung to our arms, our clothes, our boots. It took the whole camp to control the burn. The heat prickled the hair on our arms. We could only take the heat for two hours at a time. After two hours, a crew would return to camp to rest, drink water, eat something, and then go back out to relieve the last shift. We did this all day.

By dusk, we were fatigued and making reckless decisions. I saw Tony out of the corner of my eye, heading in the direction of the fire with nothing but the pack of water on his back. Did he think he was going to put out that fire? Was he delusional?

"Tony," I yelled, "You're getting too close to those trees." I motioned overhead, the flames spewed in the air, and with the shifting winds, it was hard to tell which way they'd burn.

Tony stared at me, bewildered. I watched as an ember floated in the wind, landed on the hemlock about five feet from where he was standing and lit it up like a rocket.

"Tony!" I tackled him to the ground, covering his body with mine just as a limb from the tree fell two feet from our faces. I bolted up, grabbed his shirt collar, and dragged him away from the fire that erupted all around us.

We sat catching our breath watching the fire lick away at the edges of our fire break, our lungs ready to burst.

And when we got back to camp that evening, smoke hung over our barracks. The air was dense and my lungs felt squeezed. Trucks lined up to transport us to another camp for the night. They had pitched tents for us and laid out some grub.

The day's events upset us all, but Tony was remarkably quiet.

"You ok?" I called to him in the tent we shared.

"Yeah," he rolled over.

"Tony?"

"I'm sleeping."

I left it at that.

The next day we got news that the last shift had controlled the fire. It was quelled for now, the area just a heap of smoldering ashes. Our crew was told to get chow and head out to keep watch on the perimeter with our fully-loaded water tanks.

It was a monotonous job. We sat around, swatting away at the flies buzzing around our heads. I expected Tony to be happy it was over and return to his animated self, but he was unusually quiet.

"What's eating you?" I asked him.

"It's my mother," he said. He pulled a letter out of his shirt pocket. "She's ill."

"Oh. I'm sorry."

"Yeah. I guess it was that fire that spooked me a little. My dad's dead. All she's got is me."

"You need to go home and see her?"

He shook his head, eyeing the distant mountain. "Not sure I can yet."

"Why's that? If she's sick, I'm sure Captain Blake would grant you leave…"

"It's not that simple."

"Why not?"

"Because I'm not who you think I am. My real name is Vincent. Vincent Armerino."

Stunned, it took me a moment to register what he was confessing. My jaw dropped. "You aren't Tony Delaney?"

And then he told me a story. The truth of who he really was.

"My father was a tailor for the army. We did pretty well, lived in a nice apartment building in South Bronx, until my dad got sick with influenza. Ma had to do something to keep us all from starving, so she took in laundry.

I hated it. I came home from school, and the apartment was steamy, the air smelling like lye. Her hands were always red and raw while my pa sat on the couch wheezing, coughing, and spitting blood into a bucket by his side.

One day my ma sent me to the market to pick up sugar and eggs and the owner, Mr. Giovanni, told me we didn't have no more credit. I asked him how much my ma owed, and he said it was around three dollars. I had to bite back tears 'cause I knew my parents didn't have three dollars, and I knew my ma needed eggs for dinner. The sugar was just so my dad could wash down his medicine.

I went back home, my head hung low. When I walked in the apartment and saw my ma spoon-feeding my pa his medicine, him dribbling it all over himself and her with that worried look always plastered on her face, I just couldn't bear to tell her the truth of it, so I ran out before she could ask me if I got the groceries.

I went back and asked Mr. Giovanni what I could do to earn some of that money my ma owed, and he told me to stick around, and if someone called, I could deliver groceries for five cents.

So that's what I did whenever I could. I even skipped school sometimes to wait by the phone in the corner of the store. Sometimes the phone would ring, and it wasn't a customer, it was somebody who wanted to talk to a friend or family who lived on the street. Those times, I'd run a message to the apartment and let them know they had a phone caller waiting for them at the corner store, and I'd get a few pennies for the effort.

I was walking back to my apartment one day with a small box of groceries for my neighbor when I saw this lady sitting on the stoop of the building, smoking a long cigarette. She was new to the building, 'cause I would've noticed her before. She wore a slim-fitting silk dress that touched her knees. I remember that dress was real pretty blue—like the color of the blue-bells that grow on the mountain. She had curly black hair that she bobbed, a string of pearls round her neck that landed at her waist, and bangles on her wrist as if she were going somewhere special. Her skin was delicate, the color of cream. Because of that she didn't look like anyone else I knew in the neighborhood.

'Excuse me,' I said as I worked my way around her and into the building to deliver the box to my neighbor, Mrs. Rizzuto.

When I came back outside, she was still sitting on the stoop. She nodded at me and said, 'Are you the boy that answers the phone at the corner store?'

I nodded my head yes and tried to avoid looking at the long slender legs stretched out in front of her, crossed at the ankles.

'Good then. I tell you what, I know a way you can earn some money.' She folded her legs under her, dipped her long fingers into a small coin purse and brought out a nickel. 'Every Tuesday and Thursday I will receive a call at noon. I need you to bring me the message.'

'You don't have a phone?' I asked. I figured if she could afford them pearls round her neck, she might've owned a phone.

Her laugh was soft. 'Not many people do.'

'Yeah, guess you're right 'bout that,' I said. I shuffled my feet in place and stared down at 'em like an idiot to avoid looking straight at her.

'What's your name?' she asked.

'Vincent,' I said, puffing out my chest. I knew lack of food made me look scrawny, and I wanted to appear older.

'Hello, Vincent,' she smiled. 'I'm Mrs. DeLorenzo.' She extended her palm with the nickel sitting in the center, glinting in the sun.

I eyed it suspiciously. 'Who's gonna call?' I asked.

'That's none of your business.' She pursed her lips and curled her fingers over the coin.

I watched that nickel slip away from me, and I didn't think twice, I just said, 'Yes.'

I knew it meant missing more school, but I wanted that nickel. I had our debt at the store down to two dollars and Mr. Giovanni was more generous with his credit. He wasn't mean or nothin', but he couldn't keep extending credit to people, even if they were sick.

Like clockwork, the phone rang on Tuesday just as Mrs. DeLorenzo said it would, and I rushed to answer it as Mr. Giovanni finished with a customer.

'Hello?' The man on the other end had a voice that came out of the depths of the ocean.

'Yes?' I said into the receiver.

'You the kid who's going to deliver my message?'

'Yes.'

The man gave out a small laugh and then said, 'Okay. Tell Mrs. DeLorenzo to ask for Mr. Smith, two pm Wednesday, the Tallmidge.'

'That all?' I said. The phone clicked. He had hung up.

Mr. Giovanni was leaning over the counter with his hands spread out wide, his expression curious, waiting for me to tell him something like an order, and I blushed and said it wasn't a customer, and ran out of there. When I reached her apartment, she was wearing red lipstick so dark it made her teeth look shiny when she parted her lips.

'What did he say?' she asked.

I thought she appeared too anxious, so I tried to sound nonchalant when I told her Mr. Smith's message. She clicked her teeth, and some of the lipstick rubbed off on them.

'Thanks,' she said and shut the door.

On Thursday the phone rang exactly at noon, and this time, the cracker on the other end told me to relay the message: three pm Friday at the Wickwire Hotel. I placed the phone down in the handle and turned around to find Mr. Giovanni standing with his hands on his hips studying me.

'What was that about?' he said.

I shrugged.

'You taking messages for somebody?'

I gulped down the contents of my stomach, which was rising to my throat and said, 'Yes, sir.'

'Who is it then?'

'One of my neighbors.'

He stood over me, thinking I'd tell him more.

'You wouldn't know him. He doesn't shop here.'

'Everyone shops here, young man.'

The bell over the door alerted us a new customer entered, and Mr. Giovanni reluctantly left me to conduct business.

I waited a few minutes in the hallway after knocking on the door to Mrs. DeLorenzo's apartment. I heard some muffled voices, then a shout, before a man came to answer it. He had on a white t-shirt without any sleeves, and he smelled like the after-shave Mr. Giovanni sold in the store.

'What do'ya want?'

I poked my head around him and saw Mrs. DeLorenzo motioning at me to stay quiet. Her arm had a nasty looking red mark, her mascara was smeared under her eyes as if she'd been crying, and her hair was tossed all over her head like she hadn't combed it that day.

'Wrong apartment,' I said and ran out of there.

That night I was tossing and turning thinking about what I saw at Mrs. DeLorenzo's apartment and wishing I hadn't gotten mixed up in her mess.

But on Tuesday, I skipped school again to catch Mr. Smith's message at noon. His voice sounded like fog as he told me when and where Mrs. DeLorenzo should meet him. I placed the phone back on its hook, turned round to leave, and barreled right into Mr. Giovanni.

'Who's calling every Tuesday and Thursday at noon? Eh? You running numbers for somebody, Vinnie?'

'No, sir, Mr. Giovanni. It's nothin' like that.'

'Then what?' He had his arms crossed over his broad chest and wouldn't budge outta my way. I had to think fast.

'It's my neighbor, Mrs. Donelli. She's gotta sick son in the hospital, and he calls to update her.' I figured using Mrs. Donelli's name might work because she was an old battle-ax that didn't get out much, and everyone, including Mr. Giovanni, disliked her. Mrs. Donelli accused him once of padding his grocery bill, and she refused to pay. My ma wondered how she fed herself because there wasn't another grocery store for blocks, and we all knew she was too cheap to have them delivered. One day I figured it out when a young man in nice clothes came up the stoop with a box of groceries, tipped his hat at me, and told me he was Mrs. Donelli's son.

'Mrs. Donelli's too cheap to ask you to deliver messages,' Mr. Giovanni said.

'Her son pays me,' I blurted and skirted past his bulking figure out the door of the store before he could ask me another question I had to answer with a lie.

That day I must have looked guilty because when I took the nickel from Mrs. DeLorenzo, she asked me what was wrong, and I had to lie to her too.

'My dad's sick, that's all.'

'Wait a minute,' she said with a concerned look on her face. She reached into her purse and handed me a dime. 'Keep it,' she said as my mouth fell.

My dad started getting better and my ma was even hoping he'd get some work back. But the army didn't need him because there was no war going on, so he continued to just sit on the couch all day, staring into dead space as my ma hunched over piles of laundry from the rich ladies uptown.

She'd take a train to pick it up each Monday morning then bring it home and put it in a big tub of boiling water mixed with lye. I'd help her string it up on a line outside the apartment window that stretched all the way across the alley to the other building.

My ma did the best she could, but we were still hungry, and my dad's medicine cost a lot of money. So, I kept at it with running the phone messages for Mrs. DeLorenzo. As the weeks wore on, she started appearing more and more anxious when I showed up at her door to give her the message.

Then one day I got to the phone too late, and Mr. Giovanni answered it. The man on the other end asked for me, and Mr. Giovanni said, 'Who is this? What kind of game are you playing with Vincent?'

I gestured to Mr. Giovanni to just let me have the phone, but he slammed it down before I had a chance to get it away from him.

'It's no good. No good, Vinnie,' Mr. Giovanni yelled. I was going to answer him when a customer came in, and he left me to help her.

Then the phone rang again, and I picked it up quick and said, 'Vinnie here."

'Tell her to come to the phone.'

I didn't think that was such a hot idea and I told Mr. Smith so, and he barked at me. 'Get her to the phone in five minutes!' And hung up.

I went to her apartment to tell her, and when I got to the hallway, I heard some yelling coming from the other side of her door, and I knew it was Mr. DeLorenzo doing the yelling.

I hesitated for a minute outside the door, wondering what to do when I heard her scream and a loud slap. I pounded on the door, shouted her name. The door swung open violently, and there was the bulk of Mr. DeLorenzo standing in my way and smelling like whiskey.

'What the hell are you doin' here again?' he yelled.

I saw Mrs. DeLorenzo sittin' on the couch, crying into her hands, and I couldn't help myself; I just pushed past him and went to her.

'Are you okay?' I said.

Before she could answer, Mr. DeLorenzo gripped my arm and slung me around with such force I went flying across the room, knocking over a chair.

Mrs. DeLorenzo bolted off the couch and started pummeling his chest, and he backhanded her so hard she fell into the table and crumpled on the floor in a heap. He was standing over her, his leg lifted in the air as if he might kick her in the gut. I jumped up and flew at him with the first thing that came to my hand—a glass vase filled with roses.

Her eyes widened in disbelief at what I'd done. 'Get out of here. Now!' she shouted at me.

I hesitated. Mr. DeLorenzo was moaning on the floor. I wanted to make sure he was okay, that I hadn't hurt him.

'Get out! Before he gets up,' she said.

I ran. It took me two whole blocks before I figured out where to go. I couldn't go home, so I went to my Aunt Viola who lived in the Irish neighborhood. I knocked so hard on her door she thought I was the police or something.

'What is it?' she said. 'Is your father dead?'

I shook my head.

Aunt Viola held the door open for me, and I tumbled inside and told her what happened.

'Christ in heaven,' Viola said. 'I've got to get your ma.'

She sent one of her six kids scurrying over to my apartment to get my ma. I was already feeling guilty, but when my ma came into the apartment, her eyes were rimmed with tears, and I felt even worse.

'Vinnie, you have to go somewhere,' she said. 'The police are looking for you. That man, Mr. DeLorenzo said you hit him with a vase, and you blinded him in one eye.'

'Where'm I gonna go?'

It took a couple of weeks and me sleeping on the floor of my Aunt Viola's apartment before my Uncle Mike brought home a flyer from the Corps.

'Found this in one of the shops. They're looking' for young men. You just have to show you don' have any job prospects, and that yous family is poor and they'll take ya.'

I took the flyer and read it. 'But it says here I gotta be seventeen. I'm only fifteen.'

My Uncle Mike just shrugged. 'Your ma's gotta figure that one out. But it'd be worth it. You get three square meals a day and send home money every week. Just think kid, it'd be your chance to see the world.'

'See the world?' I scanned the flyer. It didn't look like no fancy places I'd be going to visit, just looked like tents in the woods.

My ma and Viola figured it out. Viola's oldest boy Anthony had died from a fever the year before, and she gave me his birth papers that would make me eighteen. I enrolled the next day. They couldn't tell how old I was anyway cause so many of the boys signing up were underfed and skinny.

. . .

Tony, no Vincent, gave me a sly wink. "And that's how I became Tony Delaney instead of Vincent Amerino."

My mouth went agape. What he just told me could get him in a lot of trouble. It could get him kicked out of the Corps.

He sighed, rolled back over, and stared up at the ceiling. "I told you 'cause I know you won't say anything to get me in trouble. We just saved each other's lives today in the fire. Why go ruin it all now?"

"But what happened to Mr. DeLorenzo?" I asked.

"I can't go back home is all," Tony said.

"Does Mary know?" I knew he and Mary snuck around together. After that dance, Mary was transferred to a new camp and Tony met her in town every week. My Ma had written me a letter asking me in confidence what I thought of Tony and whether he was a stand-up kind of guy. I assured her, yes. Now I wasn't so sure. But I understood why he always appeared younger than the rest of us. He was younger than me by five years.

24

I didn't know what to make of Tony's revelation. I asked him if Mary knew. He said yes. This concerned me. Taking someone else's identity and lying about it to enroll in the Corps was surely a crime. What would she do if he got caught and sent to jail? I didn't want to see her hurt.

I didn't get too much time to dwell on it either. I got word that I was accepted for a position with the Corps Administration in Washington, D.C. They liked my writing so much they wanted me to craft their message to the Congressmen in charge of the Corps' budget. My position was titled Public Relations for the Corps. It meant I could marry Emma and we could live there together, maybe buy a house. Which was timely because she had informed me she was pregnant.

I went right to Captain Blake with the news of the appointment. He had highly recommended me, so it came as no surprise to him I was hired.

He slapped me on the back. "Good for you, Ben. I knew you'd go places."

Emma and I got married. We held a small ceremony at the church in town. Ma and the girls came, Doc Sloane and Lila, a few of the fellas. Tony was my Best Man. Mary was Emma's Maid of Honor. Emma had made a crown of black-eyed susans and a bouquet to match. Ma was now gray-haired. The girls had grown like reeds. Sarah, the youngest, was going to school. I was so proud of our family. I wished Pa were there to witness our marriage vows.

■ ■ ■

I spent the last few weeks preparing for my eventual departure. While I was in town with Emma for a few days going over some paperwork for our travel plans to Washington D.C., Jimmy Beaufort was put in charge of breaking up a mile-long stone wall and crushing the stone for gravel. We had been putting off the project all summer. Captain Blake demanded

Jimmy get it done before the weather turned. The wall bordered the McConnell homestead. What none of us knew was that it was put up by Mr. McConnell with the help of Finn when he was just a boy.

Finn didn't know the wall was being torn apart and crushed until he happened upon the crew while coming back from another excursion of 'checking' on the safety of the abandoned buildings. He was on a horse and pulled up to see what they were doing.

Jimmy was hacking away at a large chunk of rock while the others tore the wall apart. Finn shouted at him to stop. Jimmy cussed at him. Finn grabbed the stone hammer out of Jimmy's hand, and in the process, it dropped on the foot of one of the men and broke his big toe.

Finn was the safety instructor. Of all people, he ought to know better. At least that's what Jimmy told Captain Blake when he got back to camp to file a complaint. Jimmy didn't stop at just the wall while listing Finn's digressions. He mentioned the scouting trips to inspect abandoned buildings in the park and told Blake that Finn was a derelict. I heard all about how Jimmy undermined Finn when I got back to camp, and Tony filled me in. I went in search of Finn first, to make sure he was all right. But when I reached his cabin, I found it empty. Captain Blake found me there, searching for Finn.

"He's gone, Ben."

"What happened?"

"What happened? He wasn't following orders; that's what happened. And I ripped him up one side and down the other for it. He couldn't take it, and he left."

"Resigned from the Corps?"

Blake stood in the doorway. "I'm putting Jimmy Beaufort in charge. He's going to take over Finn's duties."

I pushed past Blake. "It isn't right," I said.

Finn wasn't hard to find. He was walking down the road in the direction of town, nothing on him but a pack on his back.

"Finn!' I called.

He turned around and squinted into the sun. When he saw me coming, he just kept walking.

"Finn. Hold up!" I ran after him.

When I finally reached him, he slowed his pace. "What do you want, Ben?"

"Why are you leaving the Corps? You've done a fine job with the men. They need you still."

"Ain't my kind of place. I don't like it no more," he said.

I knew that wasn't true. Finn McConnell had proved himself to be invaluable to Captain Blake. After running his father's mill for so many years, he knew his way around machinery. He had set up an engine repair shop and trained a group of men in mechanics. When things broke down, these guys fixed it. They'd show up on the work-site and get things running again. It didn't matter if it was a motor for a saw, a truck, or a front loader. Under Finn's tutelage, they became experts. When he directed the men, he did it in a quiet way. They respected him.

It took some time at the Camp, but Finn was a new man. Our infirmary numbers dropped precipitously under Finn's guidance. He showed the men how to handle an ax, so it didn't go flying out of their hands and impale a fellow worker. He explained how to operate the trucks so that they didn't put it in the wrong gear and run over someone's foot; how to predict the direction of a falling tree; how to handle a horse and mule so they didn't kick you in the head. His measured tone and easy patience won the confidence of the men, and Finn thrived. I tried to remind him of that.

"But the fellas really take to you, Finn. Look at all you've taught 'em already."

"Leave it be, Ben. I ain't going back."

"But where will you go?"

He stopped walking. "I've been saving up some money. I'm planning to buy a farm in a place where no one's gonna bother me."

"What about your ma and pa?"

"They're coming with me. Nobody's coming to Pa anymore to grind their corn. Hell, nobody is even growing it anymore. They just go to the General Store to buy their food now."

"But Finn, you don't want to just grow old on a farm with no one but your parents. Think about what you've been able to do here. And the people you've met. And the social life, the schooling. Everything!"

"Don't glamorize it, Ben."

I was taken aback by that word. First of all, because it was not a word Finn would typically use, second of all, because I didn't like the connotation.

"What are you talking about?"

"You and all your trumped-up writing about 'the Corps does this, and the Corps does that' in your Happy Times news. Like they're some kind of heroes."

"Well, we are, Finn." Yet, hadn't I thought the same thing at one time? That Captain Blake was making me write propaganda. How had I changed?

He turned dark. "You don't know what a hero is, Ben. But the men, they're just pawns. They're being told these mountains are for tourists so they can come in their expensive cars and pull off at the lookouts we're building so they can say they've experienced the wild. Hell, they don't even know what wild is. And in the meantime, people like my parents, your kin, they've all been thrown out, given less money than their land is worth. And then the government folks—who you're working for now— they hire poor young men, pay 'em one dollar a day to rebuild after letting the lumber companies destroy everything."

He was huffing by the time he was done.

I was speechless. Although all of his points were valid, and I agreed with them, I felt there was something missing. For instance, if it weren't for our work, Hickory Run would be a ghost town. Our folks back home wouldn't be able to buy food or fuel. We wouldn't have electricity in the mountains, or phone service. The men wouldn't have gotten their High School diplomas, or like me, college classes. Many may have died from illness or gotten into a life of crime. There may have been downsides to our work, yes, I understood that, but I couldn't agree with everything Finn said. I just didn't see it the way he did.

He walked away.

"So long, Finn."

He back-hand waved. It was the last time I ever saw him.

•   •   •

I was angry beyond words when I got back to camp, and I went in search of my cousin Jimmy.

I found him with his brother John jack-lifting the tool shed to adjust its rock foundation. Jimmy struggled with the jack. It was one of our Joyce jacks, a relic from the railroad. It was a good jack for lifting equipment like skidders or cars that went off the rails. The jack had a lever where you inserted a steel bar, cranked it up and down to lift the jack, and when you needed to bring the jack back down, you clicked the release to reverse the direction of the lever. The release wasn't working right. It would jam periodically; Finn had been meaning to fix it and had warned Tony and me not to use it one day when we went to the supply shed to retrieve it.

As I approached, I knew it was that jack Jimmy was working with because he was grunting and groaning and cussing while John fiddled with the release.

"Go get some blocks to hold up the shed while I work with this thing," Jimmy barked at John.

I tapped Jimmy on the shoulder. "What the hell did you tell Captain Blake?"

Jimmy swung around and narrowed his eyes. "I told him the truth is all. Finn was not doing his job. He came up to me and the men, trying to get me to stop doing what I was told to do with that wall. And he cussed me out in front of the guys. I couldn't have that."

"You're a mean son-of-a-bitch, Jimmy. Always were. Can't you see what that wall meant to Finn? You could've just stopped what you were doing. You could've found another god damn wall to take apart. For God's sake, there's hundreds of them in the fields around here."

Jimmy threw his shoulders back and got in my face. "Don't tell me what to do. You're just soft on Finn is all. You know as well as me he wasn't doing his job. I just did my duty."

"What the hell are you talking about?"

"The squatters," Jimmy gestured to the mountains. "All those people in the cabins. Don't tell me you didn't see them. Living in those cabins that the Park owns now, squatters. They don't belong there. We were supposed to kick 'em out. And Finn wouldn't let us do our job."

John came back heaving two large blocks of wood. When he heard Jimmy and me yelling, he put them down and got between us.

"You guys need to cool down and stop your bickering. We're on a job here, Ben. Take it up with Jimmy later," he said without a stutter and a pleading tone. He knew what it was like to get in between Jimmy and me in the middle of a fight.

"You're such a bastard," I said to Jimmy.

"Go to hell," Jimmy said. He and John rolled the blocks up to the shed and wedged them under it to hold it up while they tried to pull the jack out. It wouldn't budge. They would need another jack to raise the shed a few more inches and then slide this malfunctioning one out.

I meant to tell them that, but I watched with smug disdain instead, taking pleasure in Jimmy's frustration. Finn had shown me how to release the lever. You had to pull it out, twist it counter-clockwise and yank hard. Problem was the lever released quickly, which it wasn't supposed to, and the force of it could be dangerous if you happened to be close by and the bar was still in place.

"Jimmy," I started to say.

"What now?" Jimmy yelled as he tugged at the lever trying to get it to trigger and go in reverse. "You gonna tell me how to do my job? You gonna tell me I'm wrong again about something? You Taylors are a bunch of self-righteous assholes. You're just like your Pa that way."

I meant to tell him: give it up, I'll go get another jack. I meant to tell him it wouldn't work right and could be dangerous. I meant to do these things. But then I stared into those icy blues and remembered that day in Taylor Grove, the look in his eyes—was it pleasure?—to see Pa killed. He could have stopped cutting down that tree that meant so much to my pa until the sheriff came or one of the Lavery company men. From his vantage point, he could have warned Pa to back off when he saw him coming over that knoll, called out that a tree was falling. But he didn't do any of those things. He killed my pa as far as I was concerned. He deserved to be punished for it.

"Let me show you," I said. I walked up to the jack. Jimmy stood with the bar in his hands leaning over and watching me as I fiddled with the lever. One pull and twist and the lever would release violently, the bar would fling up and hit him in his teeth, maybe knock him off his feet. I don't think I wanted him to die. I wanted him hurt.

Just as I expected, the lever snapped back. But what I hadn't expected—Jimmy stepped away, letting go of the bar. It flew out of the holder in a trajectory toward John's face. In one desperate moment, John tried to get out of the way but tripped backward. The bar landed on his forehead with such force we could hear his skull crack.

"John!' Jimmy ran to him.

I bent down and held his wrist, my head pounding from the rush of blood. His pulse was weak. What to do? Stay calm, they told us. "Quick, we need to get him to the infirmary."

We manufactured a makeshift stretcher out of tree branches and some boards that were lying around, placed him on it, and walked him down the hill to the infirmary.

Someone went to town to find Doc Sloane. A few of the men waited with me by John's bedside until Jimmy told us all to leave. John had stopped moaning. We assumed that was a good sign.

I went back to my bunk. In my head, I tried to piece together what had happened, what I had just done. I was wrestling with my thoughts when Tony came in and told me John was dead. "Captain Blake wants to see you," he said.

He followed me to Captain Blake's office. It took everything I had not to faint on the trail leading to his office. Sweat was brimming on my forehead. My palms felt clammy. I wasn't sure what I would do. Confess everything? My life was ruined.

I stopped walking. I couldn't breathe. I bent over, hyperventilating. "Tony," I said between gasps of air. "I've gotta make a run for it."

"What? What are you talking about?"

"It was all my fault, Tony. I did it. I killed my cousin John."

Tony stood in front of me, his fists on his hips. "Are you crazy? Jimmy's the one that let go of that bar."

"Yes, but I knew it could happen, and I didn't warn them. It was that jack. You remember? The one Finn told us not to use anymore. They must've gotten ahold of it somehow. Finn must've forgotten to put it away. I knew what would happen. I knew the lever would fling back and hurt somebody. I was thinking it would've been Jimmy. I hate him. I was so angry with him... I...I wanted to hurt him." My knees buckled and I knelt on the path, smelling the crush of pine needles under my knees.

"Get up," Tony said. He pulled at my armpits. Then he slapped his hands on my shoulders and leveled his eyes on mine.

"Listen to me. John didn't deserve what happened to him, but it's not your fault. We'll take care of this. I'll take care of this."

Blake was frantic, pacing the floor, and raking his hands through his hair, which was standing on end. He was puffing on a cigar like a fiend, clogging the room with smoke. He wanted to know what transpired before John's death. When I told him about the jack, he wanted to know why Jimmy was working with a malfunctioning jack.

"How'd it trip and reverse direction?" he demanded to know. He had to file a report, and someone had to take responsibility for John's death, and it wasn't going to be Jimmy because he told Captain Blake it was my fault.

While I tried to conjure up a defense, my mind kept flashing back to that moment when I was about to tell Jimmy to get a new jack. I hadn't wanted to kill him, just hurt him. Did that make me a murderer? What about my future with Emma? How would she take it if I were to go to jail for my cousin's death? What would I do for a living? My whole life was set. I was going to a new job working for the Corps. I was going to be a father. While I searched for the right words, Tony spoke up.

"It was my fault, Captain."

We both stared at him and said, "What?"

Tony didn't even look at me, just kept on going. "Yeah. It was an accident. Finn told me that jack was no good. I was supposed to take it to Coop to repair, and I got so busy I forgot. So, when Jimmy came to pick up a jack, he must've seen it there, it was the first one on the shelf. I left it there because I wanted to remind myself to take it to the blacksmith."

Captain Blake sat down at his desk, let out a big sigh. "Sit down," he said.

We sat across from him.

Captain Blake looked me in the eye. "Is this true?"

"Sir, I…"

"Yes, sir. It's all true," Tony broke in. "Just like I told you. I'm awful sorry. It was an accident."

Blake's gaze leveled on Tony. "You know what this means then?"

"Yes, sir."

He dismissed us before I could say another word.

"What the hell were you thinking?" I said to Tony when we were a safe distance from the Captain's office.

"It's all for the best, Ben. You can't be taking the fall for that asshole cousin of yours. And besides, I've been meaning to quit here anyway and join the army."

"What the hell are you talking about?" I yanked his shoulder back, so he was facing me. "They won't let you enlist in the army when they find out you were kicked out of the Corps."

"They won't let *Tony Delaney* enlist. But they'll let Vincent Armerino enlist. I just turned eighteen."

"But I thought you couldn't go home?" I said.

"That was before. My mom told me that man got his eyesight back and moved away, and all charges against me have been dropped. It's safe to go home now, Ben. It's the right thing to do."

"But what about Mary? What are you going to tell her?"

"I'll send for her after I've saved some money. I couldn't marry her anyway right now. She makes more than me, and I want to be able to take care of her."

We stood in the woods on the path leading to our barracks. The trees were a naked, dull brown. A dusting of snow covered the path. Our breath became vapor in the cold air. His eyes were clear, sincere, and determined.

PART FIVE
WASHINGTON D.C.
1938-1942

25

Emma and I moved to Washington D.C. and I started my new job working for the Corps Administration. We rented the bottom floor of a townhouse on the southeast side of the city close enough to my office in one of the federal buildings so that I could walk to work. My view of the mountains was replaced with a view of granite and marble monuments dedicated to former Presidents and museums that bordered the grassy plain of the National Mall. As the days passed, I felt the pull of the mountains give way to the pressing matters at hand. Emma had a baby girl and we named her Eliza after her mother. Having a newborn and a new job while getting used to the rhythm of life in a city was enough to shake me out of homesickness.

As busy as this time period of my life was, I often thought of Tony and what he did for me and wondered how he was doing. It would happen at odd times. Emma and I took Eliza out for a stroll through the Botanic Gardens near the Capitol building one Saturday afternoon in the spring. The heady smell of flowering trees filled the air. And I remembered the first time Tony witnessed the redbud blooming in the forest. "What's that pretty tree over there?" he asked me. I remembered telling him it was just the beginning. Because the real glamor girls of the forest, the azaleas and rhododendrons hadn't put on their show yet. A pang of guilt hit me when I looked down at my baby girl and Emma who was pushing her along in the carriage. Eliza was gurgling and Emma was inhaling the new spring air, positioning her face to the sun. I was so lucky. Was Tony living a good life?

Right after he left camp, he sent me a letter from New York telling me he'd signed up for the Army. I sent a letter back, but I never heard anything afterward. I waited a few more months and tried again and there was still no reply. When I broached the subject of Tony with my sister Mary during our infrequent phone calls, she became evasive about her feelings which wasn't surprising given within a year after Tony left, she married a man she met in the Forest Service and lived in the same neighborhood as my mother. She had a baby boy.

I envied Mary for being able to live in Hickory Run. I never adapted to life in the city. I couldn't get used to the swish of tires on the pavement as cars and trucks passed our street-facing windows. Or the people. So many people. When I walked to work, I had to contend with the bustle of people, hats on, heads down, rushing to wherever it was they had to go, not bothering to notice their surroundings much less the other people passing by. And the summer heat had me dragging my feet to work every day. While I was used to the heat in the Smoky Mountains it was nothing like the city. On the weekends we'd draw our shades and close all of the doors after the morning sun started to rise and batter the windows. The large elm tree in front of the townhouse cast some shade but it was never enough. The heat penetrated our façade and we'd wait it out inside our townhouse until the late afternoon, when an inevitable light rain would cool things down. Like a horse let out of the barn we'd grab baby Eliza and stroll through the steamy streets where the air smelled of boiled cement and blanched rosebuds.

"It's because they built this city over a swamp," my friend Mac at work told me. He sat at the desk directly across from mine and was from Virginia. He'd done a stint at the Corps camp in the Shenandoah Mountains and we often had lunch together.

One day we sat on a bench under a tree overlooking the reflecting pool by the Capital Building and he told me about the swamp.

"A swamp?" I said incredulously.

Mac took a huge bite out of his hot dog and contemplated the throngs of congressional aides and tourists coming in and out of the Capitol Building in front of us. "Sure is. This here pool was once a pond of scummy water. They had to do something, so they dug down to the clay and cemented it."

He finished off his food and brushed his hand over his balding head as if he had hair to comb back.

A trickle of sweat worked its way down under my collar but I was in no hurry to get back to the office because it was just as bad there with only two fans blowing hot, humid air around the office.

"You ever been in a swamp?" I asked.

"'Course I have," he said with a southern drawl. "How 'bout you?"

"The swamps I knew back home were in the forest, full of dead tree trunks and created by beavers who flooded the lowland rivers. Some farmers might try to drain them with channels to grow onions or potatoes. But they weren't places I liked to explore."

"So, this whole city was built on a swamp?" I decided to look up whether Washington was really built on a swamp because I couldn't believe it although it did feel like we walked in cream soup during the summer.

His eyes slit against the glare of the sun reflecting off the pool. "Hard to believe ain't it?"

Mac always said everything was hard to believe, which was ironic given that his job was to feed me the statistics I needed to string together a narrative to feed to the congressional aides so that their bosses could send good news back home and keep the Corps funded. Mac and I had to entertain a much larger audience of people than I used to have to entertain with my Camp Happy Days newsletter and press releases to the Hickory Run news. We dealt with facts about the work of the Corps that came in from all over the country: a new amphitheater built in Madera Canyon Arizona, hiking trails through Acadia National Park in Maine, a camp of all black veterans built a stone water tower in Abilene State Park Texas. The Corps planted hundreds of thousands of trees in the state and national forests. They worked side by side with farmers in the heartland struck down by the Dust Bowl, tilling fields, planting windbreaks and grasses to control soil erosion. They assisted towns with recovery after hurricanes and flooding. There was no corner of the country where the men of the U.S. Civilian Conservation Corps didn't leave a mark.

Like me, Mac was a product of the education system afforded by the Corps. When he first got to his camp in the Shenandoah Mountains, he was put to work like all the other guys, digging latrines, and breaking up rock to build roads. But the teacher at his camp school took note that he had a knack for numbers, and they put him in charge of inventory. He worked his way up and like me found himself a desk job in the administration.

He smoked a lot of cigarettes and his voice took on this gravelly timbre as he spoke, telling me stats. "The men at the camp in Watkins Glen State Park just completed building eight hundred and thirty-two stone steps through the gorge. Hard to believe, ain't it?"

"Yeah, Mac," I'd reply.

Or, "The Corps camp in Manchester Ohio has pumped three thousand dollars into the local economy this quarter, hard to believe, ain't it?"

I'd type away at my desk using the facts and figures he fed me to compile the latest report.

We often sat by the reflecting pool eating from the street vendors reminiscing about our days at the camps. Even the food, we told each other, was better in the camps than from the street vendors.

I regaled him with stories about my days growing up in the Smokies and my time at the camp. He enjoyed hearing them and I found that I enjoyed having someone around to listen. Mac was a temporary replacement for the people in my life I had lost. My brother Sam and my friend Tony. They always paid attention to my stories with a cock of the head and a smile on their lips.

One day we sat by the pool at our usual bench and he asked me about Tony.

"You sure talk about him a lot."

"I guess I do," I said.

"What happened to him?"

"Not sure. I tried to find him, but he isn't answering letters."

"Why'd he leave the Corps again?"

I paused, my gut flip-flopping as the guilt gnawed away at me. Tony could be with Mary now if he hadn't taken the fall for me. "He wanted to join the Army," I said.

His thinning brows lifted in surprise. "But what about your sister Mary? I thought he was going to come back for her."

I considered how to answer and wished I hadn't revealed so much to him on our daily lunches.

"Well, Mary moved on. She got married. So hopefully that's what he did too."

"Humph," Mac said as if he thought that couldn't possibly be right.

I left it at that, neglecting to tell him that I didn't believe Mary really ever did get over Tony; she named her son after him.

■ ■ ■

Mac was really the only friend I had in the city because he and I had the most in common. Besides our rural background, he had a family back home that depended on his astuteness with numbers, and I had Emma and the baby who depended on my ability to sell things with my writing. One similarity to our experience at camp; Washington D.C. was filled with outsiders who came there to work. And they came from all over the country.

We got a kick out of the fact that people went into a tizzy the year there was an invasion of the seventeen-year cicadas. People over-reacted to their presence. I knew enough about their special life cycle not to be alarmed at their numbers. My Pa had told me their story and I had lived through it once. Besides, I always loved the sound of them in the trees, their low hum evening background music.

Our neighborhood in the city had some old trees and that's where these insects thrived. Every seventeen years their larvae crawl out of the ground from the tree roots they've been living around, molt and sprout wings. Then they explode in the air. Their big black bodies and wide set, red eyes make them ferocious, pre-historic-looking creatures. But they are harmless at this stage, only looking for a mate, which gets clumsy. They land wherever they can and on whatever they want.

Emma and I walked one afternoon in the park near our house and the cicadas swarmed in the air. People batted them away with their hats, cursing at the wind. Emma put a screen of linen over the carriage so they couldn't get in, but we didn't last long outside. They flew around like banshees out of hell looking for mates. One landed in Emma's hair and she shrieked. I laughed and managed to wrangle it out. "You remember these don't you? We were in grade school when there was an outbreak," I said to her.

She batted at the air. "No, I don't remember it being this bad."

A car screeched to a halt on the street corner and the driver got out of the car to swipe away the insects coating his windshield.

"They're going to cause an accident," she said. "Let's go home."

It was times like the outbreak of the cicadas that I longed for the mountains. I'd never felt lonely growing up, even when my siblings were my only playmates. And when I lived in the camp for the Corps, I never had a moment to myself. But living in Washington D.C., even with people bumping into me on the sidewalks and at the corner grocery, and in the parks, I felt very much alone. Even with my small family waiting for me after work, when I walked home in anticipation of seeing little Eliza in her highchair and Emma fussing over a roast, I felt I was missing something. I thought often of Tony and what he would say to cheer me up. He was from a city and he would know what secrets the streets held for me; he'd have been able to tell me why I would be ok here just like I explained to him how to not be afraid of snakes. He'd be able to decipher the strange smells wafting from my neighbors' kitchen windows. It was something I couldn't talk to Emma about because it was hard to define the emptiness that would creep up at the slightest provocation; this need for a best friend. Other than this feeling that came upon me without warning, we were happy.

We loved our little home. It was the first place we both had that we could call our own, even though we rented, and the furniture was part of the deal. Emma nested right away. While I was at work, she made curtains and slipcovers with the sewing machine she had shipped from Hickory Run. She loved being a mother and within a year of our move was pregnant again.

"You don't mind, do you?" she asked after telling me she was pregnant.

I smiled. "Of course not," I said.

"I know you don't love it here but if we have to, we can always go home and live with my dad until you find other work."

I squeezed her hand gently. "Don't worry about it. We'll find a way."

26

As reports came in from all over the country about the Corps, I paid special attention to what was happening back home in the Great Smoky Mountains National Park. The Park was experiencing a steady increase in visitors each year. The infrastructure was in place and most of the people who had lived there had either moved or been evicted. Those that stayed had signed leases requiring them to abide by the new Park rules. That included no hunting or fishing or cutting wood for fires. I couldn't understand why anyone would want to stay—my aunts included. But they did, for years, until people started to die, and their descendants moved away. The last church closed its doors and then there was no one left. Mary said the Park was considering keeping most of the structures in Taylor Valley and McConnell's Cove intact as a cultural heritage site.

My life in the mountains was now considered a cultural artifact. Part of me found this distasteful. I remembered what Finn had said about what I was doing. "Writing propaganda for the Corps" was the way he had put it. And as I sat at my desk each day pounding out statistics about forest fires squelched and bridges being built, I wondered if what I had lost in the mountains was for a greater good. Would our small community have survived the Depression anyway? Or would the lumber companies, after strafing the land for their own profits, have just left a wasteland? I would never know. Neither would Finn. But I understood his desire to keep what he had. I knew one day I'd be back in the mountains, and I wanted it to be the same, but I knew it never would.

As the impacts of the Depression began to wane, the popularity of the Corps plodded along, and even though unemployment was low, men stilled joined the Corps, that is, until the war broke out in Europe in 1939.

Slowly my work became less relevant because the population's attention turned to what was going on over in Europe. Those that had survived the last war worried the country would be dragged back into another. I felt the buzz of anticipation all around me. Our bosses held closed-door meetings while Mac and I wondered whether we might lose our jobs. After work people scurried to the newsstands to find out what battles were being fought and by whom in Europe. The city was wound tight and you couldn't help but feel pulled in by the rope.

Then the government passed a conscription law in 1940 that required all men between the ages of twenty-one and thirty-five to register for military duty. Emma was due with our second baby.

"What will I do if you get sent away?" she asked.

I didn't have an answer. I went to work and tried to focus on the facts that I knew, not the speculation that I could do nothing about.

The mission of the Corps bent to the changing times. Instead of working in parks and open land, the Corps sent men to military bases to shore up the infrastructure. The economy improved, and with a war pending we lost recruits. Everyone's attention was on the war in Europe. After the attack at Pearl Harbor in 1941, the Corps lost all funding.

■   ■   ■

Because of my bum ankle injury from the Corps (the one thing I could thank my cousin Jimmy for) and my advanced age, I enlisted as a correspondent for the Army. By now we had two girls and Emma was pregnant with a third. She wanted to move back home. Her father was ailing, and she missed the mountains. We figured since I could be transferred anywhere with the Army, she might as well head back to Hickory Run. With the money we had saved and a loan from her father, we bought a small house on Main Street for her and the girls while I stayed behind in Washington, D.C.

It was heart-wrenching to say goodbye. We traveled by train back to Hickory Run and I got to see my sisters and my ailing mother. Mary showed up at our new home with a basket full of cookies and bread and her toddler Tony— my godson—clutching at her skirt.

"Good to see you," she said. "You look like you've lost weight."

I picked up Tony and swung him in the air until he laughed. "And this little guy has gotten so big!" I said. "How's Frank?"

"He'd be here but he had to travel to Knoxville for work," she said.

Her husband Frank still had his job with the Forest Service. He had tried to enlist in the military but was denied because of an old hand injury from a saw that made it impossible for him to handle a gun in combat. I was glad he would be around for Mary, and Emma if she needed anything because he was the only man in the family to help. Emma's father was too old to help if there was an emergency and I had lost my only brother. Now I wouldn't be around, and it soothed me that Frank and Mary lived nearby.

I stayed for a couple of weeks to make sure Emma and the girls had settled into our new home. I could already see Emma's mind working over where she'd place the furniture, what type of fabric she'd need for curtains, what wallpaper to buy for the rooms. I wished I could be there to help with all of it. But I would have to rely on my family of sisters to assist. I knew I was leaving Emma and the girls in good hands. The community at Hickory Run would look out for them. But that didn't make it any easier.

"I'll come back once a month," I said the morning I had to leave as we lay in our new bed staring out at the tree turning crimson in the yard. A cool fall breeze fluttered the lace curtains in the window.

"It won't be too long," she said, stroking my hair.

"This war can't last that long," I said, rolling over to face her. Her auburn hair had a few streaks of gray now and her body had lost the sharp edges of youth to a roundness that suited her. I felt so lucky to be married to her. My first and only love.

Eliza clung to my legs as I pushed open the door to leave that day. "Don't go, Daddy!"

Emma picked her up. "Shush now. Daddy is only going away for a little while. You'll see he'll be back before you know it." Tears glistened in her eyes as I waved good-bye and got into the car that was taking me to the new train station.

I settled in my seat and choked back my own tears. It wouldn't help the girls to see me break apart. I had to keep in mind this was only temporary, until the war was over.

. . .

My duties shifted from promoting the work of the men in the Conservation Corps to promoting the war effort. It wasn't that hard. Everyone was upset about the attack at Pearl Harbor. None of us had any idea just how long an ordeal the war would become.

While I missed Emma and the girls, I had no time to think about them. I spent my time writing reports for members of the Congressional Armed Services Committee. And when I did have some downtime, I spent them searching for Tony. I knew his real name, Vincent Armerino. And I knew he had enlisted in the Army. How hard could it be to find him? Very hard, as it turned out. I'd find a clue of his whereabouts and send a letter off to the camp at which he was supposedly stationed and get nothing in return.

Part of me wanted to just let it go. Forget the past. My life had taken a trajectory that I would never have imagined growing up as I did in the anemic yet sumptuous environment of the Smoky Mountains. Besides my immediate family members, most of the people I knew growing up had either left or died. Maybe Tony was dead. But that couldn't be. That was something I'd be able to track down. Because as the war picked up speed, so did the deaths of young men sent to fight. My job once again changed, and to some degree stayed the same. I began to write obituaries for decorated service members to send to the press. And I had to make them endearing because the people in charge knew that this war was going to last quite some time if we were going to win.

PART SIX
DECEMBER 1944
BATTLE OF THE BULGE
THE ARDENNES MOUNTAINS

27

I'd never seen mountains so foreboding as the Ardennes in the winter of 1944. Dawn didn't arrive until eight, and the sun left the sky by four every day. Fir trees clung to the sides of ravines carved by rivers that wound their way through valleys dotted with towns and villages.

South of Brussels and only thirty miles from the North Sea, the mountains are targets of the sea's prevailing winds which bring fog and rain so dense you could swim in it. If it wasn't raining, which it was for most of December, it was snowing. The snow pelted the forest, blanketing it in a deep, wet layer. It was one of the worst places on earth to do battle. Tanks had to travel single file on the narrow roads made even more treacherous by the hairpin turns every few miles. The twisting road network was familiar to the Americans from the highlands of Virginia who named it Skyline Drive, which traverses the Shenandoah Mountains in Virginia.

In the Ardennes, I learned the art of writing obituaries. Among my many jobs was to tell the stories for the men who could no longer tell them. My task was to write and send the next of kin the Western Union telegram: *The Secretary of War deeply regrets to inform you that your son, your husband, your only brother…*

Sometimes, if the young man was especially brave or loved by members of his platoon, a soldier would come to me asking if he could send along a letter to the family. Or he'd ask me to write it for him, knowing my knack with words, my ability to make things up if I had to, might lessen the pain back home. I'd sit there and conjure the image of a woman, Ma maybe, hunched over the stove, stirring a pot of soup she has made from the rations. A sharp rap on the door sends her heart thrumming. She brushes her hand on her soiled smock, shuffles to the door of the apartment, and when it swings open, on the other side is a man in uniform, holding the telegram. He stands silently and for one brief, beautiful second she thinks it's her son, returned home from the front. She sees the telegram in his hand. Her eyes go heavy, and she reaches out to the man with one hand, then pulls it back to cover her mouth so she won't scream and scare the neighbors.

The soldier steps inside, apologetically hands her the blue envelope with the telegram inside it. She falls backward on the couch and rips it open. She reads my words and keens. There is no one to feel her pain but me. And that is why I write to her and every other poor creature that has to open one of my telegrams a follow-up letter, hand-written because she deserves one moment of happiness in the darkness, one glimmer of hope that her Jonnie or Frankie, the son she bore and clothed and cooked for, didn't die a worthless death on the battlefield. Even if he did. I tell the story that his mother wants to read. Call it fiction, call it bending the truth. In the end, there comes a time when a story has to be told. Because of that, I weave the truth out of memories and stretch them into a cord for people to grab hold of and hang onto in the belief that their loved one's life mattered.

"Your son died valiantly, on the fields of...." "He died quietly in his sleep after sustaining an injury to his..." "He will be remembered fondly by his......" "His heroic acts and character will be remembered by all...."

Even if it's not all true. Even if he died in agony, with half his body torn to pieces after tripping the wire of a Bouncing Betty. Or crying out for mercy while bleeding internally in a field hospital without any morphine. Even if he ran away from the enemy, shit all over himself in the process because he hadn't expected it to be so brutal, to be so god damn hard to stay brave while under enemy fire. It doesn't matter. Because I'm a storyteller. That's what I do. And ultimately, what really matters is the solace I might provide in the longer term to the loved ones remaining. Every one of the letters I write reminds me of my own loss. I know their pain.

I was stationed at the regimental headquarters in an abandoned hotel in the town of Clervaux in Luxembourg.

The town sat next to the Clerve River in a narrow valley. Only one road which led to Bastogne and eventually to Antwerp ran through town. From all angles, one had a view of the mountains: they hovered over the town and made some men claustrophobic. I was used to it. I'd grown up around mountains and wasn't put off by the way the winds blew through the trees like a melancholy song or pelting rain and snow which turned the trees into green icicles.

I worked for Colonel Hurley Fuller, who took over the main hotel in town as his headquarters. Fuller was an ornery son-of-a-gun, but I had plenty of experience after working for Captain Blake. Fuller, like Blake, was a veteran of the Great War and had a propensity to smoke. His favorite was a pipe. When he lit up, I was immediately reminded of home: of Pa sitting next to the fire after a long day of work, lighting up his corn cob, the tangy smell of tobacco filling the cabin. The war did that. Anything and everything made me miss home. Maybe it was a woman walking hand in hand with her child down a street. I'd think of Emma back home with our girls. The smell of turkey roasting, when we had special meals, would remind me of Ma and my sisters preparing for a holiday. My mind would wander to our conversations around the hearth. It was the only way to survive.

Colonel Fuller had some unfortunate events unfold during his time in the second war and was demoted. His position at Clervaux was supposed to be his chance to redeem himself. Besides the headquarters for commanders, Clervaux was a rest stop for soldiers in between battles. They could get a hot shower, warm food, and some rest. The atmosphere in the town was one of relaxed anticipation. The men had a chance to recuperate, but they all knew at some point they'd be back in the trenches, and all they wanted was to be home for Christmas. The men built snow forts in the streets with the village children, and helped the townspeople put up Christmas decorations in the church.

Many of the soldiers who arrived in Clervaux had seen battle in the Hürtgen Forest. That battle had wiped out most of the 28th and many of the 110th Divisions.

The ones who'd survived straggled in. Defeated. Vacant eyes. Wincing in agony from trench foot. Most ended up in the infirmary we set up at the castle in town. It was there I got to know many of them, heard their stories, checked to see who was still living, who needed last rites, taking notes for their obituary before their buddy in the next cot over died as well.

If I knew a man was dying, I stayed with him through the night knowing all he wanted was the warmth of a hand on his arm, murmuring soothing words to bring him back from a nightmare.

I listened to their raspy stories.

"They moved like wraiths (meaning the Germans). In and out of the fir trees. In the blinding snow it was hard to tell what was real anymore," one soldier told me while gripping my arm and wincing in pain.

"The forests were like nothing I've ever seen! Like what you'd picture in a fairytale. The kind that doesn't end well."

I heard estimates that over twenty thousand men had died in the battle in the Hürtgen Forest since October. The fog and rain severely hampered our air power, and we never gained a foothold against the Germans, who had the advantage of knowing the forests well.

In the weeks before Christmas, I checked the packages that arrived daily to see if any needed to be returned to sender. I had a list of the dead, and I'd check that list against the addresses on the packages. They came from all over America.

On one of my usual rounds, going through loads of packages dumped at headquarters in the mailroom, sifting through, checking off names, and with a heavy heart, writing Return to Sender on too many of them, something caught my eye. A package addressed to Vincent Armerino. My heart skipped a beat when I saw that name.

Tony! It was addressed to Tony from an address in Brooklyn, NY. The brown wrapping paper was tattered, the postal date stamp indicating it had been sent in September and had traveled to numerous places before arriving here. I scanned my list of the dead. Tony wasn't on it. Sweat broke out on my brow. It meant he was here. He was in Clervaux.

I raced to the regimental headquarters to check the names of the men who had come in from the 28th and 110th, and there he was: Private First Class Vincent Armerino of the 110thDivision. Wounded. He was in the infirmary. I could only hope he was still wounded and not dead. I scurried across town to the castle and scanned the rows of cots in the infirmary, searching for his familiar face. How much would he have aged? How had I missed him during all those days I'd spent in there? Maybe he wasn't critical. I spent time with the men in critical condition, following the Chaplain around as he did Last Rites, recording the last words of the dying.

I found the chaplain praying over a wounded man, his chest bandaged and bloody.

"Is there anything we can do for you, son," the chaplain asked.

The man's breath came out in heavy gurgles. His eyes were shut.

Suddenly a hand shot out and grabbed my arm. His eyes fluttered open. "Am I going to die? Here?"

The chaplain mumbled a prayer.

"I've really gotten myself into a mess here, haven't I?"

I sat down beside him. "Is there someone I should write to for you?"

He nodded. "My wife. Tell her I love her and tell her how much I will miss her and my son.

His face broke out in a sweat, and he gritted his teeth in pain before his eyes clamped shut and his grip tightened on my arm. Then, just like so many others, he let go. While the medic came to cover him up and wheel him away, I didn't linger. I'd grown numb to death.

My mind returned to the task at hand. Finding Tony. I grabbed the arm of a passing medic. "Did you ever attend to a man named Vincent Armerino? From the 110th?"

He displayed a sardonic smile. Was I kidding? You know how many men I've treated here? His eyes were bloodshot and baggy.

I kept looking. Nothing. If Tony was wounded, he'd have recovered enough to give up his cot to those who came trailing in from the Hürtgen.

My search went on for days. I kept the small rectangular package addressed to Tony tucked in my breast pocket, hoping to find him and deliver it myself. During mail call, I stood on the sidelines of the men hoping for a letter or package from home, scanning their desperate faces for a glimpse of him. Nothing. His name was never called. Finally, as I passed by soldiers milling about, one called out to me.

"Sergeant Taylor. I hear you've been looking for Vinnie Armerino?"

I pivoted around. "Yes. I have a package for him."

I found myself suddenly afraid. Could it be this would be the day I finally found Tony, faced him, and thanked him for what he did for me? What would I tell him about Mary? Did he know the truth?

The soldier's cold breath lingered in the air. He cocked his head toward the Castle. "I was in the 110th with him. We came together. I practically carried him here. He was recovering from a bullet wound to the leg, but I heard he was moved and was bunking somewhere in the cellar of the Castle."

"Why, thank you. I'll go look for him."

I picked up my pace. Would today be the day?

I checked my breast pocket to make sure his package was there. It wasn't. Damn. I must have left it on my desk. Each day after searching for him, I put it there to remind myself to keep looking for him.

I was in my office, reaching for the package when it happened: German soldiers started popping out of the Ardennes forest like ants from a hill. Astonished by the numbers, our men radioed to headquarters. Fuller came rushing into my office. "The Germans are attacking!"

For weeks the men saw no action and became complacent. They hoped the war would be over soon, and we'd all be home in the New Year. The commanders believed there would be no action and left only a skeleton crew of men on look-out during the night watch along Skyline Drive. What we didn't know, what the commanders didn't know, was that we'd be in the thick of battle with the Germans on December 16th.

We found out later the Germans had assembled a vast army of men, tanks, and artillery. They had 27,000 men ready for battle to our 5,000.

Their objective: to reach Bastogne and then on to Antwerp to target our supplies and ammunition. Our Army stood in their way.

In the ensuing hours, the Germans destroyed and severely damaged communication lines , creating a sense of panic. The onslaught destroyed most of our tanks and created heavy casualties. When Fuller sent word to his commanders we were under attack, there were no reserves or air power to help us. We were told to "fend them off."

Fuller told all of us—clerks, cooks, medics—to grab a rifle and defend the town. It became a street fight.

"Taylor," he said, "Work your way to the Castle and tell the men of the 110th to hold their positions."

I grabbed a gun and followed a group of men out through a back window. We slid to the ground, and as soon as we did, a German sniper shot at us. I ducked for the cover of a nearby tree. From there, I managed to make it into the woods. Panting, I watched from my hiding spot as German tanks chugged down the main road toward the hotel and headquarters.

Our men, outnumbered, courageously tried to stop the advance, throwing grenades, running for cover as the German tanks blasted any building where they sensed enemy fire. The heavy artillery sent shards of rock into the air and then raining down on the streets. Civilians screamed and ran for the protection of the castle. German soldiers, following behind the tanks, strafed the houses with gunfire to flush out any enemies. I watched men fall from windows onto the street, their bodies riddled with holes.

The Germans continued like this all day, creeping their way through town one building at a time. From my perch in the woods, I was useless. Too far away to get a good shot, I bided my time until I could reach the Castle and watched in horror as the Germans blew out the first story of the headquarters, wondering what happened to Colonel Fuller. I heard later that Fuller escaped with some men through the rear window and climbed a steel ladder up the cliff next to the hotel.

When the skies dimmed, I left my position in the woods and crawled on my hands and knees toward the Castle. I found a back window, knocked, and pleaded my case to be let in. No one inside from the 110th Infantry knew who was winning the battle outside the safety of the walls. Wounded civilians and soldiers came pouring in. We moved them to the cellar.

Snipers positioned themselves in the turrets and picked off cocky German soldiers who opened their hatches to grab a smoke. The Castle was the last hold-out, and there was only one hundred or so of us left to defend it. We were outmanned and outgunned.

The last night of the battle, I was trying to sleep with my back resting against the cold stone wall of the hallway. I could hear the cries of small children and the moans of the wounded. Men called out to their loved ones in delusional nightmares. I must have found rest because I woke to a gray dawn punctuated with searing flickers of light. I must have been dreaming about a fireworks show back home. How pretty, my muddled mind thought. Half-awake, exhausted, it took my mind a few moments to sense the danger of these stunning lights flickering in the morning sky.

The Germans launched white phosphorous onto the roof. The moss-covered slates smoldered; flames trickled along the Castle's walls. I was used to fire, but I also know the terror it evokes. People flooded out of the cellars, women clutching their babies, crying, screaming at our men. Surrender, surrender!

By noon the next day, the old wooden beams of the Castle smoldered like a campfire, the heavy stench making it hard to breathe. Everyone gasped for air. All around me people hacked up blood. Finally, we put out a white flag. Sergeant Kushner, one of the crack snipers, exited first to talk to the German soldiers, while as many of us that could fled from the back entrance. That's when I found Tony.

28

In the chaos of fending off the Germans, we'd missed each other. But when a group of us groped our way out of a small opening in the cellar, I heard his voice, unmistakable, encouraging a fellow soldier to carry on, even though he was injured, shot in the leg.

"You can do it, Les. I'll carry ya if I have to."

I knew it was him in front of me. I reached out, took hold of the other arm of the wounded soldier he was helping, and draped it over my shoulders.

"Tony," I said.

His dark eyes registered mine, and he smiled. "Some reunion, eh?"

We crept into the woods, avoiding the German snipers positioned along the ridge overlooking the Castle.

There we sat and listened as tanks rumbled into town, German voices echoing off the cliff walls behind us. We rubbed our shoulders to stay warm and cupped our hands over our mouths to keep our fingers from getting frost-bitten. My mind was racing. Would I survive this? How was it I was here with Tony? All of the questions I had wanted to ask him were now pointless because the only thing that mattered now was how to survive this onslaught and make it out of there alive and once again see my Emma and the girls. Les was leaning up against Tony, groaning.

"We need to head west, toward Bastogne," I whispered. "We'll eventually meet up with another regiment."

It was slow with Les. We dragged him along, his feet sliding across the frozen ground, his head hanging. Drool came out of his mouth, froze to his face. I was pretty sure he'd die on us, but we held tight, slogging along. We hid amongst the trees, or what was left of them, as we snaked our way westward.

When we first entered the forest, we'd hardly noticed the scene; we were so caught up in escape. But as the day dragged on into night, the forest took on a primeval feel, reminding me of the tale of Red Riding Hood. I always hated that story. Ma would read it to us at night. Scared the hell out of us all. I think that was her main objective. Don't go off in the woods without one of your siblings, especially to visit Grandma. She never got along with Pa's mother. I sensed it. Anytime we had a family gathering, Grandma would make a snide remark when Ma stepped into the room. She thought Ma was 'uppity'. Or at least that's what I guessed many years later. Grandma died when I was eleven. But her presence lingered on at my aunts' cabin. Her quilts, her cookware. Her recipes.

"Christ," Tony said. "Will you look at that."

The canopy had opened, and we had entered an area where there had been a skirmish. The land mines had twisted and gnarled the trees reminding me of the after effect of a terrible wind storm in the mountains back home.

Shredded uniforms, shirts, helmets, boots, and body parts hung from the tree limbs. Dead, frozen bodies littered the forest floor.

"Watch out," Tony said, motioning to the forest floor. His breath turned immediately to frost in the air. His short beard had icicles hanging from it. "Those needles mask tripwires."

We finally reached the edge of the forest and waited until dark to continue in the open. Along the way, we picked up a few other men. By the third day, Les had died. We woke up, and his lips were blue, his eyes frozen shut. We buried him with broken boughs from the evergreens and said a quick prayer. I noted mentally how far we were from Clervaux in case his next of kin wanted to know where he died. I took off his tags, someone took his boots. And we left him, a frozen corpse, buried by snow and pine boughs, which was all we could manage on the rock-like ground.

After a couple more days of walking, I couldn't feel my feet. But I kept going. I did it for Emma, for our girls, I did it for Tony. We hadn't talked yet about anything but survival, but I ached to know what had happened to him. As the bleak days wore on, the only sounds were of distant gunfire and explosions, our feet dragging through the thick, wet, snow, and our laborious breathing. We couldn't talk. It would have taken too much energy. But why had he stopped answering my letters? Did he know about what had happened to Mary?

The temperature dropped precipitously. At night, stars scattered across the achingly clear sky. If I were back home in the mountains, it would be breathtaking. But each gulp of air stung my lungs and made it hard to breathe. A few of the men said they had no feeling left in their hands or feet. I gripped my rifle so hard that my fingers froze to the metal. Finally, after trudging through the fields one evening we spotted an abandoned hunting cabin tucked away at the edges of the forest. It was a godsend.

Snow filtered through a hole in the roof, coating the kitchen table. I propped my rifle against it and stretched my fingers. There was a stack of cut wood, and one of the men started to make a fire in the fireplace.

"Don't do that," Tony said. "They'll find us."

"Way out here? I haven't heard any gunfire in twenty-four hours. We're far enough from the battle," the man said.

"The battle is all around us," I said.

"I don't give a shit," he said. "I can't feel my feet."

None of us had the will to dissuade him. We all longed for heat.

After he started a small fire in the hearth, he took his boots off and the small cabin filled with a putrid smell.

"What's your name, soldier?" I asked.

"Private Markham." He rubbed his feet, clenching his jaw in pain.

"You had your feet checked back at the infirmary?"

"You got trench foot!" a soldier named Sanders said.

Indeed, Markham did have trench foot. His toes were red, swollen. The rest of his feet were warped, wrinkled, blue. It happened to men while they sat in the trenches or on long marches through wet conditions. The wet snow had seeped into his boots, and over a prolonged period, numbed his feet and stopped the blood supply from reaching his toes.

"I got that guy's boots. They were in better shape than mine. I just need some new socks is all." His socks were limp, black with mud, ragged with holes. "I spent four days trudging through the snow and ice to get to

Clervaux, only to find the town surrounded by Germans. I thought I'd get some rest." I had to look away from his bloodshot eyes as his voice cracked.

"Throw those socks in the fire! They stink!" Sanders said.

I contemplated my feet. Dry. "Here." I took off my boots, handed my socks over to Markham. "Put these on."

He was hesitant at first, incredulous maybe. But when I insisted, he gratefully took them and put them on his feet. I saw his face relax a little.

We scoured the place for blankets, table cloths, sweaters, anything to protect us from the biting cold. The cupboards were bare, long since evacuated of any food, and we only had a few candy bars and tins of rations we'd grabbed before evacuating the Castle.

"Even the mice must've given up," Tony said.

We rested on whatever hard surface would hold us. Since I was the highest ranking, they looked to me for leadership. It was like the Corps all over again. I found myself head of a ragtag group of men. Malnourished, exhausted, freezing, missing home.

"We'll take turns keeping watch. I'll go first. Get some rest. Give Markham's feet a chance to heal. We'll get going again when this cold snap breaks."

No one argued with me.

"Tony," I said.

"Tony," I whispered.

"Let the man sleep, why don'tchya?" said another of the men with us, Private Firth.

Tony's eyes fluttered open. "Ben? Ben, don't call me that. I'm Vincent."

"Vincent. What happened to you? Why didn't you answer my letters?"

"Didn't Mary tell you?" he said.

"Tell me what?"

"Forget it, Ben. I'm married now. I have a kid. I named him after you."

A rat-a-tat-tat in the distance made us all perk up.

"You two. Shut up." It was Sanders.

"Ben, we've really gotten ourselves into a mess here, haven't we?" He made an effort to smile, and it broke my heart because it was half of what it used to be. Like me, he was scared.

I felt the package in my breast pocket. "Here," I said, giving it to him. "I found this in the mail. I was hoping to hand-deliver it to you, but I never saw you at mail call."

He smiled and took it from me. Tears glistened in his eyes, reflecting off the embers in the fireplace. "From my son, Ben. I never made it to mail call. I sent a friend for me. I'd been wondering why I hadn't heard anything from home."

"Mail was slow."

"Yeah." He examined the package.

"Well, aren't you going to open it? I already opened mine. My girls sent me a sweater. I'm wearing it under my coat. Sheep's wool from my aunts' sheep. Remember my aunts?"

"They still alive?" He chuckled.

"Oh yeah! Those socks I gave Markam? My Aunt Peg knitted 'em. She's still shearing sheep and making her own thread."

"Jeezus. Like nothin's changed." He turned the package in his hands and then gave it back to me. "Can't open this before Christmas. Bad luck."

"Don't say that," I said.

He punched me in the arm. "You never had bad luck."

My eyes locked his. "That's because I always had you by my side."

"You hold on to it for me. When we get out of here and are sitting in front of a lit-up Christmas tree, you can give it back to me. We'll celebrate together. I promise."

"You two know each other from somewhere?" Private Firth said.

"Oh, my God! Can we get some sleep here?" Sanders bitched.

"We were in the Civilian Conservation Corps together," Tony said.

"I was in the Corps," Firth said. "Stationed in the San Juan Islands. Ever hear of 'em?"

"No," Tony said.

"Yeah, well me neither. I'm from Ohio. They sent me and a bunch of guys from the mid-west to this port in Seattle. And when we saw this ship that was going to take us out there, some of the fellas panicked. They thought they were being deported or something. They fled."

"Huh," I said. Looking back at my time in the Corps, I could believe it. I'd never been any farther than Knoxville myself when I enlisted.

"Hey Tony, I mean Vincent. Remember when the guys panicked because of the War of the Worlds?"

Tony laughed.

"I never made it to the Corps," Sanders said. "I had a job working at my uncle's store."

"How about you, Markham?" I said.

"I was too young."

"Oh. How old are you?"

"Eighteen."

"Christ!" Sanders said. "We got a baby here."

In the dark, with just the faint glow of the fire, I looked at Markham. If his brow hadn't been furrowed in pain and worry, he might well have looked eighteen.

Markham's trench foot made it impossible for us to leave immediately. I don't think we wanted to either. Not right away. The fighting was off in the distance, and we were exhausted. The next day I went outside to scavenge food and spotted vestiges of turnips poking out of the snow. I went out again and pulled up as many as I could salvage from the cold ground. They hung limp in my hands.

Sanders scoffed. "You expect us to eat those things?"

"We're out of rations. And it will help prevent scurvy," I said. We boiled them in melted snow and drank the broth, chewing on the softened root.

Even with the relative warmth of the cabin and the rest, Markham's trench foot wasn't healing. In fact, I could sense it was getting worse. Once a day, he stifled a cry as he took his boots and socks off to air out his feet, and the smell of decay permeated the cabin. His feet had an awful purplish-blue hue. I was worried when the time came, he wouldn't be able to walk out with us. If gangrene set in, he'd need to have his foot amputated, and then what would we do?

Although I had decent boots, my own feet felt ice cold. I made some makeshift socks out of my sweater. Using a pocket knife, I ripped off one of the sleeves, cut that in two and wrapped each half around my feet. My toes stuck out, but the base of my feet would stay warm.

I consulted with Tony while outside taking a piss.

"We might have to carry him out of here if we wait much longer," I said.

"Yeah. I say we leave tomorrow. The moon is only going to get bigger."

"Tony, before we go, I need you to know something. It's about Mary."

"Hey, look at that," he said, his eyes went wide with wonder.

A shaft of sun had escaped from the slate-colored sky and was beaming on the mountain face ahead of us. The trees, coated in ice, shimmered.

"If you didn't know any better, it's like a picture postcard ain't it?"

"Yes," I whispered.

It lasted only a moment as the clouds closed around the sun, and then a rumbling sound reverberated on the wall behind my head.

"Shit," I said. "Go inside and tell the men to prepare to leave. I'm going over there to scout." I crawled on my hands and knees in the heavy snow toward a knoll where I could use my binoculars to get a better view. In the distance, German tanks crossed a stretch of river. I went back to the farmhouse to report.

"There's a river to cross," I said.

"How deep?"

"Up to our waists. The Germans are ahead of us. We should work our way north and cross further upstream."

"Let's wait it out," Markham said.

"That's crazy! They're right outside our door," Sanders said.

"If they knew we were in here they'd have flushed us out by now. They must have more pressing concerns. Like making it to Antwerp before the Allies."

We had a restless day listening to the tanks and men marching in the distance. I prayed they wouldn't look back and see this cabin and check it out. I didn't want to become a prisoner of war. I just wanted out of there.

We waited until nightfall to leave the farmhouse, keeping to the woods wherever we could, darting behind hedgerows, stone fences, and old cattle troughs. Every now and then, a sliver of moon peeked out from under dense clouds that rolled over the fields. The river glimmered in the distance. Chunks of ice bounced along in the current. After a few miles, we reached the banks.

"We should cross here," I said.

"How do you know it's not too deep?" Sanders said.

"He knows," Tony—no—Vincent—said.

Years of fishing at night with Pa taught me how to gauge the depth of a stream. You had to know these things in order not to fall under while trying to scoop up unsuspecting fish. We'd go to Hickory Run at two a.m. with a lantern and swing it around our favorite pools. The fish would mistake the light for dawn and come up to feed.

"This may be the shallowest part. Follow me, and we'll steer clear of any pools that are deeper than our waist."

"I...I don't know how to swim," Markham admitted.

"Ah, shit!" Sanders said.

"Quiet!" I shushed them then checked the swirling, rapidly-moving water. With care we should be okay. "We'll form a human chain then. Me in front, Ton...Vincent, then Markham and the rest of you fellas behind."

We didn't want to get our boots wet, so we took them off and slung them over our shoulders. Then we strapped our rifles high up on our backs and formed a chain. I went first. My feet shrank against the icy water. I pushed my toes forward, feeling for a steady rock and found purchase. I grabbed Tony's hand; he took hold of Markham. We went forward. And then, about halfway across, Markham cried out as he stumbled on a rock and fell backward, losing his grip on Tony. He yelped and landed face down in the water. Instead of shooting back up and reaching for Tony, he panicked and flailed. This made him lose his grip on the guy next to him, and he went under. When he came back up, gasping for air, he was yelling. Just as Tony went to reach for him, a chunk of ice flew past us and hit Markham on the head. He went under again. In the weak light, we could only make out the shadow of his body as it was tossed and tumbled downstream, out of our grasp.

"Hold on!' Tony yelled. Before I could say, 'wait, don't do it', he went after Markham.

"Tony!" I called. I started after him, but Sanders vise-gripped my arm. "You aren't going after him. You'll die. Get us out of here!"

I led them to the other side then scrambled in the snow, my feet still bare, numb. I dragged myself along the edge of the stream bank, calling for Tony, gasping for air between sobs. I didn't see him anywhere in the ebony colored water. Suddenly I felt two hands under my armpits, pulling me up. It was Sanders and Firth. They had my boots and rifle.

Sanders threw down my boots. "Give it up. You'll never save him. That water is too cold. If you want to die too, go ahead. But we're moving on."

We walked for another day. My big toes rubbed against the top of my boots, and each step felt like a knife was stabbing my toes as my toenails ripped to shreds. My mind went numb with grief and pain. I had a bleak hope of seeing Emma and my girls. Tony. I'd lost Tony. Again. Had I told him about Mary? I couldn't remember. The time with him was all a blur. I had lost my best friend, not just once, but twice. Nothing seemed right. Life was too cruel.

We arrived in a small village that had recently been bombed. The houses were charred, smoldering and vacant. A few stray dogs wandered the streets scavenging for food.

"Look," Firth pointed.

A church stood at the end of the village road. Still standing. We stumbled inside.

There was a gaping hole over the altar, and light snowflakes pirouetted through, dusting the statue of Jesus like powdered sugar.

"We can sleep here," Sanders said. "On the pews. At least we're off the cold ground." He had taken on an air of command which didn't bother me one bit. I was tired of being in charge. Tired of making mistakes. Tired.

"Remember to take off your boots. Air out your feet," Sanders said.

It was agonizing to take off my boots. In the process, my big toenails slid off. My feet bled; my makeshift socks were torn. I gasped in pain and then lay back, looking up at the church rafters. I placed my hands over my hammering heart and felt it, Tony's package.

"What day is it?" I said.

"Christmas," Firth said. "Can you believe it? I thought I'd be eating a turkey dinner by now."

"Yeah, well Merry fucking Christmas all," Sanders said.

I pulled the package out. There was no way I was going to return this to sender. When I sent condolences to Tony's family, his son, Ben, I'd tell him his dad loved the present he sent. I'd tell him he couldn't wait until Christmas, opened it, and was thrilled. I ripped the package open. Inside was a pair of wool socks.

Tony had saved me again. And I never got to tell him what happened to Mary, or that he was the father of her son.

HICKORY RUN
1959

29

Emma stopped in my office to accompany me to the Grand Opening of my cousin Jimmy's new furniture store on Main Street. I was supposed to write an article about it for the Press. The door swished open and in she walked like a breath of fresh air, her hair neatly done, her lipstick in place, her dress pressed.

She pecked me on the cheek. "What did the doctor say?"

"Nothing to report. I'm doing fine," I lied.

"Ready then?" she said brightly.

We walked arm in arm.

People gathered around the storefront, peeking inside the large windows. Balloons festooned the front entrance, large banners telling folks to *Come on In*!

We wiggled our way past the on-lookers and entered.

Jimmy's wife, Betty, was standing by the punch bowl. She had on a tight pink dress that was cut low. We went to her first before finding Jimmy.

"I love your dress!" she gushed at Emma. Betty had a way of putting other women at ease because she really did outshine them all when it came to fashion. If it wasn't what she was wearing, it was how she was wearing it. No one slid into a dress like Betty could.

Betty bent over slightly to dip the ladle into the big crystal bowl filled with sherbet-colored punch, allowing a birds-eye view of her cleavage. "Punch?" she asked, holding up a cup.

"No, thank you," I said. Emma took one from her hand.

"Where's the man of the hour?" I said, trying to sound jovial. Really, I hated this assignment and was mad I had to do it. My boss requested it because Jimmy was my cousin. We got along for the sake of propriety and our families, even though we shared a mutual disgust for each other.

"Here I am!" Jimmy came up behind Betty and threw his arm over her shoulders like he was tackling her. He squeezed her into his mighty chest, and she laughed and batted his arm.

"Jimmy, you're going to ruin my dress."

"Emma, Ben. Glad you could make it! How are the girls?"

Emma told him the girls were doing well. One was on her way to college. Jimmy's gaze drifted.

"That's great. Could you excuse me, please?" He sauntered off toward an unsuspecting customer.

"He's such a smooth talker," Betty gushed. "I'll bet he has that young couple buying up half the living room department." When another couple walked over, she said, "Punch?"

"I'm going to look around the store," I said to Emma.

"I'll stay here and help Betty."

I wandered around. I had to say this about my cousin: he always came out on top. After the incident that killed his brother John, he was promoted. Partly, I think out of pity, partly because Captain Blake was afraid he'd cause a ruckus and it was the only way he knew how to keep Jimmy silent about the malfunctioning jack.

It'd been a long time since I thought about that day. If I had warned Jimmy, would he have all of this? What would John be like as he aged? I imagined he would have married a nice girl. He'd settle for a mediocre job and do just fine at it. Or else he'd have gone off to war and died like half the men in this town. That was another way Jimmy was lucky. Because of his connections with the Lavery Company, he was hired as a contractor for the War Department. Lavery had diversified and had a major contract with the U.S. Government supplying machinery to build bridges.

Yes, Jimmy did well for himself.

"Are you feeling all right?" Emma asked, taking hold of my hand and squeezing it gently.

"I think I've seen enough to write my article," I said. "I can talk to Jimmy later. He's busy now."

"Oh, I'll say. He has that young couple pulling out a checkbook as we speak."

I glanced over at my cousin. His icy blues landed on the young wife as her husband rubbed his chin with concern. The woman blushed at something Jimmy said. Betty's chirpy voice could be heard above the din: "More punch?"

"I think that punch is spiked," Emma said. "I'm feeling a bit giddy." She pressed her palms into my hand again.

"Are you flirting with me?" I said.

Her eyes sparkled. She nodded.

◦ ◦ ◦

I met Mary for lunch a few days later.

"I'm dying," I said.

"You always were melodramatic."

"Mary, look at me. I mean it."

She set her fork down. "You're dying?"

"Yes." I rested my hand on hers.

"From what?"

"Lung cancer."

"But that can't be."

"I have cancer growing inside me. It's so large and has been growing for so long, there is nothing the doctor can do. All those symptoms I've been ignoring because I thought I had bad lungs like the rest of us. It wasn't asthma, it was cancer."

"It can't be right. You need another opinion."

"I've got an appointment to see someone in Knoxville next week."

"What's the prognosis?"

I was about to answer not good when Glen Potter stopped at our table. "Howdy, folks! Ben, how are the girls?"

"Fine, Glen. How's Flo?"

"Doin' just fine. Thank you. And Mary, how's that young man of yours doing at college?"

"Great, Glen. Thank you."

"Now that's good to hear. You folks coming to the gala?"

Glen was talking about the gala celebration for the twenty-fifth anniversary of the founding of the Great Smoky Mountains National Park. Glen was the mayor, and it was his brainstorm to host an event in the community hall to celebrate all of the commerce that the park has brought to Hickory Run. The men who worked at the numerous Corps camps planned to attend as well. Or at least those who were still alive and I could find to contact and invite. We planned on having a reunion at the site of Camp 46.

"Sure will, Glen. Looking forward to it." Now I wondered if I'd even make it to the gala. I suddenly realized there was a litany of things I'd have to remember to decline, back out of, or tell people to plan to do without me.

Glen smiled down at us, caught Mary looking down at her plate, and said, "Well, I'll leave you two alone."

"Let's get out of here and talk," I said. "Too many people know us in this town."

On the way out I ran into Alice Reed. It brought back memories of the day we scoped for squatters in the mountains. Finn had told the fellas he would report the Reed girls' status to Captain Blake. He never did. For years the thought of those girls getting lost or eaten by a bear while making their way to Bird Town haunted me. But when I ran into Alice in town she remembered and thanked me for my kindness. She told me she and her sister stayed in the cabin until the weather broke in March, and then Finn showed up at their cabin. He led them on their journey to their aunt's house in Bird Town. She was working on her college degree after serving in the army as a secretary.

It made me happy to know they found their way, but I never did find out what became of Finn. Some say they saw him in town a few years back, but no one knew for sure if it was really him or someone who looked like him. He remained a mystery.

Mary and I wandered outside and walked down Main Street. "Let's drive up to the old homestead," I suggested.

We got in my truck and drove the paved roads into Taylor Valley. As the car careened up a winding road, we viewed those distinct landmarks Pa used to point to and tick off names like one would a grocery list: White Oak Sink, Turkey Pen Ridge, Fodderstack Mountain, Crib Gap. We stopped at a look-out pull-off on the side of the road, one I had helped build in the Corps. In the distance sat my aunts' cabin. Now in their late sixties, people considered them a tourist attraction. Visitors hiked to their cabin to watch them card wool, weave cloth, spin thread. They sold honey, quilts, and wool thread to anyone who made the trip. They were a living museum of sorts. A magazine had contacted me because they knew I was related and asked if I'd do a piece on my aunts and their peculiar way of life. It made national news.

"Does Emma know?" Mary said.

"Yes. I told her and the girls last night."

A hawk circled in the sky, riding a draft of warm air.

"I want Tony to know the truth." Those words had reverberated in my head for years. When Mary first told me she was pregnant soon after Tony left; while I stood beside her at the courthouse as she recited her wedding vows to her husband Frank; when I stood up at church to be Tony Jr.'s godfather, bundled in lace, his skin the color of toast; while I watched young Tony play with my oldest daughter, Eliza; while he watched over my youngest daughters, making sure they didn't get into trouble, as if he was their big brother. As if a sense of duty is an inherited trait. How many times I watched as Tony grew to be a man did I want to tell him the truth? That his real father died a war hero. That his real father was the reason I was able to live a happy life.

"You can't, Ben. He can't know."

"Mary, he's twenty-one now."

"No. He can't know. It would crush him to find out. There's a reason I never returned Tony's letters. We had no chance at a future together. I could never leave this place and he couldn't ever come back. I married a good man. Frank's a good father to Tony. That's all that matters." She sighed and sat down on a bench. "Besides. I made a choice. I could have chosen not to have his son."

"What are you talking about? You regret your time with Tony?"

"There were other options, Ben. You forget I studied under Aunt Bertie. I went to her when I found out. She kept a canister of pennyroyal for women who found themselves 'compromised' or too sick or poor to bear any more children."

"Does it smell like mint?" I said.

Mary nodded and looked away. "You extract the oil by steaming it."

I was reminded of that fateful day when I handed Ma Aunt Bertie's satchel of herbs and then the evening when she came out of the outhouse, bathed in blood. I wondered if Mary knew Ma had aborted a child.

"Don't look so shocked. She used to distill it into an oil and sell it to the pharmacist in town, Mr. Beyer. He'd put it into a pill form and sell it to his customers for 'female troubles'."

"Mr. Beyer depended on the Taylors for a lot more than Aunt Bertie's herbs. Cousin Floyd and Pa supplied him with moonshine," I said.

Mary chuckled. "That was a well-known fact." She turned serious. "If you think telling Tony about his real father will make things right, it won't. You can't change the past."

"I know that, Mary. I'm just trying to honor Tony's legacy."

"You've done enough for him," she said. I wasn't sure if she meant her son or my good friend.

We got back in the car and drove to a trail that led to Pa's grave. It was a short hike from the road, past trees emblazoned with markers to guide hikers to the waterfalls. We cut off the path at a place we knew well, a point where a big boulder protruded from the ground like God dropped it there. We walked a short way until we reached the spring, turned right, and passed the site of our old cabin, now long gone and demolished by the park, the remnants of our rock foundation the only evidence that we ever lived there.

Pa's grave was covered with moss. I went up and swiped it away then clapped my hands to release the warm earth. Next to Pa was Sam's grave marked by a small slab of rock, and on the other side of that, Ma. We had to get special permission from the Park Service to bury her next to Pa and

Sam, but we knew that's where she'd want to be. I was glad she wasn't around to witness another one of her children's deaths.

"They'd be proud of us," Mary said.

"I know."

* * *

I was cleaning out my office desk and pulled out a file. Tucked inside were some old photos and news clippings from my days in the Corps. Also inside was the carbon copy of a letter I sent to Tony's wife after me, Sanders and Firth finally found our regiment and recovered from our long ordeal in the Ardennes.

I read the letter I wrote to his wife again and wondered what to do with it.

January 20, 1944

Dear Mrs. Armerino,

By now, you have received the notice of your beloved husband, Vincent Armerino's death on the battlefields in the Ardennes Mountains. I knew your husband well and was there when he died. I want to assure you that he died a hero, trying to save a comrade.

I also wanted to tell you how I came to know your husband and what a dear friend he was to me.

[I went on to explain how Tony and I met but did not tell her about his secret identity, fearing he may never have told her this himself. I told her about the Corps and all of the hard work we did. I told her that Tony saved my life, but I didn't tell her how, and then I told her this...]

There are few people in a person's lifetime that one can truly call a friend. In my case, I was blessed with a true friend. He was always looking out for me, my constant companion, my cheerleader when no one else wanted to have anything to do with me. He brought joy to the lives of the men in the barracks with his charm and good nature. I will miss him because the loss of Vincent takes some of the joy out of living in a world without him. We only have our memories now. And that will have to be enough. He told me to tell you he loves you, and he loves his son with all of his heart. I am sure Ben will grow up to be as great a man as Vincent.

• • •

A few days later, I was climbing the steep terrain to the top of Taylor Grove with my nephew Tony. I wondered what I'd find up there. My lungs seared with pain from the effort. Tony sensed when I needed to rest and waited. We could have taken a car and driven on the road to the grove, but I had wanted to relive the memory of the climb while I still had enough strength.

"You ok, Uncle Ben?" Tony placed his hand on my shoulder, a look of concern in his dark eyes.

"I'll be fine."

We continued climbing. It wasn't as treacherous a hike as I recalled it was when I took this trail with Pa those many years ago, and I was able to look back down without fear. But it was rather steep, and a few times I lost my grip, my foot faltered and stones cascaded, and I thought of how glad I was to be in sturdy hiking boots instead of bare feet.

We got to an opening. It was now a secondary forest, mostly planted by the Corps.

"Wow!" Tony's attention was on the canopy. "Look at all these trees!" He pulled his camera out of his pack and started snapping pictures.

"Yes, your father and I…" I caught myself and stopped.

He looked at me quizzically.

"Your Pa and I hiked up here a few years ago, and it looks like it's grown significantly since then. I planted a lot of these trees twenty-five years ago when I worked with the Corps. My friends, Tony, Stan and Matt, my cousin John. We crouched down for weeks up here planting seedlings and heeling them in."

A small gesture I had thought at the time, compared to what was lost. But now the next generation of trees was growing back with a vengeance.

I sat down on a dead tree trunk and caught a waft of decay. "Tony," I gestured, "sit down here next to me while I catch my breath."

Tony's brows knit with concern. He sat down. "You ok, Uncle Ben? You look peaked."

"I'm not feeling well is all."

"Yeah, Ma told me you were sick. You going to be all right?"

He said it with such hope that for a moment, I thought, yes, I will.

"I'm going to get another doctor's opinion."

His face relaxed. "Well, that's good." He patted my thigh. "This place is neat. I'm so glad you brought me here."

"It used to be filled with big trees. You couldn't even see the sky." We both looked up. Pink clouds floated by, breaking up the cornflower blue sky, the depths of which was endless. Like what lies above, I thought.

"Tony," I said. "I want you to have this." I pulled a letter out of my sack. "It's a letter I wrote a long time ago. I made a copy. I want you to have it. It was addressed to the wife of the man you were named after, Tony Delaney."

"The address here says Mrs. Armerino."

"Yeah, I know. Tony had an alias. And I want you to have this too." I retrieved some pictures that we had taken for my editorials. "These are pictures of me and the guys planting seedlings right here in Taylor Grove. See how big the trees have grown since then?"

"Wow," he said wide-eyed.

I pointed to a picture of Tony and me, arms slung around each other's shoulders, shovels in hand. "That there is Tony."

"And this. This is him with your Ma." I handed him the one and only picture I had of Tony and Mary. I had taken it about a week before Tony left. It was at an event we held at the recreation hall, a going away party for Mary as she departed to her next assignment with the Park Service. I had meant to give it to Tony as a gift, but then he left in such a hurry, and I was in a tailspin over the events surrounding my cousin's death. I'd forgotten about it. Life went on, I moved, Mary moved on. The picture sat in my box of personal items left over from my days with the Corps.

"They were close, huh?"

"Tony was in love with her. He worshipped her. But as things go, it wasn't meant to be. He died in the war. I was there. That's when I wrote this letter to his wife. I want you to keep the letter. And if you could one day, take her one of the pictures of me and him. I want her to have them. I want her son to have some pictures of his dad from his days in the Corps."

"Why not mail them to her?"

I shrugged. "It would be nice if they were hand-delivered. I know I won't be able to travel anymore."

"I wouldn't know how to find her," he said. "Besides, when will I be in New York City?"

"You'll make it one day. I'm sure of it."

I wondered if when he did, he'd see what I saw—the resemblance between him and his half-brother. Or maybe after a while, he'd examine these pictures and figure out who his real father was. If he did, so be it. I followed my sister's wishes and didn't tell him the truth he deserved to know. But I did want him to know one thing.

"The man you're named after, Tony. He saved my life."

"Oh yeah? How?"

For a moment I thought I was looking at my friend instead of my nephew. What could I tell him? That Tony took the fall for me and that was why I was sitting here and not his real father? Would it have mattered? Would he have died in the war anyway? Would Mary have remarried? What was the point in telling him the truth? Maybe he'd figure it out on his own. After I was dead and gone.

"During the war he saved my life."

"But I thought you were a war correspondent?"

"I was. But he shielded me from some incoming gunfire, threw me to the ground just in time before I was hit."

I went on with a made-up gun battle, and Tony's heroic deeds. Storyteller to the end. We hear what we want to hear. We say what we know will please. I wanted Tony to know the essence of the man who was his real father.

We grew tired of talking and sat listening to the forest.

Tony broke the silence. "Take a look at that one!" He pointed to a tree in the distance. It was a hemlock that had somehow escaped the Lavery

Lumber Company ax. We hiked up to it, and Tony stood next to the trunk. "Take my picture!" he said.

The trees whispered in the wind, birdsong echoed in the distance, I heard the drumming of a partridge and an insect flicked my ear. I thought for a moment I heard Pa telling me it was going to be ok and he and Ma would meet me in Heaven. Sam was there waiting for me too.

I lifted the camera to my eye and captured Tony's explosive smile.

AUTHOR'S NOTE

Although this is a work of fiction the story is loosely based on actual events and people. Specifically, I found inspiration for my story from reading about William Walker and Walker Valley as well as the residents of Cades Cove before the Great Smoky Mountains National Park was founded. William Walker died in 1918 and was one of the last hold outs to the Little River Lumber Company. On his death bed he signed over his remaining acres to the lumber company with the agreement that they would not cut down the old growth trees on his property. Years later, the lumber company sold all of its land to the National Park system, with the caveat they could continue cutting trees until they had exhausted the supply. In 1936, the company cut William Walker's old growth trees. His land is now part of the Tremont Institute in the park. I found inspiration for Ma's story from the transcribed diaries of Emma Bell Miles who also wrote about the Smoky Mountains in the early 1900s. The lyrics to the square dance songs were altered slightly but otherwise came directly from her book *The Spirit of the Mountains* (1905).

I found stories about the people who lived in the region after visiting The Great Smoky Mountains Heritage Center in Townsend, Tennessee, the Cades Cove Heritage area of the Smoky Mountains National Park, and the Cherokee Museum in North Carolina. They have quite a collection of journals, books, and diaries with oral histories of the residents who were removed from the park in the early 1930s. I took fictional liberties describing Ben's aunts—the Taylor sisters—from the story of the Walker sisters, who remained in the park until their deaths. In 1946, The Saturday Evening Post published an article on them titled: *Time Stood Still in the Smokies*. Aunt Bertie and her knowledge of local herbs is entirely fictional.

Another source I used extensively was the Civilian Conservation Corps Legacy website. Many of the camp newsletters are digitized at various libraries. I used some of the exact language found in the 1937 camp newsletters now part of the Indiana State Library Digitized collections.

If readers are interested in learning more about the Civilian Conservation Corps, I recommend the books: *Nature's New Deal* by Neil M. Maher; *In the Shadow of the Mountain: the Spirit of C.C.C.* by Edwin G. Hill; *Rightful Heritage: the Renewal of America* by Douglas Brinkley. *My C.C.C. Days* by Frank C. Davis chronicles his experience at Camp NP5 in the Great Smoky Mountains National Park. Finally, Studs Terkel's compiled oral histories from people who lived during the Great Depression in *Hard Times: an Oral History of the Great Depression*.

Other sources about the lives of the people living in the Smoky Mountains include *Spirit of the Mountains* by Emma Bell Miles, *Our Southern Highlanders* by Horace Kephart, and *Our Appalachia: an Oral History* by Laurel Shackleford.

Thank you to all of those people who helped me on this journey including Alex Beldon, Robert Hilliard, and Amy Nye for their editorial input.

Finally, I am grateful for all of the first-hand accounts from the Battle of the Bulge. Sources include the History Network, The U.S. Army military history website; *The War: an Intimate History 1941-1945*, Geoffrey C. Ward and Ken Burns, Knopf 2010; *I'll Be Home for Christmas*, Library of Congress, Stonesong Press 1999

ABOUT THE AUTHOR

Sheila Myers is an award-winning author of four novels. Her essays and fiction are published in *The Stone Canoe Literary Magazine, Embark Magazine, The Adirondack Life Magazine*, and *History News Network*. Her last novel, *The Night is Done*, the last in a trilogy about the infamous Durant family, won the 2017 Best Book of Fiction by the Adirondack Center for Writing, and received a Kirkus starred review. She is a professor of ecology at a small college in Upstate New York.

You can connect with her on her website at
https://www.sheilamyers.com/.

ABOUT THE AUTHOR

NOTE FROM THE AUTHOR

Word-of-mouth is crucial for any author to succeed. If you enjoyed *The Truth of Who You Are*, please leave a review online—anywhere you are able. Even if it's just a sentence or two. It would make all the difference and would be very much appreciated.

Thanks!
Sheila Myers

We hope you enjoyed reading this title from:

BLACK ROSE

writing™

www.blackrosewriting.com

Subscribe to our mailing list – *The Rosevine* – and receive **FREE** books, daily deals, and stay current with news about upcoming releases and our hottest authors.
Scan the QR code below to sign up.

Already a subscriber? Please accept a sincere thank you for being a fan of Black Rose Writing authors.

View other Black Rose Writing titles at
www.blackrosewriting.com/books and use promo code
PRINT to receive a **20% discount** when purchasing.

CPSIA information can be obtained
at www.ICGtesting.com
Printed in the USA
LVHW031235190422
716605LV00016B/921

9 781684 339341